AF528916

## Advance Praise for *Girls Who Stray*

'The protagonist of this story is empowered in an effortless and unconventional way, her thoughts leave you with a sense of restlessness, her desires are uncensored, there is always a feeling that anything can happen at any moment. And even though the story explores themes that are familiar – power, fear, anxiety, love, existential angst and death – we feel that we haven't been here before, that the unexpected has gotten the better of us and that we must urgently turn the page to discover what happens to this young woman who repeatedly fails to fulfil society's expectations of her.'

**Kalki Koechlin**

'Edgy, acute and insightful, this disquieting novel, full of hurt and learnings is told with style and élan.'

**Namita Gokhale**

'Suspended between the memory of a tender, familial past and the breathing proximity of a near-dystopian future, this novel speaks the erotic language of contemporary Indian youth with remarkable candour. Asserting a powerfully unsettling sexual agency, it brings India's most striking urban spaces remarkably alive.'

**Saikat Majumdar**

# GIRLS WHO STRAY

# GIRLS WHO STRAY

*A Novel*

ANISHA LALVANI

B L O O M S B U R Y
NEW DELHI • LONDON • OXFORD • NEW YORK • SYDNEY

BLOOMSBURY INDIA
Bloomsbury Publishing India Pvt. Ltd
Second Floor, LSC Building No. 4, DDA Complex, Pocket C – 6 & 7,
Vasant Kunj, New Delhi, 110070

BLOOMSBURY, BLOOMSBURY INDIA and the Diana logo
are trademarks of Bloomsbury Publishing Plc

First published in India 2024
This edition published 2024

Copyright © Anisha Lalvani, 2024

Anisha Lalvani has asserted her right under the Indian Copyright Act
to be identified as the Author of this work

This is a work of fiction. Names and characters are the product of the author's imagination and any resemblance to actual persons, living or dead, is entirely coincidental

All rights reserved. No part of this publication may be reproduced or transmitted in any form or by any means, electronic or mechanical, including photocopying, recording or any information storage or retrieval system, without prior permission in writing from the publishers

This book is solely the responsibility of the author and the publisher has had no role in the creation of the content and does not have responsibility for anything defamatory or libellous or objectionable

ISBN: HB: 978-93-61315-90-9; eBook: 978-93-61315-20-6
2 4 6 8 10 9 7 5 3 1

For sale in India, Bangladesh, Bhutan, Maldives, Nepal and Sri Lanka only

Typeset in Minion Pro by Manipal Technologies Limited
Printed and bound in India

MIX
Paper | Supporting responsible forestry
FSC www.fsc.org FSC™ C016779

To find out more about our authors and books visit www.bloomsbury.com and sign up for our newsletters

# Prologue

*In bed, taut and naked, it creeps into the place of certitude, of love; it says – what are you doing to yourself?*

*The sting on my face is sharp. And although just a game, it takes me by surprise.*

*But this time I don't turn the other way.*

*Then there is another sting, and then another, and for the first time the pleasure is not, not even the idea of it, and for the first time I realise how much I fear the man.*

*The cold metal clasping my wrists, the stockings tied twice around the eyes, the knot of the gag cloth pulling on my hair. The weight of it now, something real. I see myself through his eyes – spread wide open, the body in light and shadow, the blast of the AC making the fine hairs stand on end.*

*The music plays on, saxophone and tabla.*

*He twists my face to the right at an angle, then does nothing.*

*I wait.*

*He might have slipped away to the window for a smoke, to his laptop, his phone. I move my face back an inch to face him, breathe easy, and immediately there is another sting with the back of his hand, the sharpest one yet. Calculated, on mark.*

*He must be able to smell my panic now. Sweat on my forehead, lining the palms; that stench from my armpits he tells me is the loveliest smell in the world, and now his hot breath on my face as he comes closer, my heart a time-bomb as he puts his ear on my chest.*

*But I don't turn my face to the other side, don't rattle the cuffs, don't cry out or tell him to stop, don't do anything at all.*

*I can picture him – confused, worry hovering close. Beginning to anger.*

*But still, that smile on his face.*

*He wraps me in his arms, holds me tight. Kneads his fingers through my hair, clutches from the roots. Then yanks my head to the right, taps my forehead against the headboard slowly. Tap tap tap. Now, with his hands still on my head, he lowers himself to my right breast and licks the nipple, a lioness cleaning her cub.*

*His nails dig into my scalp. His cold metal trishul on the bone between my breasts. That trickle of spit on me, his flopping, and I realise I can't bear him – his musk cologne, the scratch of his coarse chest hair, the dead weight of him on me.*

*I shut my eyes through the blindfold. Try to think.*

*I could run away now, tell my family about it. It could be over, just like that, a bad dream I could train myself to forget. Or I could go to the cops. Nothing will happen of course, but at least it will be off my chest and I could carry on. A million possibilities, and it could all be over tomorrow.*

*But for the first time, something else.*

*Beneath the fear is a tranquillity. For the first time – after a long time – I feel calm, a stranger to myself. I squeeze my eyes and plunge into the dark inside, reach out for it. Hold on to it by the skin of my teeth, the edge of my nails scraping.*

*Blindfolded, with my mouth gagged and body in open exhibit, I turn straight to him.*

*I keep my face aligned straight.*

# One

I have been wandering these streets all day. Driving around Delta, through sectors Alpha, Beta, Block A to J, in circles. Biding my time, rolling up the tinted windows against the white sun.

Driving past his construction sites, past the white apartment complexes, their foundations obscured by billboards. Svelte blondes in yoga wear meditating in serene forests, gleeful gap-toothed children. Corporate types shaking hands. One by one by one, I drive past them all.

'Casablanca: A World Apart', I read once again at the entrance. He may be inside right now on a site visit, approving raw material, doing any one of those unnameable things that is making all this happen, or he may be in the corporate office in Gurgaon.

And on the other side of the highway – there it is as always, the entrance to the village. I screech to a stop in the middle of the highway, echoing the gruff volley of abuse in my head. Look back at the men driving past, plaster the sweetest smile I can at heads that poke out of windows. Crazy fucking bitch –

I let them pass, one by one. Let them all pass. Let it all pass.

Then, before the next car can overtake, I make a hairpin U and turn off the tarmac into the village. Relieved for no reason, I bump along the open drains of plastic and sludge. Past, once more, the kirana stores of paan packets, ladoos and kachoris leeching oil and flies, advertisements on crumbling walls – ointments to increase the sex drive, astrologers to revive your business, an unused post box with a dozen fluorescent bills saying 'PG for girls', 'English Tushuns', 'Repair Electronix Items' . . .

Today as well, I take it all in – the women in their pallus and bangles, boys in acid-washed jeans, children sucking jellied lollipops. The Wah Ji Wah restaurant in slumber now; it will blink alive tonight, blasting Haryanvi pop from the speakers.

And the nouveau millionaires – the once land-rich farmers sitting cross-legged on charpoys, shadowed by their mansions. They flick channa into their mouths, look around listlessly, watch their sons race each other in their Lamborghinis, their Maseratis that bump off the dirt tracks to the silken highway.

Suddenly I swerve, missing the jagged rump of a cow, its face buried in plastic.

I catch my breath, tell myself to focus, focus, please just focus, damn it.

Two weeks since that night. Two weeks of aimless wandering, cruising the highway and thoroughfares of Noida, inching through the afternoons. Driving past his construction sites, and come evening, back to the frenzy of the village again. Driving up and down the gallis for hours. Watching everything, everyone – the same families, women cutting vegetables, the poorest sitting on their haunches on top of garbage mounds as high as the neighbouring mansions. Keeping myself busy scrutinising, conjuring backstories – who inherited which property from which grandparent, who secretly hates their husband? Who is plotting to kill their sister-in-law tonight?

Anything to keep the mounting dread at bay.

I feel somewhat comforted here, at watchful ease amid the chaos of everyday life. Far more than in the township that is my new home.

And today too, I buy the *Loksatta* clipped to the line outside the pharmacy. Go back to my car, bang the door shut. Sit back and scan every page, run my finger across every headline, inside and out, for any hint of that Friday night, two weeks ago.

Night now and close to the mall, I spot the wings of the angel glow against the sky.

On the bench outside with outstretched arms sits Ronald McDonald, the eternal joker with a few tricks up his sleeve. And sitting beside Ronald, he is waiting for me.

In a sharp black suit, the top buttons undone, the jacket folded on Ronald's outstretched arm. Right leg bent on top of the left, the gleaming leather shoe ticking like an alarm. He holds a burger in one hand that drops mayonnaise on his pants. Holds a toy in the other – a tiny wide-eyed doll with a thick ponytail. I can't see it from here of course, but by the swish of its hair I can tell what it is. He always teased me saying he would get it for me.

Our weekly date night and he has bought me a Happy Meal.

I park the car a little beyond sight, switch off all the lights. Watch him search these streets, scan every car for me. And even though I am the one lurking at a distance, I can feel his eyes poring over me, my body, inside it. And even though I am the one watching him sitting in this parking lot, so alone, just a man after all, I know he knows everything I have done all day, everywhere I have gone and wished further to go.

I wait. And watch him wait. And wait and watch him wait for me. Take off the ticking watch, shove it in the glove compartment. Prick my ears at the hum of the dead engine.

He's looking this way now, shuffling, rising to stand.

Our eyes lock on to each other's. I slide the sweaty key into the ignition, slipping, sliding back in, acting out a well-rehearsed script. Not looking down, back, not even shifting my eyes to the rear-view mirror, I reverse straight through, straight out the open gates and onto the highway, a deer in retreat, eyes locked on his the whole time.

Now he is at some distance and I breathe a sigh of relief. But wait – he's walking towards me now, ambling along, hands in his pockets.

He's smiling knowingly, widely.

I am sickened by him. Sickened by his arrogance, his knowing that I will fail, again and again, that again and again I will return to him, and again and again I prove him right, and I am sickened by this, by him and by myself.

I look at the road ahead that stretches empty for miles, only lit by my headlights. Now is the chance I must take. I step on the accelerator as his ambling turns to a jog, as he calls out my name.

Back on the road now, I am already speeding down the highway.

But he's running behind, shouting, gasping for air, so pathetic, so sad I almost stop. From the rear-view mirror, I see him now stop, bend over, catch his breath. Flail at me with those all-seeing eyes even as he diminishes in the distance, moving further and further away, the lord and master left coughing up the fumes in my wake.

Sliding past the automated gates, descending into the parking lot, I slither past the pillars, past a few cars, past a family approaching their car. The fourth-floor A-Wing family – the kids shouting, hitting each other, the girl whining, the father on the phone . . . Chup kar! Chup abhi! Past all this, weightless, I drive to our designated yellow box at the very end.

Turn off the engine, look at the white wall ahead.

Slowly inch to look around. The family in their car now. Radio on, they take a lifetime, but finally they drive off.

I inch my eyes back to the white wall in front of me. Wait. Clasp my palms to my mouth, grab the air pillow and scream. Weightless, exhausted, like the Happy Meal marionette he thinks he can make me, I collapse on the steering wheel as another day seeps away, as the horn blares a warning that echoes through the parking lot across the night.

---

Three nights later, a notification drop-down and the passport photo of a missing schoolgirl flashes on my phone. Her eyes frozen, already witness to her future. Thankfully, just a WordPress blog of a citizen-journalist type, I realise, and put the phone away. A week later, a small report in the bottom right of *Navbharat Times*, third page under the city beat, three children missing on their way back from school. The son of a dhobi and two sisters – daughters of a peon from a nearby warehouse.

But there's nothing major yet, nothing out in a big way. Still, I keep my eyes peeled, my ears to the ground, trail the gossip of maids and watchmen, the conversations of aunties and uncles on their evening rounds discussing rising oil prices or the scams of the newly elected MLA.

Picking up every hint, stitching it all together. Making mental notes every minute. And he knows I am doing this, I know, his antenna always alert, although he pretends not to, continues with his calculated aloofness, always business as usual, a satellite in a distant orbit.

And he is letting me do this right under his nose too, granting me these little liberties, allowing me my imagined victories. Calls me his doll. Tries to make a fool of me. But I am picking up his ways – does he know this? Playing the ingénue – clueless, dripping with honey.

Secrets buried beneath more as we scrutinise the other in secret. I can be good at this game too, he must have realised, enjoying it as much as he is, relishing it, conjuring up new tactics with every manoeuvre. How I love a good game. Hidden chambers of the mind, everything open to speculation – every conversation, every smile, every wink, a gentle caress, groove marks encircling the neck, a faint wound on the flesh – could this be a sign?

But sometimes I become weary of all this; don't you tire too, old man? Sometimes I want to just plead with him to stop, to let our guard down with each other, to expose my game and his, to let go once and for all, to finally tell him that I know what all this means, what he is trying so hard to do – the sideways glances, his lingering gaze, the sudden concern, fast-food date nights, electric-blue bowling nights on the weeknights in lonely malls.

I know what all this means, I want to tell him. I know.

But I don't. I play along.

I go to him, despite that night and what I saw, what I did.

Old man, sick man, dead man. I kiss his eye, his eye, and hungrily his mouth.

---

This morning too, I watch him chant at the doorway of the bedroom, and as he leaves for work I make my way home.

Rising in the elevator of my building, I fix my eyes on the CCTV, knowing I am making eye contact with him right this very moment as he sits in his office, tie askew, legs dangling from the table as he puts out one cigarette, lights another, glances at something on the iPhone, but inside, invisible to all but me, there is a definite tension, the nerve that throbs at the corner of his eye. And maybe, as he looks at my grey-and-white projection, maybe for a moment, he is overcome by tenderness. This tenderness that laces our affair like a threat – it comes from nowhere and wraps itself around him, and maybe, just this once, he lets go of his vigil, granting himself this one indulgence.

His finger touches my face on the screen, traces down my body, and I can feel it here and now as I exit the elevator on the seventeenth floor, Kenny G's saxophone lending to this moment a forced insouciance, and I get back home to the newscaster announcing the Nifty has closed at an all-time high yesterday as my father flicks the channels and my grandfather drifts to who knows where inside his room.

Down the passage, straight through the door on the left into my room. I draw back the curtains the maid opens every morning, striking the sun on my face. Now it is dark again. I collapse on my bed, yell through the closed door to my father that the school friend I spent the night with at the other end of the city, in Dwarka, is just fine, as am I.

Everyone is just great.

Then shut my eyes.

Still chilled by that night. It won't go away, even now, a whole month later. Not the click and reel, although I hope it will get better with time, that even if the pictures remain, the fear will pass.

But it hasn't. And when I close my eyes, I can see everything that happened that night. Him, with those men, in that house, with those children. Creeping at the back of the house, shovelling, smoking, looking tense. I could see it all from the window. At first I had doubted myself, wondered if I was too high, too drunk, too drugged, too something, but they kept coming back, over and over again, those images, like a click and reel. On my morning and evening walks; as I half-heartedly applied to, readily rejected, job offers in the middle of online interviews; at the dining table, in the middle of conversations about nothing with my father; and through those aimless afternoons driving through the neighbourhood, always his construction sites in the foreground.

And finally, I faced the fact that they were too real, I could not have made them up, even if half-deranged. There they were again, those images, speeding through my mind with full force, each sharper, clearer, more vivid than the one before.

So mouth firmly shut, too scared to change anything, any one thing that might cause any kind of disruption, the tiniest disequilibrium, to the perfect universal order of things, I continue as though nothing has changed. During the day, I saunter through the malls, the highway cafes – to buy time, procrastinate, postpone, defer. I concern myself with the task at hand – the mall rats to observe for hours, the infinite entrapments on my phone, the right perfume to suit my mood, my personality type, the right body mist to match my sun sign. The right topping for my cappuccino, the right pickles for my Sub sandwich.

And as I wander I construct elaborate plans in thin air – when to give my testimony to the cops, what I will say, the specifics of the night, the images in my head finally exposed to another, the fear finally shared. I imagine what will eventually happen to him – no sentence or incarceration perhaps, but the media will hound him for sure, and he will be left with a ruined public image for a long, long time.

But at night I still go to see him in places where we have always met – the bowling alley, the parking lot of McDonald's, his property sites of the future, his penthouse in his unfinished apartment complex, racing in his silver Jaguar on the highway to keep the game going, a barrage of sweet nothings to one another. Or driving in his BMW through the gates fitted with hoardings of even more svelte women in white tights meditating against the hills. The gates open for us and he parks before the giant pits fitted with foundation slabs. We walk up the fifteen–sixteen flights of stairs of his tower block still wet with cement. We reach the top floor, and then . . . only a staircase jutting out into the sky.

I look at this staircase. I look at the night sky beyond. Turn around to him, fear up my spine like a thousand mice let loose. Wait. Has he brought me here to push me off? To finish me off once and for all, his only witness to that night? Unsure of what I would do, of who I was?

He's a thick mask to me since that night, one month and three days ago. I once thought I knew him, for a brief window of time. But he's inscrutable to me again. And I'm the same to him.

So I come to see him at night, fearing him, wanting him, unsure if he will in fact finish me off. And as I drive home every morning, relieved to be alive, back to another day of wandering, I know there is no other way for now.

And the fear swells as I drive home – what if instead I am eventually found out? Witness to, accomplice, co-conspirator. But then I placate myself, tell myself not to worry, we are cocooned by the web of his networks and his money, will always be. There is always somebody that can be paid off, hushed up, even permanently if needed. This is child's play compared with what he faces every day.

But still, I scan the newspapers, cover to cover. Look online frantically, search for children, murder, filthy, depraved rich, again and again, but very little, almost nothing shows up, even now.

A few more poor dead children mean nothing to this city.

I am a coward, I know this of course. This should have stopped a long time ago. I have enough evidence now to put him in the white glare of the world's radar. But I don't, and I don't even try, don't wrestle with myself even once.

Instead, I continue to play these mind games with him, as he does with me, gripping tight the rope, making sure it never slackens. And so, as the days drag on, the months, we carry on in this strange tautened limbo that we keep testing, like pigeons pacing gingerly on livewire, cooing to ourselves in respite.

But for how long can we go on like this with suspicious minds, I wonder, as I walk to the kitchen for a mug of black coffee, as I nod in passing to my father, as I overhear my grandfather snoring, as I firmly shut and then lock the door of my room behind.

And it comes back of course, it does, this morning, as it could any morning, any evening – after my avoiding it for days, roaming the city in firm denial. Me crouching next to her on the ground, them digging frantically. Then me lifting her up with them, even though there was no need. The two men would have managed fine.

Me throwing her into the pit with them. Then turning around and scraping dirt from the inside of my nails as I heap the mud on top of her, bit by bit, layer by layer, burying the dead girl in the backyard of the brigadier's house.

---

One year ago.

My father and I sit on the orange sunflower plastic cover of the sofa-cum-armchair set in the living room. It's a little past eleven. The clock ticks so loud.

Our first night in the new apartment. The living room empty, except for this furniture on which we sit. Everything else will be unpacked tomorrow, in the days to follow. Now we stare at the blank TV screen still not connected, and face each other's reflections.

This room in which we sit dark, except for the white tube light in the kitchen, the only light fixed in the house yet as we wait for the clear bulbs to arrive with yellow light tomorrow.

And it is now, when there is nothing that must be unpacked or ordered, no one to call, no packer-mover to tip, nothing to move or set down or replace, that the weight of all that has happened stares us in the face.

I wait for him to say something, as I know he waits for me. I am itching to finally speak out what the silence has been saying all these months anyway – that he's a retired divorcee now, confined to live the rest of his days in the isolated outer suburbs of this massive city. Relegated to solo games of indoor squash, to evening walks in the park lined with pruned frangipani trees, to home-delivery apps and to keeping tabs on the latest offers for superfluous medication, routine groceries, his domestic retirement delights, the door-to-door collections for the annual society gathering.

But of course, I can't say any of this, and really there's nothing to be said. And so we keep to ourselves.

My student debt is mounting, and he has a few more years of EMIs before this house is his. And looming large on the horizon, the fact that this apartment is a major chunk of the collateral for my student loan – the loan I took to complete a degree in England, from where I have recently returned. This apartment, his first home after years of government housing, his only real possession, still not entirely his. We haven't spoken about any of this, at least not in any direct way since I got back three months ago.

Three months in the other house first, the one taken on rent. A house of quiet men, without her. He misses my mother, but will not make this known, not to me, not even to himself.

Three months of browsing through job postings, emails, text messages and updates on all the latest job search apps, noting down numbers to call, politely turning down offers on emails and phone calls. A friend's friend has a new startup and they need a content editor, a magazine in Gurgaon is having staffing trouble. Browsing job-engine websites – Naukri, Monster Jobs, LinkedIn – online courses to learn, ORACLE, Java, SAP, Linux, online MBA do-it-yourself courses, part-time courses in finance and accountancy, HR.

Devouring self-help books, highlighting the suddenly inspiring extracts with lemon and orange felt pens, leaving important pages dog-eared, with fluorescent post-it strips sticking out like breadcrumbs, signposts to refer to in the ambiguous haze of the future.

And sitting in front of my father's reflection like this, I know the talk to follow will be of the job market, of so much time that has been wasted, of skill sets that must be honed, opportunities not to be missed. And after this, it will move to the need to tighten our belts for the sake of family. To grow up, take on some responsibility finally. You're twenty-three now, not a child any more by any means. You have had your education, studied what you wanted, much against my advice. And almost offhandedly, dropping mention of the loan at the end of the conversation, just a casual afterthought.

But I have my set responses prepared.

I know that he has been waiting for this moment – to talk about my education loan – every day of the preceding three months since I got back.

Nice view na, he says instead.

Yes, nice tennis court, nice rock garden, nice recreational-cum-party hall, I think, then pause.

Nice indoor gymnasium, nice, helpful gym instructor, nice table tennis court, I mouth the rest in my head.

The heater is making my mouth dry, I respond, and get up to switch it off.

And before he can say anything in response, we hear the static from inside the room, the music now louder.

The radio again, the late-late night programme on 102 FM Gold, my grandfather's favourite. The anchor in a slithering voice evoking a sense of nostalgic romance in exquisite Urdu. I can't stand this voice that I hear every single night – this anchor who makes a living off his listeners' heartaches, my grandfather's delusions. Encourages them to call in with stories of broken marriages, an old affair remembered, the death of a husband. And every night they call. Women mostly, middle-aged, widowed, holding tight to their longing. He encourages them this, urges them to tell their stories, responds with an air of inevitability.

The conversations between the anchor and callers in between songs end with a hint of flirtation, a soft sigh, a quick shayari on the illusions of the ways of the heart or some such, some musing I never understand, something I'm sure passes through my grandfather too, though I hear him say waah, waah, but always at the wrong junctures.

Dasht-e-tanhai, cries out Iqbal Bano, to the open night in charged lament – in the desert of my solitude, beneath the dust and ashes of distance, blooms a field of roses of your presence.

I sit back on the sofa. We listen to him – his thin voice that struggles to sing, an embarrassed cough, and then as he hums the rest of the song. And although I don't hear it now, I know that he whispers her name to himself as the song ends, as the retro English programme comes on and my father gently nags him to put it off, please Daddy, enough, draws back the curtains, covers him with a thin sheet.

Now my grandfather holds on to the rails of his bed. Clutches at the walker, creeps to the window past the male nurse asleep on the mattress on the floor. He looks out the floor-to-ceiling windows at the half-finished building opposite, at the black boxes of empty houses all around. To the right, he sees the metro rail slicing past, the pits of construction that stretch beyond. Workers in fluorescent orange jackets and yellow helmets break rock inside, a thousand hammers strike like rain. They work all day, all through the dead of night.

He sees all this, and whispers for her again. Shahbanoo.

Out of bounds all his life, now she is everywhere. Beneath his eyelids, at the breakfast table, as he pretends to use his walker, as he sits down to pray or listen to the radio, singing to him, imitating his movements, teasing him, following him inside his memories, following him from house to house, from room to room in this new house, as he ages to infirmity.

And in this new house we watch my grandfather speak to ghosts, and each plays its part in his drama that carries on from dawn to nightfall, and on again.

As we listen to the weak medley of Iqbal Bano and my grandfather, we look at each other, my father and I, knowing we will hold on to this long after he is gone.

---

A little more than a year before this, I left the country so as not to face the fact of this shifting – the numerous trips to the faraway suburbs, all the paperwork and unnecessary practicalities. My father so anxious with all the bank work, pacing up and down. Breathing down my back as I was constantly made to check for better rates online, read articles on honest builders, on brokers that levied hidden costs, dig up old contacts and associates who could advise, sometimes for a fee. Obsessively calculating property tax and this tax and that tax in untitled MS Excel sheets all over the desktop.

I had gone with him the first few times. Sat in the car beside with all the brochures of the new townships on my lap. Would you like a swimming pool? he asks. Wouldn't you like to be able to go rock climbing whenever you liked? Imagine a sauna in the middle of winter! I look at him and say yes, sure, of course, tired of telling him again that I wouldn't be coming back, I'd get a demanding job, live an exciting life in London, or if not London then New York or Hong Kong – as a squatter maybe, in a council flat, on the dole perhaps, living off the taxpayers of the great nations that actually care – living poor and hard, but free. Far away from here anyway.

Bright and early we set off from our home in Jor Bagh, driving past colonies of pale pink housing, over the toll bridge that cuts across the Yamuna, right to the six-lane expressway. On our first trip I sat reluctantly, sulking at my father, sulking at the passing cars, staring out the window and trying not to listen to my father as he couldn't stop talking about all the wonderful amenities at our doorstep, and such conveniences! We won't have to step outside our complex at all! And how wonderful that the new metro line that will connect right to Rajiv Chowk, the super grocery store not even one kilometre away. Not fazed by my monosyllabic replies, strangely encouraged instead. We drive past the blue double archway into Noida, past the Buddha sitting calmly at odds with the world. Past the park of giant elephants with upturned trunks saluting every visitor.

Suddenly scooters of hooded men and women on bikes – a pillion turns around, a swoop, a howl as my father screeches to a stop.

And then they're gone.

He keeps to his lane at the far left the rest of the way, letting the others zip past.

Now to Greater Noida – construction sites flank either side of the expressway. We whip past billboard after billboard – a new school, a hospital. Billboards for new townships as far as the eye can see. I read out each name as quickly as they pass – 'Rosa Gardenia', 'Regalia', 'Solitaire Splendora'.

Imagine myself on the highest floor, the penthouse apartment, there, and then there and there . . . looking down on the traffic, this dark blue Maruti Swift Dzire driving cautiously past, that truck up ahead blaring hectic Haryanvi beats . . .

And then, in a disembodied American drawl, Google Maps tells us we have reached our destination, and my father parks and we get out.

There's a shimmer in the air as gravel soot rises from vats. Cement mixers churn sludge thick and grey. I fix my sunglasses firmly to block the day, this white new world, so unreal. Workers smoke beedis on the divisions between the roads, beside saplings caged inside iron gratings. A young boy is writing with chalk on the rusted giant rollers lined back to back. Makeshift slums line the edge of the apartment complex. Now stepping into the office, a balding portly man with a wide grin, rounded glasses and straight tie walks towards us, slightly bowing. Namaste-ji, namaste, namaste . . .

The sun pours in through the glass, yellow fluorescent tubes on the ceiling gleam hard. The AC is on full blast. Surrounding the office are three tall grey towers, their shadows on this office site in the middle. A touch of Chopin through the speakers, the smell of instant coffee in the air, servile young boys in bowties and smudged white gloves from the neighbouring hotel management college present us with coffee, green tea and thumb-nailed butter cookies every five minutes.

We sit on the chairs. I smile back brightly. Some banter about the state of the market, some polite conversation about the clean track record of the builder, the occupation certificate, property tax, maintenance charges. Then the executive puts his palms on the glass, leans in and whispers – I'm telling you sir, no good time like now, just before festival and puja season, go for it!

I glance at the faux alabaster statues of naked Venus, the Roman columns at the entrance of the office. While the men talk shop, I excuse myself, amble to the centre of the office site. A mini layout of the complex lies under a glass casing, a doll's township, an elaborate birthday cake. A presentation is being made, red laser dots swiftly point here and there to a rapt audience of two – newly-weds who look at each other seriously every time the executive makes an announcement, her red glass bangles jingling with every nod. Other executives mill about busily, looking serious, whisper mythic secrets to one another, their heads downcast.

In the next cabin, an old mother and son talk mutedly with an executive. He tells them the retail and business zones are just two and a half kilometres away, the airport just fifteen kilometres away, the best schools and hospitals just . . .

I walk past.

I glance at my father still filling out some form, walk to the plexi-boards at the end of the room. Bright blue boards with smiling white children, one Asian peering at butterflies, skipping, doing their homework. Another board with white women in perfect yoga postures on pink yoga mats, expressions of inner peace as the sun sets behind their long golden hair, a group of white men playing snooker and golf, drinking whisky, giving each other hi-fives in the den. I amble to another section with the sample flats, with Italian marble flooring, gleaming Jacquar bath fittings and sparkling modular kitchens. I walk around the bed slowly, and then look up to make sure no sticky executive is around and undo the pillows, mess up the sheets, and I'm out through the back door into the lawn, back into the main lobby again, smiling at my father.

After green tea, after our fill of butter cookies, we walk up to the sixteenth then seventeenth floors to see empty flats, the lifts not yet ready. Slowly, on freshly dried concrete, my father pants, chatters on about the dishonesty of builders, government interjections, contractors, real estate litigation, pants some more. The executive chatters away in response – this land has been developed by X builder but then Y minister is creating trouble, and there, on that land, the villagers won't budge. All land a site of contestation. Is there any free land in this damn country that nobody is fighting for? I want to ask these men, but don't of course. Keep my mouth zipped tight, push back the sunglasses slipping with sweat.

We step into hallways caked in sawdust and drying paint. Painters flecked in white turn to look at us vacantly through hooded faces, drills bore through walls, bore into the brain, and with it the smell of new paint.

Now inside the whitewashed silence of new apartments, in each of the three blocks.

Down fifteen floors now, my father still chats with the enthusiastic executive. He takes us to the multipurpose garden-cum-children's play area on top of the parking lot, beside the pool. We walk past gardeners in uniforms and matching caps clipping the violet edges of amaranth leaves. Figures of a monkey, a giraffe, a lion and a baby elephant made of shredded leaves stand in the centre of the play area.

In Block II, cleaners in uniforms and matching caps, the same design as the gardeners but in different colours, scrub the tea-rose flooring, spotted with black granite. A woman segregates the garbage. The chatter stops as we walk in and everyone salutes and continues to work in silence. My father and the executive ignore them, I nod awkwardly. Now up the elevator that works in this block, teetering violently up the seventeen floors. Richard Clayderman still on the elevator station, Kenny G always. Om Jai Jagdish as instrumental. I hum this muzak in my head to distract myself from this elevator that shakes too dangerously. The executive does not seem too worried, my father of course making a grand joke of it all, though I know he is as worried as me.

The L-shaped corridor extends to the right here. We enter a door to the immediate left. The executive tells my father it's of perfect vaastu compliance, there are built-in cupboards in the passageway, finishing for the taps and fixtures, actually you know what Sir, he wanted to choose this flat himself, but customer satisfaction is priority, he's ready to sacrifice, and also, he chuckles, his wife told him there was no need to invest any more, he has already invested in two properties in this complex, and really God has given them everything in life. The men chuckle some more about nothing at all and entertain talk so small I begin to predict their responses in my head and give myself a point every time one rings true.

I walk further into the apartment.

From the other end of the passageway, my father looks at me. Nods his head vigorously, smiles wide. I look all around and above, at the flooring, the built-in cupboards, the taps. Inspect the kitchen cabinets, the bathroom and the commode with the dusty plastic covering.

Walk into the master bedroom that will soon be my father's. Glance out of the window. Beyond the unfinished towers of this complex, I see the silhouette of a labourer sitting on the highest spoke of scaffolding in the distance. A flimsy green net below him billows in the breeze. He stares straight into the sun, against the sky still blue with light. From a temple somewhere in the dry plains that stretch beyond, bells ring, the aarti rises very faint. He takes off his helmet, folds his palms as the sun sets.

The knot inside me loosens a little. This could make a life, I think. And finally, I take off my sunglasses, walk to the edge of the room, squint my eyes through the grill to look at him properly, survey the land. I close my eyes with the ring of the aarti and say my own prayer.

In the elevator shaking wildly on the way down, I laugh despite myself, laugh at my father's stupid jokes and the sales executive's exaggerated enthusiasm, but really laugh at my own silly sense of dread, my haughtiness, my whiny arrogance, the unnecessary contrivance of it all.

Behind the multipurpose garden-cum-children's park is a fountain we hadn't noticed on the way up, maybe because it was switched off. Mermaids, nymphs and Greek sea gods in Italian marble look down imperiously at us. A faux nouveau Europe in the outskirts of Delhi, in perfect sync with the rest of this world.

The executive asks us to wait, scampers off.

I quite like that last one, what do you think? my father says, and then, before I can answer, the water ejects sky high, disco red and blue and purple lights flash in unison to Beethoven's rising sonata, and all we can do is watch and contemplate the grandiosity of life in silence.

Two minutes later, the water patters back into the fountain bowl, and I turn around to find my father firmly shaking the executive's hand. As we walk back to the car, it strikes me how a few short hours can mark the outline of all the days to come.

---

On the ride home driving down the highway, the streetlights watching guard, the dread that I'd managed to keep at bay for some time now, that I guarded with such care, seeps in again.

From the pit of my navel, it laughs a hollow laugh back at me, and suddenly it becomes all too real, this new apartment at the end of the city, my father's retirement, their divorce, my grandfather slowly losing his mind, bit by bit, day by day, me going away to acquire an obscure degree in an obscure university in the unstable economy of the West, though never openly admitting so to myself, and of course especially not to my father. And the gaping hole of the student loan on the other side of my degree that envelopes all this. Meanwhile, the Indian economy that erupts all around, values questioned and discarded before any hint of understanding, disruption that shatters through. My own future that could be anything, anything at all, a thing to be feared, so wide open in its possibility.

A life without her, with only half of her.

I look out the window and see bodies huddled around fires – watchmen, labourers, street kids, slum folk – wrapped around each other, lying on the streets, this city, this country, snatching back your moments of self-pity before they can become a great big wallowing sea.

I close my eyes and see my future, in the middle of dreamy England, moors that undulate all the way to the stormy ocean.

And anyway, I pacify myself, I will only visit him as a guest, during Christmas holidays with my husband and beautiful mixed-race children, twittering in charming clipped English accents, on the way back from a visit to the Golden Triangle, or from camping in Rajasthan or Kerala, on the way to visit an elephant park in Thailand.

I look at my father, so happy, babbling with genuine excitement, humming to the latest Bollywood hit on the radio, a song he definitely hasn't heard before and definitely doesn't care for. I give him a weak smile. He turns to me and beams, ruffles my hair.

And later, when later has already arrived, when later has turned to now and I find myself leaning against the ice glass of the aeroplane, I look down at this city below like a giant star cluster, so huge, this city I call home that I now leave forever – spreading manically, surrounded by parcels of farmland till the ends of the earth. Wheat fields of stubble, some still scorched black, not a patch of wilderness in sight.

And there, at the outer end of the cluster, where the city gives way to the dark beyond, I can see the faint trace of our apartment complex and in it Block B rising to its full height, the only apartment on the only floor of the building lit.

And I see tomorrow, and all the tomorrows to follow. My father scampers about with his free khadi grocery bags saved through his years in government service. He chats up the watchman, the maali, tries very hard to find a maid. On his morning walk he sees the busy site manager approach his car – the manager of the new Infotech Park that will attract the technology companies, the multinationals, the giant Indian conglomerates, the feisty startups with their glitzy, generic jargon, like a foreign language from the future. He walks quickly to him. How is wifey? Kids adjusting? A quick nod, a perfunctory smile, back to the iPad, and then the manager is off in his sleek gold Nexus.

I look down at my father from 40,000 feet. See him lay out the table every evening for dinner, at noon for lunch, back to the kitchen now for the matching cups, a soup spoon at the side, a three-course meal every Sunday, matching crockery for himself and my grandfather but not the male nurse who sits on the floor beside my grandfather's feet like a puppy and no one questions it. But they, my father and grandfather, sit at the dining table, eat their meals to the screaming matches on the 9 o'clock news. In this three-and-a-half BHK house, yet another day passes and my father and grandfather retire for the night to their respective rooms, the male nurse unrolls his gadda in the alcove in the remaining half room – the servant's quarters.

And not until after I reach Heathrow – walking speedily out of the terminal, the suitcase wheels tapping smartly against the walkway, airlifted to the super-speed bus now straight out of a London of wide, smooth highways that spill over up to the corn and barley fields that roll bright on each side, past chocolate-box towns of brick and stone and storybook houses with black trim for windows, chimneys and back gardens, a shy red fox peeking out from the middle of a bog – not until all this and straight to the pristine university town in the serene heart of England do I think of her.

My mother takes me for the last Nirula's brownie-fudge and ice cream outside Delhi airport. She tells my father formally to please wait outside, if he doesn't mind, an instruction, not a request. She buys me the ice cream and we sit on the red plastic chairs inside the parlour white-lit in hospital glare. I say nothing, keep my eyes fixed on her to express my anger, resentment, accusation – knowing all along this is her idea, her doing. I stare at her stone-faced, tell her how selfish she is, how she's abandoned him once and for all for good, it's all over now at least for him, and just how does she feel about that?

But she doesn't look up. Instead, she slowly mixes the ice cream with her little red plastic spoon, sucks on the ice cream and fudge playfully, drags the spoon away as those words – expected, avoided, skirted around for so long – now drop out of her mouth casually.

She has decided to leave Delhi for good, the old house in Bombay needs her. As if on cue, as though I have prepared for this all along, I cut her short, ask her if it's really *she* who needs *it*. She clenches her jaw, looks at me with a world-weariness that tells me I am not the only one who has mentally prepared for this conversation. It's all I have, she says with resignation, the same words, always, when speaking of that house, Bombay, her glorious wild past, her tamed domestic 'situation', making me feel again the weight of the great sacrifice she has made as my mother. Then she looks past me. A hazy look clouds her face. Take care, baby, she says, take good care of yourself. She grabs and squeezes my wrists, suddenly overcome.

I look back, surprised as she almost tears up.

As I leave them and present my ticket and passport at the gate, I glance back at my parents, my father blowing air kisses as though I was five, waving energetically. My mother stands a few metres apart, clutches her arms to her chest, tight-lipped. They still stand, still wave to my back even as I check in, collect my boarding pass, mannequins repeating motions.

They dissipate into the night only as I take the escalator up to immigration.

That night my father drives back to the rented apartment in Saket. In my mind's eye, I see him check if my grandfather is all right, covers his open toes with a thin sheet, turns to leave and then turns back and covers him with another blanket. Stumbles over the feet of the male nurse. Then retreats into his room in this makeshift house, lies down, feels somewhat proud of his only child, a bit anxious, but mostly hopeful for her future. He picks up the pillow from under his head, and hugs it very tight, waiting for sleep.

The next morning he goes to the furnishing stores nearby, those recommended by his colleagues' wives, and busies himself with new matching table mats, crockery sets, new wallpaper print, considers colour schemes, the right fabric for curtains.

And my mother, I see her drive back to her friend's house in Vasant Kunj. She drops the keys into the glass bowl on the table, walks upstairs to the guest room she has been using all these months. She takes off her sweater, her pants, kicks off her boots. Crouches into a tight ball.

Is devastated and finally, free.

---

In England now, in cultural studies class, taking down reams of theory, abstractions that bounce off my head even as I write everything down meticulously, nod vigorously at the impassioned lecturer, at my impassioned classmates from all over the world and their raging debates in class and in the warm, plush, red pubs, I think of them.

A background film reel to these days that blur one to the next, lived by another ghost self.

I walk through the gothic facades of this university town, up and down the pebble streets as the musicians play Bach, or an old Queen number, or some wayward Beatles song long forgotten. Through the meadows, by the banks of a river that trickles to a ditch, always sparkling clean.

Along the streets of this charming textbook village that surrounds the university, a stranger to myself. And back in the university halls, and sometimes in the classroom, or the cafeteria, and mostly in the immense library, to fill my sense of the real, I collect memories of him, sometimes her. I wonder how he will live without her, wonder what the need for this divorce was, how much of a difference it would make. Couldn't they have continued on as they had all this time for the rest of their lives?

Live across cities on and off, as they have done for years now?

I left not because of the approaching divorce, but because of the silence surrounding it, how smoothly it would be handled, almost with a sense of relief. No banging doors or vessels. No fits, no silent tears or my father's brooding at night when he escaped to his telescope on the terrace. None of this at all. My mother and father treating their divorce as just another stage in their lives, inevitable, to be humbly accepted, freeing themselves up for the final withdrawal, before the final renunciation into the forests, the caves in the mountains.

I see him in the apartment in outer Delhi, looking skywards, ready to give up the ghost. But not her, not at all; she's Bombay-bred through and through, and that's where she will remain forever.

---

All my life they have been drifting apart.

She in her flamboyance, her joie de vivre, her need to be the centre of attention all the time, to surround herself with admirers, pushing him away. And he in gradual retreat, his unquestioning acceptance of defeat.

And he knew of those men, he must have – it was a mutual understanding they shared, although they never talked about it, never to me, never in front of me. The extended family, the colony whispering. And she knew we knew – flaunted it like an open secret. He held on, believing he was above the possessiveness of other men, jealousy and other such domestic dramas. He strived to be someone better, bigger, to fulfil his duties to his family, yes, but also to the larger project of the nation, its communities and districts, its development bureaus and committees.

This should, eventually would, pass.

He worked for the Central Pension Accounting Office of the finance ministry, and later for the Department of Social Justice and Empowerment, where he kept track of the delivery of schemes that emerged every election cycle – pensions for war widows, rations to BPL families, support to jobless youth.

Let her do what she wants, these family matters are to be tolerated. He had a family to provide for. Bigger things to think about.

I saw him grow to accept this situation as just another fact of his life, like the changing seasons, old age, the endless cycles of government.

She yearned for him to show his possessiveness, but he never did, and so she continued her flirting and serenades with God knows who, with a sense of urgency and abandonment and, eventually, defeat. But he needed her, no matter what she did he needed her. Even through her absences and her cruel carelessness, even *for* it. Her breeziness, her rushing in and out, the underlying drama of her life spilling onto us all – he needed it and so did I.

And she must have needed us too, in her own strange way, otherwise why stick around for so long? He must have expected it all along, but when the final divorce papers came, it must have come with a shock. And me, I expected it all my life, but when it came it sank me from inside.

I never brought it up with them together or separately, biting my tongue at the dining table on what was so clear – the fewer and fewer nights we ate together. I never brought this up with my friends, with anybody. And of the three of us, I seemed to be the one most concerned about their growing distance while they seemed at such ease in their own lives, she spending her afternoons and evenings drinking at the gymkhana with whoever happened to flirt back – a building uncle's brother, the strung-out trombone player from her racy past as the belle of Bandra, the owner of a new restaurant down the road – growing raspy as she drunkenly belted out an old blues number no one knew in the bucolic towns of our postings in Pune, Vadodara, Mangalore and, finally, Delhi, as no one did outside of the close group of people she called friends in the Bombay of her youth.

And he – in his free time collecting donations for the annual colony mela – ensuring the residents paid their society charges at every cooperative housing society we lived in, ensuring that all maintenance charges were paid, all the residents complied with electrical norms, paid dues to the watchman every month, and to the gardeners, plumbers and maids.

Them meeting, night after night, behind the closed door of their bedroom. I never understood it. Maybe there were other things that drove them apart, things they'd never tell me even in their odd, oblique ways.

Perhaps I was never meant to understand.

My mother, my father, my family, I love them.

Then how and why has it come to this?

A father withdrawing into himself, a mother rushing around, filling herself with senseless chatter and garbled music, with any old wayward man she meets in the bar, with endless drink to fill up the glass that will always remain half empty. Full of words, the thoughts in her head racing against each other, inane conversations about acquaintances neither of us truly care about or even really know – Aunty Rosy, Uncle Gerald – inventing this cacophony to delude herself into feeling alive, to convince herself her days are well spent, her life worth the while. A foil to the father-and-daughter duo crouching in the shadows. Without realising it, slowly being buried by the chaos of her own mind.

And my father? My father sees everyone slipping away – he is losing his wife to life, his father to old age, and his daughter, his mirror image, to the very thing he is losing himself to. And what is this 'thing' – a hidden and quiet losing of his ability to attach words to things, ideas to feelings. Not quite being able to come to terms with what he is feeling, not being able to put it in words. Not seeing it as a cause of concern, the slow but definite withdrawal of his own mind.

---

And one day, long after she left us, a thunderbolt we had come to expect, they sat me down in the living room of his makeshift house in Delhi. By then she had been staying with her friend in Vasant Kunj for over a year, and he in this rented apartment in Saket with my grandfather. A forced lunch of rice and dal, the sun streaming on the coffee table through cheap cream curtains, they finally told me, very matter-of-factly. A so-called family meeting after years. I knew it was coming – there was nothing else that could have called for such formality.

She said they were separated, had already applied for a divorce, which would, hopefully, be granted within the next six months. That I must carry on with my dreams, my ambitions, my future, etcetera, etcetera. I listened carefully but was looking at him throughout, the silent one, the stargazer, so like myself – this passive outline of a man I wanted to shake up, instil a fighting spirit into. I wanted to draw the carpe diem-ness out of her and shake it into him. All the while I was looking straight at him, and he looking at the wall behind, or the TV, shaking his feet, looking at her blankly from time to time, nodding but not looking at me even once.

And the next few months followed as if in a dream – packing, repacking, in and out of houses, sealing boxes with duct tape, stripping them off, new addresses and old, Bombay–Delhi, Delhi–Bombay, helping my mother take her belongings back home, my grandfather limping like a towed car at the rear end hand in hand with his male nurse holding the catheter pole gleaming yellow in the sun.

And then finally, after all the arguments and discussions that went on into the night, after finally convincing my father that this degree would prove beneficial, would definitely lead to a bright career, assure me of a financially stable future – ignoring the gnawing uncertainty inside – I decided to plough on and apply.

After all the essays reflecting on why I was best fit for the course, after the scholarship rejections, the bank work for the loan . . . after all the paperwork, uploading of documents and teachers' references, one of the universities – not the one I had been vying for, not even the one I reserved as back-up, but the university that was my third-to-last choice – sent me an invitation letter. Still, when I received it, I was elated. I knew it was time for me to leave.

And so here I was then, in England.

And all that remained unsaid seems so obvious here, in plain sight in the crisp English winter – the fact that they dragged their marriage on for me. I can almost hear my mother say it – we stayed together for you. But now that I was finally gone, they'd settle it once and for all.

I zone back into the class, bored with my boring family and their humdrum sorrows, bored with this professor and my classmates so enthusiastic about who-knows-what, bored with myself. I set my pen down, zone out of my thoughts as the professor goes on.

Glance out the windows, the casements lined in gold.

The British countryside rolls on and on, green and drenched, the sky forever grey. This is a glorious life, a sublime way to be. A dream world, floating like the curled clouds above the earth. I am heady and numb at its possibility. A whole year left of days like these, happily marooning myself in the library, the course taking up ten hours a week, the rest of the year left for research, for exploration, for 'personal development'.

India is very far away, a long time still coming.

---

In the university, I forge a few faltering friendships with my reticent, scholarly friends, some so well-travelled and well-read and worldly they could be twice my age, but they're not. I check their student profiles on the intranet and confirm this from their Facebook pages. From wealthy parts of London, from Paris, rich American families, a few on scholarship from Kenya and Pakistan, others sons and daughters of scions of big businesses – shipping, retail – or of well-established high-ranking civil servants of their furiously developing economies, still having earned coveted scholarships.

I seem to be the only one here with no endowment, and with a loan.

In cafes as white and quaint as the snowy world outside, I stir muscovado sugar into my coffee with a stirrer made from recycled plastic, listen to their raging cultural debates in awe, watch as the words dissipate with the sugar into the black vortex below me – 'hypermodernity', 'late capitalism', 'simulation', strung together to form sentences that declare the decline of the nation-state, a breakdown of all standards of art, a renewed focus on subjectivity. The technological revolution and AI are ripping all notions and standards apart, they proclaim, almost cheering. Some chip in on globalisation's ultimate triumph, a simultaneous celebration and lamentation of the homogenisation of the world.

My mind jolts, charged with all this discourse, this banter, this place so foreign and cerebral and alluring. Listening to them, their thoughts articulated in a faux-posh West London accent, a thousand vague ideas pass through my mind every minute, so fast I am left speechless. And all I can do is muster up some courage and offer some kind of occasional fillers – 'Yes, but Derrida's deconstructive stance' or 'the all-consuming proliferation of the media' or 'neoliberalism and free-market capitalism are dissolute' – before someone else relieves me of the burden of ending that particular thought.

And so I offer such fillers occasionally, but more rarely as the months pass, volunteer a line or two I think sounds original but not offensive to anyone present, or to the favourite thinker of anyone present as I imagine. I quote any intellectual who surfaces in my mind at that moment – Camus, Nietzsche, Sartre – hoping to contribute meaningfully in some way, to add value, to strengthen the fuzzy idea of what my argument might be in this fog of postulations and positions that every word, every occurrence, only makes more obscure.

I walk on eggshells, afraid to offend – knowingly, or worse, unknowingly – worried something I might or might not say will anyway. That my silence will be construed as rude. I feel vague and doubtful about the very meaning of the sentences that leave my mouth, wishing very much that I can stop talking, take these words back. Lock them up inside my mind for good.

But after I do speak hesitantly, there are a few nods, some silence, quizzical looks, then someone changes the subject altogether. I am good for fillers only, I realise one day during such a conversation when I have embarrassed myself, but how exactly, or why, I can't work out. I decide to occupy the role of this side-act, this filler person, in these daily dissections of the state of the world and the global economy at the local coffee shop.

But I tire a bit at the end of these conversations, feel the urge to block out this chatter that feels from the gut up increasingly irrelevant.

And so one day, breaking off from a filler, I ask what I have been wanting to for so long now – what do they actually plan to *do* with this degree? And as I ask my father's forewarning dawns on me, that this degree is simply too obscure, that it will find no currency in my life, not the one

I come from at least, not even the one I can make, although not in so many words.

There's an uncomfortable silence. Nida from Pakistan smiles knowingly, or maybe I imagine it. Most are unsure but confident in their lack of surety. Nida wants to go back home, maybe join her father's textile business, start a forum for the workers on art appreciation. Chege from Kenya says he would apply as cultural relations officer to the Tate Modern in London, and if that doesn't work out he can always go home and work on his writing. The others are toying with journalism, teaching, criticism, say life is for exploration and that it's important to keep experimenting.

Life is all flux.

And you? they ask.

Same, I say coolly, with a shrug of the shoulder. Maybe I'll work on my writing back home, taking a cue from Chege.

I keep quiet for a while as the conversation turns back to something I can only pretend to understand. Then lapse comfortably again to my fillers.

What will I do when I go back home, I begin to wonder as the first term passes into the second. Sitting in my class, tapping the pink rubber of my pencil against my notebook, half listening to the professor discuss the evolution of aesthetic sensibilities in the latter Tudor period. Because even though I very much want to stay on in this country, though to do exactly what I have no idea, it's likely I will have to return to India soon.

I look at Mila and Alex, my classmates from Spain and the English midlands, respectively, who sit in front of me in class. All rumours indicate they have been dating for the past two weeks. I look at their backs sliding closer to each other and wonder what they would do if they were me. What would they do with this degree in India?

In the student bar one late evening, tapping my card as the bartender looks up and tells me it's not going through. What? I shout to her through David Bowie screaming.

Not. Going. Through.

After three more tries, embarrassed to the bone, I walk back to my gang, bend over and quietly ask my classmate Nina if I can borrow three pounds, just as the music stops and everyone at the table overhears. Sure, she smiles casually. After she pays up for me and I mutter my thanks, I rush back to my room, not daring to make eye contact, and immediately message my dad to send me money.

The next morning, the first message I see – Maybe it's time you get a job?

I blink my eyes – once, twice. It seems the obvious thing for him to say, the natural thing for me to do, but I still can't quite believe it.

After four days of not a single penny in my account, telling no one about this, walking to the other end of town to stand in long lines full of students and junkies to eat the free mashed khichdi doled out by the Hare Krishnas, I think it might not be too bad to actually get a job.

Walking back to the hostel, I glance up at the vacancy sign outside the first Sainsbury's I see. I saunter in, ask about the opening.

Immediately the signing of the contract, me being ushered into the store room to try on the purple fleece jacket. The training for shop floor assistant, the tagging of new groceries that come into the store, the 'may I help you' badge and the smile I put on every time I walk in for work.

I sink myself into university life. I write my essays, labouring over formatting the footnotes. Drift through the presentations and workshops and seminars. I go to my job at Sainsbury's thrice a week after class, all too aware of the student loan approaching, tightening with every turn of the calendar.

But for now, I try my best to push my anxieties back as I get out of bed, brush my teeth, read up my notes for class or the café filler contribution sessions.

And I believed, honestly believed the lie that this place, the trusts and scholarship granters that had denied me funding so far, that the great and good British heart, would present me with several opportunities, perhaps even sponsor a research scholarship post this degree to me, yes me, with my average test scores, my timid presence in the classroom, only talking when spoken to; to me, with my half-hearted interest in the subject of my master's that I never seemed to really understand, never truly considered worth studying at all, if I was honest with myself.

I believed they would sniff through my mediocrity, eke out some underlying interest, help me develop it, make it come into being.

That they'd forgive me my desperation.

And so, as the months pass, although busy with activities and events of the year – gardening, cheap gin-n-tonic nights that turn to ink-blue dawns in the college canteen, Halloween socials and Christmas fetes – I increasingly wake up every morning to the sinking feeling that all this is just a fantasy, a break year from real life that lies on the other side, across a continent and the Arabian Sea. And then onwards to what I was dreading, what my father predicted, what my mother defended me against – clocking day in and day out to a cubicle, content writing for eight hours, plagiarising, copy-pasting, spellchecking and grammar checking. A sell-out to corporate greed, enticed, like everyone else, by capitalism's twinkling handouts and the promise of a steady, medically insured, provident-funded future.

Meanwhile, my father buys the apartment in Greater Noida, hoping to move into it the day he retires and has to give up the spacious government housing apartment in Jor Bagh. But the builder delays – the land falls under some litigation. My father pleads with his superiors to defer his retirement, at least for six months, rents the flat in Saket for the time being.

But I know the real story. He has been waiting for me to come back to move in there with him, so sure that I will. So sure I will not find a job in London, or New York or any grand European capital of my imagining, so sure of the futility of my degree. But mostly, a sinking sureness – as I faced the honest truth myself too – of my not trying hard, not trying at all, of the mediocrity in me as a testament to his own little failures and quiet little fears.

---

One year, two months and twenty-three days since I left, I return home. Still floating in fever dreams of an England of powder snow, of curlicue clouds, of libraries of ancient volumes stacked to the sky.

With a head full of half-baked understanding of Foucault, Derrida, Deleuze and Heidegger, I return to an India of start-ups erupting out of conversations over cappuccino, angel investors and equity firms floating past billboards leaving crores in their wake, an India where anything produced anywhere in the world can be bought at throwaway discounts during festival seasons, during discount seasons, during the space between that makes up ordinary life. New pipelines, coastal roads, new metro projects like gridlocks over and above every city, transportation hubs, expanding airports, underpasses, smart cities sprouting in every corner. I come back armed with a degree in Philosophy of Cultural Aesthetics, or Anthropology of the Mind, or Literary Criticism circa 1880, spouting opaque theories I barely understand, deconstructing every sight and sentence, battling the hegemony of the world outside the university.

When the wheels hit the tarmac, when I see my father wave outside the glass gate at Arrivals, all the postmodern posturing bandied about with my university friends bounces straight off my head.

I am jolted awake.

I come back to India seeing everything as portentous and symbolic, assigning more meaning than necessary, a nervous wreck.

My father immediately sends me to get my Aadhaar card made, my irises snapped, fingerprints inked solid.

And the source of much of this anxiety, blissfully avoided for nearly a year now – the loan. I come home to the student loan I have to pay off tightening like a noose around my neck.

---

India is a Nokia handset from the early 2000s, retrofitted with a shiny flip cover.

The malls are swanky, global restaurants popping out of every corner – Japanese ramen bars and sushi makis, moussaka, beetroot hummus and guacamole on tacos. Puppy bakeries and puppy spas delivering snow-white pooches with ponytails that spill like fountains from the top of fluffy heads. The highways have stretched longer, cars zipping through FastTagged tolls, apps tracing parking violations, zipping orange scooters on the road delivering food, groceries, medicines, furniture, personal parcels, just anything you please. Spa services with the click of a button at home, an army of deep-cleaning warriors with deep-cleaning weapons – green apple-, lavender-, lemon-scented – for every stain. Doctors available 24/7 on video calls for consultation for any real or imagined illness. A new IKEA to ogle at six floors of well-designed, ergonomic furniture and swallow Swedish meatballs whole in the basement restaurant. Decathlons at every corner offering wide indoor pathways to try your electric bike, your skateboard, to buy your diving gear.

But behind the blingy facade I sense to my bone the outdated oldness of the city, the loose cement mixed with water, the makeshift corrugated iron sheets falling on top of filth beneath the metro pillars, tarpaulin tied in every corner, buildings in a perpetual state of repair lined with bamboo poles, cratered potholes everywhere, dried gutka splatter, backs of broken bus stops housing the blankets of neighbourhood beggars. Children with no hands, women with no hair and men with no eyes, with outstretched hands and nasal pleas at every traffic signal. Garish pink-and-red 'Heppy Birthday' posters wishing the ruling MLA's son put up by the neighbourhood sycophant. The city a site of constant construction, slums spilling out of the sides of roads, on pavements and monuments and upscale buildings, the cops scratching their crotches, water tempos leaking, a section of the overhead bridge falling on the screen advertising the latest real estate development. And the anger of the road, every second a newfound threat as a Mercedes rams into an SUV into a Hindustan Unilever truck into an autorickshaw and the shakarkand cart topples over. Passing this scene every morning in my car, reading 'Mera Bharat Mahan', reading 'Jai Mata Di' on the back of the truck crashed by the wayside.

Every day feels provisional, a temporary phase till my permanent return to the first world. It will pass, I tell myself, it will pass, as the days slip one to the next.

It will pass.

---

My grandfather lets out a moan, my father's footsteps shuffle to him, the male nurse wakes up with a cry. Daddy, are you OK? Daddy? Daddy? I stay still under my blanket till it is quiet again.

On the white wall opposite, the reflection from the electric-blue swimming pool ripples. I watch the watery shadows make hypnotic patterns. The chlorine pellets dissolve to the bottom. The motor on, on even at this hour, hums into the night. I turn my pillow to the colder side and shut my eyes again.

I have forgotten how chilly this city gets. But this is not Delhi, not the city I know but somewhere outside, a little colder. I wrap the razai around tighter, bury myself in it.

Earlier today, being a Saturday, I insisted we go out to eat, after days and days, months. Why, my father asked, what's the occasion? It is nobody's birthday, as far as I know. But I put my foot down, said I was young and needed a life, and so did they all. So my father, my grandfather, his male nurse and I, all make an expedition to the mall.

Just a regular family, I tell myself, as the children gawk and point at the yellow-green urine filling my grandfather's urine bag that rolls behind his wheelchair. I hold his hand as we ascend the elevator and stare back defiantly at the scolding mothers. Catch a place at the food court on the top floor of the mall. My grandfather is dazed here, his hands shake as he lifts up a slice of pizza. I am aware, as is my father, that the stench from his urine bag is troubling the families around us. But we ignore them and chomp through our pizza. When we get home, the men are exhausted and sleep for three hours, as though they have ventured on a grand expedition to the other side of the world.

As they sleep this afternoon, the old men of my home, I wonder, again.

What is it that I should do with myself now, I think, what would be the right thing to do? The wise thing? The appropriate thing? The smart or kind thing? The future could go anywhere at this point, lead to anything. A series of nameplate-less, numberless white doors all around – flung wide open, with no view at all of the inside. I turn to each door, wanting to peer inside, but the doors, in turn, turn with me, faster but always firmly locked, and so I bury myself back in the razai, crouch into a ball.

I wonder why I cannot open my damn mouth and comfort my father or grandfather, or even my mother in far-off Bombay for that matter, why I can't simply take up a job like my peers, like my friends growing distant from me every day, as I from them – try my chances at any one of the numerous content writing or marketing or data entry or PR opportunities that come my way through the day on LinkedIn, through the job boards and hiring agents on email, WhatsApp and SMS. Why I can't be less of a loner, what is stopping me, what inherent crankiness, what indolence, what inner guardedness, what fear is preventing me from living my life whole, being of use to somebody, loving my family back, helping them in this time of need.

And then there is the matter of the loan.

I see my father and grandfather watch me sit in my room, slouched over my laptop all day, probably wondering what the hell I am up to. Hoping I will take up a job soon, but not wanting to directly broach the topic. Glancing at me worried, and then going off to the puja room. Sitting cross-legged, staring wonderstruck at the massive pictures of Guru Nanak with his eyes half closed, tiny silver idols of Krishna and Radha blackening at the edges, pictures of gurus and sadhus and saints collected through their lives and the lives of their forebears, all gathered now in this half room that could have been a studio, my writing room, a store room, but is now this half puja room.

I see them in this room every evening at 7 p.m. for the aarti, even after I have spent all morning discussing the firm absence of any God, the lie at the end of the tunnel that is the lure of religion. The ultimate meaninglessness of life, the grandiosity of the universe, the robustness of science, scattering titbits of existential philosophy I picked up at university at the breakfast table to these feeble men, so ready to give up any trace of agency.

I watch as they bow down to their gods, offering their life's worth on a platter, their naked need so openly, to these idols.

Irritation and then guilt – tossed by that old cycle again – at the loan mounting as I sit around all day with no job, at these men decompose before my eyes. My mother far away up to her frenzied whims in Bombay, offering none of her mad distractions.

Then guilt again.

And so, once again, I do the only thing that can be done in this moment of the here and now, the only thing I know how to do. I check my meagre savings from the Sainsbury's days. Somewhat assured, I log on to Amazon and buy the weekly groceries for my household, to compensate for my aimless wandering, my wasted days. Buy shiny new glass containers to store leftovers in the fridge, melamine bowls edged with pretty blue patterns to replace the plastic pink bowls caked with the remnants of dried, yellowed dal from decades ago that my father still insists on using. I buy upright glass water bottles with spouts to replace the old plastic water bottles bought ten years ago, twenty years ago, part of a two-for-one discount deal, part of the three-for-five Diwali bumper bonus sale. I buy lacy covers for the television, newly installed with OTT channels which my father is still wary to explore. And as a special treat, fancy Italian biscuits that crumble in the mouth amidst the Parle-G and Good Day giant super-saver packs hoarded in the kitchen.

I revisit the order again and again on my phone, feel a trickle of light.

And as I read the reviews of the products just bought, of others I might go on to buy, astonished by these tender, elaborate, detailed accounts the internet offers for what is essentially a soup stirrer, I hear my father's tender fussing again, my grandfather crying out from his sleep, as though he is mid-conversation.

Shahbanoo, he says, I see the sun light up your brown hair that flows like the great river Sindhu . . . and my father saying, Shhh, Daddy, go to sleep now please . . . rubbing his back, laying him down. My grandfather coughs a little. All is quiet, and when my father turns off the bedside lamp and turns to leave, my grandfather pleads with him not to, taps the hollow on the side of his bed. And so my father sighs a sigh of mutual resignation with the male nurse. My grandfather makes room for his son on his bed. And my father stays by his father all night, repeating his questions, pausing when my grandfather speaks up, encouraging his fading memory.

After my grandfather falls asleep, I can hear my father shuffle back to his bed. But then, twenty minutes later, he is lifting something, packing it and then quietly shuts the door of his room, and I know he's gone to the terrace to look at the stars.

I long to get up, take the stairs up to the terrace and sit beside him as he points out the constellations to me. But instead I stay very still, close my eyes and try to sleep.

In the colony of my childhood, he wakes me up at 10 or 10.30 p.m. Only the rustle of the trees, a distant truck. He pats my shoulder, I drift awake, sit straight up and look at him, a finger on his lips. Then pull off the sheet, put on my chappals. In silence we tiptoe up to the terraces of the colonies of any one of the cities we are stationed in, to the telescope he has set up before dinner.

Hours pass.

We wait for the clouds to pass, for the moon to be less bright. And then it appears, Saturn ochre yellow with its rings intact, Neptune pale blue, a dream twin of Earth, a hologram, a science textbook duplicate inside the tube, under the nail of glass. They come and go, come and go, these distant worlds.

Shhhh, he says, come look.

Patience, solitude, silence, my father.

The universe is many billion years old, and we are only a tiny fragment. And even today, after all these years, I close my eyes and remember what he said – the universe is many billion years old, and always it remains, long before you, and long after.

He'd point to each faint star with a light that beamed a red pinprick into the darkness, connecting each to the other. And then I'd watch him, by the light of the moon or by torchlight, plot the constellations carefully on the chart.

They looked odd and forced to me, jutting out at wrong angles.

Now six or seven, we sit on the mildewed terrace still slightly damp after a brief spell of rain, the wide chart paper spread out in front with Big Ben, the Eiffel Tower, Lady Liberty and the broken blue ballerina as stoppers from our showpiece set at each corner. He on the left, me on the right, he still plotting against a carefully marked graph, using stencils and rulers to join the dots.

He would sketch out the constellations for hours – Big Bear, Orion the Hunter, Leo the Brave, and say the names out loud when he was done, more to himself than to me. I never did see the constellations in the sky, could never train my mind to move from star to star that he pointed out, always distracted by the limitless scatter across the universe, by their asymmetry, by their utter randomness.

So me on the other side of him, sprawled happily on my knees, excitedly joining my own dots – cats with moustaches, fish on wheels, dragons with wings, drawing arms and legs, horns and scales, and then colouring them in very slowly with Reynolds 045 blue ballpoint pen.

Then suddenly there is a distant honk, a dog whines, the couple from the flat across yell at each other, and he tells me it's time to go back, come on, come on, as if only just remembering the weight of his place here on earth, his quiet daughter so needy of his company, his cheating wife so desperate to get away. And rolling up the chart paper quickly while we walk down one floor to our flat, he chats about my drawings, casually, as though they are all real people, asks me the cat's name, no, his real name, not pet name, which school the school of fish swim to, why the dragon has broken wings. I answer instinctively, never a pause, never a moment to consider – GingerKat, oh . . . Raju Krishnan the Third, Gopal Sharma Vidyalaya school, Papa! And the dragon's wings are broken because of a sudden lightning storm!

And back at home now, he hushes my chatter gently, bas beta, bas, enough excitement for one night. And only then do I remember her again, after a million light years or more, a voyage to outer space and back with him and me,. with all of earth's species, its star cast, its mutant degenerates. And we both know, now retreating to each of our rooms, me on the right, theirs on the left, that we are dreading her noisy arrival, which comes exactly five minutes after I am in my room, and he in his, father and daughter, each pretending to be fast asleep.

I stifle a giggle as I hear him pretend-snore as my mother enters the house after another night out, shuts their bedroom door gently but firmly behind her.

Now I turn around, lie on my stomach and fall asleep to the mad antics of GingerKat or Raju flying across the stars.

---

Later that night, as the clock strikes 3.30, I wake up, dry mouthed and sore, for a glass of water.

The festival season has begun – Navratri, then Diwali, all the shaadis, all the way to Christmas and New Year. Fairy lights are wound around the necks of the construction cranes. Rising along the length of the towers, these cranes swing like prehistoric giraffes. And the towers that graze the sky – forty storeys, forty-five, black boxes refracting into each other to infinity.

I look down seventeen floors. Wonder if I jump I'll be reborn as a video game combatant in a tight balaclava slung out with an AK-47 – Call of Duty, League of Legends.

Everywhere the loose earth has been dug out, leaving dark cavities. It lies in mounds along with sacks of cement, girders, ply. Pylons line the horizon on the highway, a battalion of Soviet starships to nowhere. Tankers drive in through the night, emptying our private water supply into water tanks.

From the narrow balcony of my room, I see the male nurse lean on the vine against the grill, having a smoke on the living room balcony. I'm surprised he is up so late but he gives me a congenial nod, as though expecting my presence. I know how he feels about me; he has never told me anything of course, but I just know. Strange, isolated, erratic. Wasting away unearned privileges as the only daughter of a recently retired bureaucrat.

But suddenly the cranes whine, and we look back. We watch this strange carnival from mid-air, stuck in between other apartments, other buildings and apartment complexes, the last home my grandfather will know, and my father perhaps, but for me the newest home yet.

Casablanca: A World Apart, Phase A, Sector Delta-I, outer, outer Delhi.

I survey the land and consider potential pathways to the future, as the job portals declare, as the placement officer at my university advised us to.

I think back to *that* call.

This afternoon again – that unknown number I had been ignoring since I returned. This time on a lark, I pick up. It's the bank of course. The matronly clerk with the nasal tone, big, round specs covering half her face, hair pulled back into a bun. I see her in my mind's eye. Inquiring about the status of my job, my current income, my future plans.

I hesitate a moment.

Then the lies spill out easily, stories fashioned out of nothing like muscle memory. I tell her I am working at that startup, yes, in content management, a little bit of PR and publicity on the side too. Nice, she says, very nice. And the name of your company? Suntech Ventures – a young tech company, but will make its mark soon. Yes, I am enjoying myself very much, thank you for asking, aunty. I give an estimation of my salary, tell her I will be working for another few years, after which I might apply for an MBA in America, possibly Wharton, at which point a few college girls in the metro turn around to look at me, impressed, and then whisper to each other. I have it pat down like a chant.

She says good, it's good for young people to pursue their dreams. Good for young women such as me to make something of my life. She's glad I have given up the arts, that I am now doing something serious with my life, trying to establish a real career. Then she reminds me of the status of my current loan, our next meeting in two weeks, reminds me of the new apartment as collateral, the accruing interest.

And then, very sweetly, tells me I could borrow her son's GRE books, sure, beta, any time. Yes, he got into a good MBA degree in America and has already got a job with Apple as a software engineer in San Francisco, a newly married wife from Kailash Colony flying down to him next week. He'll soon begin his family life.

OK then, take care OK, haan chalo, tata bye-bye.

Back to the present, I shut my eyes, open them again, seek out answers to the question that is my future in the smog-filled firmament, the boxes of houses ahead, the half-built convention centre below.

The loan, floating far away all this time, perpetually deferred in England, has become suddenly all too real here.

And once again, I weigh my options.

But this time I think of the bull-cartel man.

---

Last year this day in London. The morning after with the bad boy of the stock-trading world, the bull-cartel man.

A typical grey English morning, one of my last there. The clouds race to the ends of the earth. The suite overlooks the skyline – the Thames cutting through the wide spread of the city beyond.

He is looking out the wide window facing the city, the back of his head framed by the London Eye. Tall, refined, sophisticated. He folds his elbow to pin his cufflinks, smoothens his collar. I lie on the white eiderdown mattress, watch him smoke his elegant cigarettes through a chink with my closed eyes, pretend to be asleep when he turns.

I open my eyes and hear vague traces of Spanish outside. It's the housekeeping staff. But they won't come in here, the DND still on the door, he checked this morning. I saw him do this as I pretended to sleep.

All night, the task to be performed at hand came to me so easily it takes me by surprise, although I didn't dare once to question it, to stop, to think. I did what needed to be done, performed my role perfectly. And now it was morning and one has to, as he said so vehemently multiple times last night, just get on with it.

Although I had heard this phrase a thousand times in this country and knew it to be quintessentially British, I knew he was not. His lilting accent could make him Serbian, Georgian, even Russian.

Sitting in the cafe of the student accommodation in east London my university put me on to, with a pot of black coffee under my nose. The grey-white walls, the dark green Monstera palms in pastel blue-and-peach pots lined against the wall. This clean IKEA-styled world. The spare Scandinavian sense of studio living. Far away from the university town with the ancient cathedral surrounded by patchwork sloping meadows, rolling fields and rotund, patchworked Jersey cows.

Three days left to home.

These were the days I had dreaded all along, banking on a miracle to save me. Scrolling down employer rejection emails reread a dozen times. They liked my CV, found my cover letter interesting enough, but I was neither a British citizen nor a citizen of the EU, and so they were afraid they could not sponsor my work visa. Each email a copy of the other, but still I read every single line till the end, over and over again. Now, still frantic on job portals for anything I could find, anything to stay on in this country, anything to eke out a living from the first world where I had put all my eggs in and a lot of my father's hard-earned money, his newly purchased apartment.

Now India stared me square in the face.

I overhear the group sitting next to me, they're chatting about the neighbourhood pub and how they badly need a drink. I check the cash reserves on my app earned from my Sainsbury's days. I realise I can afford one too, and definitely needed it. I follow them at a distance, and inside the pub sit at the furthest table.

Sipping my third cider, scrolling down the job portals still, much the same as in the café, I spot him staring, from the corner of my eye. Scared and thrilled to receive such definite male attention after so long, I stare back, and he smiles cockily from the side of his mouth and twists his bar stool over to face me. That's when I see he is old, unlike the others here, mostly students or young professionals or interns. And unlike them, he seems to have come from the other side of town, West End probably. I can see this in the back of his suit, the cut of his hair, the cufflinks that catch the light, even from this distance.

He is alone and I am alone, and we both know this, the only two people alone in this pub without a partner or a friend. This is why, even after twelve minutes and thirteen seconds of waiting for him to come to me, I go up to him, full of liquid courage, and offer to buy him a drink. He looks at me, my All-Star sneakers and chic, round, gold-tinted glasses that cover half my face, so fashionable amongst the young these days, my high ponytail and my backpack, and says sure, why not, and asks the barman for the most expensive whisky in the house, all of seventeen pounds.

And now it is morning and I am in bed, having slept with a strange man I know nothing about and possibly never will. He emerges from the shower, clean and white, his salt-and-pepper hair combed back neatly, his Harry Winston watch strapped on. Well then, he says and goes to his laptop bag, got to get to work. I sit up straight, covering my naked body with the sheet. He looks at me, smiles, kisses my forehead, ruffles my hair. Take care sweetheart, he says, and then somewhat paternalistically, you have your whole life in front of you. And then walks out, shuts the door and is gone, never having looked back even once.

I shut my eyes and think back to last night. That thrill like electricity up the spine, standing at the cliff edge of the unknown as he corralled me to an expensive hotel suite after the drink I bought him, and the two more he bought me after in the pub, his hand barely brushing the small of my back, making the freshly waxed hair on my arms stand on end, even as we undressed the minute we stepped into the room, even as all the fucking was mixed with an icy fear that I would be robbed, raped, murdered, liver and spleen, strangled with my own intestines, my fingers, each toe cut, smashed and scattered across the Thames, a cold case lying in some local London cop house for eternity, the fear heightened by the coke we took that he produced magically from his jacket pocket, drying my mouth further, making my heart race, making the world spin.

This grey morning, alone and naked on this giant king-size bed, the click of his exit on the door so clean, it occurs to me, as I hear the patter of the gentle English drizzle outside once again, that none of this happened. I was not, in fact, murdered last night, nor was I raped. I gave myself and took from him fully, willingly. My organs were – are – all still intact. And except for the throbbing hangover, the after-effects of the coke that kept my nerves jangled through the night, I was, am, in fact alive and well. The night as eventful or uneventful as any night like this could be. He was mildly interesting, mostly polite, but without much personality. And then it occurs to me – something that is much more plausible. He was hiding himself on purpose, behind a mask of his own making.

I began to realise that everything, or most things he told me about his life, was probably fiction – his two daughters, his apartment in Chelsea, his recent divorce.

Even his profession.

Almost all night, we were up.

What do you do exactly? I had asked after a final glass of wine.

I'm a virus of the stock market, he said.

I looked at him quizzically.

It's like a game of cards, an abacus really.

Driving the stocks up and down – that's what I do for a living, he said further by way of explanation when I did not say anything.

Like a composer? I asked

He laughed. More like a surgeon. I watch the indicator of the stock exchange go up and then come down. That makes me feel like I am in control of this life, the financial heart of the economy. I enjoy inventing the games that I play myself. I am a bull-cartel man.

He said this flatly, as though repeating a mantra he had set out for himself.

A bull-cartel man, I said to myself in my head. Bull-cartel, bull-cartel. It sounded familiar and powerful and sinister and exciting all at once.

How much money did he make, on an average day?

Money? he said. Ha ha ha.

And that was that.

He could be a Russian oligarch with political connections up among the highest ranks of the Kremlin. An IT genius with offshore companies across the Bahamas. Or he could be the bull-cartel man he claimed he was, the virus of the stock market. Either way, it made no difference. It was just a harmless, meaningless night with a strange, rich, foreign man. And that's all it would remain.

And now it is time for me to go home and get on with it.

I get up, get dressed, washed, brushed, all of the things one needs to do to get on with it. But when I go to pick up my bag, I see a large white envelope beside it. I open it and see a stack of clean and crisp fifty-pound notes neatly lined up. Five hundred pounds.

I blink. I cannot believe it. I look up at a phantom camera, some stray audio device, pull out my phone to deactivate any vague trace of spyware, but there is none.

I was not expecting this, but as I count the notes, it seems obvious, natural, like my father's suggestion to get a job and earn a living when I had run out of his money. Like me working part-time at Sainsbury's to be able to afford an occasional drink at the student bar with my classmates.

Why would he not have paid me?

Quickly, quickly, I stuff the envelope into my backpack and take the tube back to the student accommodation, checking and rechecking if the buttons of my shirt are all done, my bra strap not undone. I sit on my bunk, no roommate in sight, and count the notes again.

Five full hundred quid. I can't believe it. All this money for what? For just a dance, a performance, a silly act.

I am filled with myself. Almost on a whim, I get back up and leave the student accommodation, back into the tube, a change at Piccadilly all the way to Harrods. Still on a whim, I buy an expensive sweater, a pair of shoes, a silk scarf. I ogle at and even almost buy the expensive perfume. With a click of my newly bought leather pumps, I walk almost all the way back to the student accommodation.

And crossing Waterloo Bridge west to east, I take out the soft beige cashmere sweater from the black shopping bag and wear it right there on top of my jacket, drape the teal silk scarf around me, smiling widely at every passing pedestrian, harried-looking worker and student rushing to class, at every mother and daddy wheeling prams.

I smile widely at everyone.

I look up at the sky that has switched from grey to a picture-book-perfect blue, as only a London sky can do. I laugh out loud, take in the wide expanse of London, the south bank of the Thames out front, the city stretching all around – from the Shard like a glinting lightning bolt, a crystal ice spear on the far left, to the London Eye curving around the bend in the river to the right. The stately Somerset House looming behind. Standing here, in the middle of Waterloo Bridge, facing the city that was once city to the whole world, these soft clothes draping my body, I feel as though I am at the centre of the whole known universe.

I take out my wallet from my backpack, count my notes again, just to be sure, right in the centre of the bridge.

Keep the rest for the days back home.

And it is only while sitting in the terminal that night, awaiting my flight after the rush and the packing, the paperwork and last-minute magnet buying for my family back home, do I realise who he is.

I Google him just for a lark and see his name and face plastered all over the internet. It seems he had no reason to hide himself after all.

My first client in the escort business, it turns out, was a bear operator, the bull-cartel man he claimed he was. The founder of massive trading cartels that manipulated the price of company stocks across manufacturing, retail, but mostly infrastructure, destroying market value worth millions of pounds, creating mountains of phantom wealth for himself and his partners.

I was intrigued. I read and read, but didn't know exactly what it all meant, what exactly he did, how exactly he created all this wealth and if any of it was real, if one could actually go to a bank and cash in on this money. I wanted to know more, understand it all, be a part of his world and the spectral games he played. I flew back to India knowing somewhere, at the back of my mind, that this business of escorting, as I realised that that was indeed what I had unknowingly done, this high-net-worth game would set the course for the days to come.

---

And now, as I watch the future of this city building in front of me, too stubborn to apply for a conventional nine-to-five job, too cranky, I think of the bull-cartel man.

I scroll down WhatsApp, way, way down, and visit the links to the websites he messaged me the night I landed home a few months ago, two nights after I spent the night with him. Websites for high-class escorts, to match the wildest dreams of every high-class client. At first I didn't pay much attention, not wanting to jump into anything risky as better sense prevailed after the first rush of euphoria on Waterloo Bridge the morning after.

You're a glamour whore, he messaged me randomly, many weeks after the website links. Completely out of the blue, no hello, how are you, how is India, are you working these days. Straight to you're just a whore to the gods of glamour. I know girls like you. You chase rich men, sleep with them, grab handouts thrown to you – expensive cars, perfumes, designer dresses. It's not love you're looking for, obviously, not even money, though there's the welcome benefit of it, of course . . . but no, it's the chase you're after. You like being with powerful men. That knot of fear in your stomach, a gun under your pillow. I know a dozen or more girls just like you.

I go back to his message, read it again and again and again, furious, annoyed. Intrigued. Then go back to my room, firmly shut the door of the balcony so the male nurse cannot judge me any more as he flicks ash from his cigarette.

But before I sleep that night, I check the links to the websites he shared many months ago.

---

The lights are out. Someone must have tampered with the electricity again, drained it off from our apartment complex into theirs. Some fracas with another builder, the local corporation on strike maybe. I'm in the bathroom! I yell out, and I am only just beginning the night, I mutter to myself. I tell my father not to worry, I'm fine, to go back to bed please.

Just go, for God's sake.

Darkness, silence. I open the cabinet in the bathroom and take out the torch. Batteries in order, perfect.

From the light flashing on each breast I take photos on my phone – the curve of my stomach, the inside of my thighs, first from a distance, and then nearer, the full nipple with its gritty edge, the other one flaccid, prickled gooseflesh on pale skin. Then I turn to the mirror and take some more photos, full frontal nude, from the back. With clothes but without the bra, with just the top, then with just the jeans. All kinds of combinations. After a whole series, I put on my mobile data and upload the album on the website. I hold the small of my waist tight and marvel at my own shapeliness.

I call myself a nymph, my online moniker NymPH23052 on the website shared by the bull-cartel man, and then some less high-class ones, ones for hookers of less high-class calibre that I find after about two minutes of research.

I imagine myself to be a spirit, a spectre from beyond the mundane realms of this world, of the boring lives that these men lead, their routine office affairs and the affairs of their families and companies and governments. A teasing nymph with the power to vanish forever any second, at just a tap of a finger on the touchpad.

And as I am taking more photos, as I am uploading more, the comments trail through, first a few, a little hesitant, then more brazen. Wow! They say, Hawwwt! Show us a little more. And so I do. One eye always on the ticker that tells how many have visited my page. And before I know it there's a whole flood of men with photos, numbers, addresses. Offers for free holidays in Dubai or Phuket or Seychelles, dinners at five-star hotels, long drives and invitations for pool parties. Just half a naked breast and these men flog themselves before me, making eternal promises of togetherness, of undying love. At first I enjoy these nights, an online carnival with the insomniacs, the perverts, the lonesome, the human, each one of us hiding behind our blown-up, photoshopped, sometimes painfully wrinkled bodies. Wearing our genitals on open display like masks.

Faster and faster the men flock, leaving trails of comments: Hi baby, I love you, kudi Punjab di roxx, please baby please. More men on the internet than in the whole world. The first few nights I am surprised, excited, wondering where they have all come from, where they go in the mornings. But over time I realise that the same men are here every night, sometimes using aliases in order not to appear desperate or lonely, fooling only themselves. I know because they make the same spelling mistakes, the same grammatical errors, or use the same old baits – I have a farmhouse in Mehrauli, my friend has a stake in this hotel or that, I own two apartments in Gurgaon, fully furnished, the owner of this restaurant is a good friend, my family have been members of the Gymkhana since the British, or even hey gurl, tomorrow is Tuesday, which means Vodafone Tuesday, which means free film tickets for the late late show . . . emoticon with tongue out.

The same men, every night, approaching the same women, with the same boredom, the same need.

I do this on these nights, on and off, when the mood strikes, without schedule, without any sense of purpose or agenda. When the days are long and the nights could still be full of hope. I place photographs of myself online, sometimes tastefully nude, sometimes crassly naked, at first teasing and then later, more lurid, keep up with this slow seduction for hours, drop stale breadcrumbs on the way for the men who come, always so ravenous for any scrap.

But I keep my head about me.

I never, ever show them my face. I never give out my phone number, address, never ever tell them which city I am in. And I never go to meet them. I say I will, gleefully fix dates and appointments but never go. Instead I give fake names, fake phone numbers, fake email addresses, promising fake meetings, dates at coffee shops, bars and restaurants across the city.

Every night, legions of men abound, hovering around the women on these websites. Posting photos of their cocks, ugly, bulging testicles and hairy paunches protruding over, videos of their wedding or anniversary nights with their wives or girlfriends, with or without their knowledge. Then they rate these videos, comment, fight over them, spar, compete, make recommendations or forward references, tell each other they have a bigger dick than the other, they can fuck better, harder, give it to her good, post videos the next night of themselves doing just this.

And on and on it goes.

And so in the pitch dark night, as my father and grandfather and his male nurse lie a few metres away, separated from me and each other by a wall and a door bolted shut, I sit myself naked on the toilet and do all this. To get excited, to try to forget these mourning men outside, my mother rooted to the house in Bombay, to ring out the silence that is our family way.

And it's always like this, every night, the same routine. I sign in, upload the photos, wait. Then watch myself being watched, studied, slowly feel the desire of these men for me, individually and then all of them at once, the whole lot of them, the whole legion. I heat up, feel the sticky dampness, and suddenly I am very wet and I want to do something about it, jab something inside, fit it, contain a man within. And as I am getting myself ready, spreading my legs slowly, I see these men that keep coming through the night, these deluded, desperate, horny men, young and old, retired colonels, dutiful bureaucrats, corrupt businessmen, corporate whizz-kids, men who are members of their apartment complex committees, heads of the family, men that allow their wives to eat only after they have, never with them, who smirk silently at their wives' involvement in women empowerment projects and charities for educating the girl child, men who organise their building's Diwali celebrations, and even at sixty, even at sixty-five, still touch the feet of their dying mothers. They never stop, these men, they just keep at it, throwing free holidays and gifts at my feet, raising the bar for each other through the night as though I were up for auction, pinging me desperately at 3 a.m. . . . now 3.30 a.m.

And, looking at these multitudes, whole armies of men that wash up on the shore, a sadness overcomes me, a wastefulness. I feel sorry for them – hiding on their couches, beneath sheets, in bathrooms, so desperate for just a flashing breast, a glimpse of a passing thigh, clutching at the raw flesh of a stranger through their screens; feel sorrier for myself, my wretched self, crouching tight in the bathroom, a ghost in the bright light of the phone.

I sigh, the night once pregnant with possibility, now almost done, once again, and once again it has amounted to nothing.

I sign out of my account, turn off the phone. It shuts down with a blink.

The electricity is still out, the humidity suddenly pressing. Still sitting on the toilet, the wail of an insomniac pigeon in the nook outside the window.

Just beyond the tight mosquito net, the swollen cheese moon, too large to be real.

Offline, the night so silent.

This could be the end of the world, or already another one.

Something must be done to climb back into the one left behind.

I turn on the cold shower. Masturbate forlornly. Cry out. Exhaust myself. And finally, I fall asleep as the first bird sings at dawn.

And the pleasure, when it comes, extinguishes nothing.

---

All these nights that end nowhere, with nothing, barely pleasure even, just cheap, easy relief.

And no prospects too, nothing to gain from. I wake up in the mornings with a vague sense of remorse as I doomscroll through the job openings again. Wondering how I will face the weekend again and the unaffordable bills that came all too suddenly after those carefree margarita nights with the girls, the nights about town with my friends and their girlfriends, and their boyfriends and their combined professional and personal successes. How I can face talk of their diversified investment portfolios, the astute financial plans they are making, the insurance schemes they have already invested in.

Wondering about the rest of my life.

And then, the spectre of the loan looming over these routine, nagging worries. My father's giant eyes behind his spectacles following me around all day in worry.

I need to lose all scruples.

Now, in the day, I take my laptop, shut the door and set to work.

---

A pimp calls me all of ten minutes after I have put out my real number. I'm surprised by his smooth English. He sounds protective almost instantly.

You should blur photo Madam-ji, he says. First blur photo, delete Facebook profile which has your number up, then we talk. Please, Madam, aapke bhale ke liye, there are just too many cheapos in this business. He talks to me like I am seventeen, which makes sense, I realise, since he has seen only my photo, knows nothing else. I always did look younger than I was. OK I say, and do everything he says.

When I call him back he says he will send me a contract, that an electronic signature will be valid, explains the commission he will take, the code of secrecy that must be maintained. OK, I say offhandedly. OK, OK, OK. And then he adds that his clients are all top class, that their lives are at stake as much as anyone else's and so they too want to keep it all a secret. He seems reliable, concerned even. But then I think of being tied up to him, business hassles, read other escorts' views on the fallbacks of networking, how the cops can trace you easily and all that, and really consider what I'm getting into. Almost immediately, I block his number and decide I can always freelance, join the growing workforce of the young hustling their way through the gig economy.

So for a few months I do this, scope through these self-same websites, this time blurring my face, targeting those I think will be reliable, prove trustworthy as my clients. Those who I can take on in the spirit of a business partner. And then I meet these men in the lobbies and lounges of hotels across the city, depending on where they're put up – The Park, Taj, Oberoi, in the heart of the city. Honchos, managing directors, and then in Gurgaon or some new four-star deluxe hotel on the wayside, in and around Aerocity, mid-level corporate honchos looking for some casual fun. I surprise myself with my acumen and judgement, always spot on. I walk into the lobby, watch the old pianist rapt on his Steinway, belt out Bach or Mozart, oblivious to the goings-on in the hotel. I stroll to the coffee shop, marvel at the choux pastry treats placed delicately behind the glass panes. Later, I begin to make an effort with a touch of lipstick, bracelets, the right kind of shoes, or a bindi. And then there is the call.

Dinner is usually brought by room service, except with the foreigners, who have no reason to hide. In the Italian restaurants I chat with them about their jobs, their industry, their home country, their serene meditation retreats in Kerala and the horror stories of what Goa has become over salad and aglio e olio pasta, sipping the finest, driest wine I secretly cannot bear, until I realise I am already drunk.

In the room there is always the same pattern – a little talk, skimming the surface of politics and the economy. My nervous babbling about the alarming ascendency of China to fill the silence. And finally, what I have been trying to get at all evening – what brings them to India.

Investment.

India, they tell me, this bountiful, bottomless geyser of plenty. This country propping up an eternal fountain of youth, such frenzied energy in the air always, such dynamism, it's irresistible. They come to invest in the megalith IT giants, the mid-level software companies, some risking their bets on the promising million startups venturing into blockchain technology and digital payments that have mushroomed across the land.

I ask them what they consider the country's potential and the crucial sectors in the coming years, ask for forecasting tips, inquire after particular sectors, some specifics about their investments – which industry, which geography, what kind of growth potential, at least who they plan to meet. But after answering a few questions, they look straight at me, sigh, already tired of my sharp questions like arrows. They give me a weak smile and then look outside the window at the black cityscape.

Ok, no more shop talk, they say.

There is abrupt silence for a moment or two, a hand on the thigh.

And then it follows.

I barely think of the men the day after and I'm sure they don't think of me too. Bland, boring men, avuncular even. Nice, model men of the global economy, good fathers and husbands. Doing their job and then going back home to their families. Moderately concerned for my well-being, wondering why I couldn't take up a decent job, do something more conventional, less morally problematic perhaps, but not inquiring much after. Leaving me alone. They make recommendations to each other, forward my referral, and so I meet more such nice, bland men along the way. I am able to support myself decently.

And the next morning, after he leaves for his 9 a.m. board meeting, I fill the tub, pour out the bubble bath soap and step inside, sink myself into the warm foam and lie back. Relax my aching body. Then head for a lavish, free buffet breakfast, filling the plate with slices of paper-thin ham, salad, rye bread a whole bowl of muesli with real raspberries, and the darkest, richest coffee. I ask the waiter for another cup. He says, certainly Madam.

I am beside myself.

How quickly these days slip by, how smoothly, without fuss or drama.

At home of course, I tell my father I am visiting friends, an old girlfriend is getting married soon and she wants me to come over every night to help her shop for her wedding lehenga, her sangeet outfit, a shimmery gown for her cocktail youngsters-only night. And then a few more evenings to buy the matching shoes. He is happy I am finally getting out of the house, mingling with people my age again. It's nice to have someone to share your troubles and dreams with, he adds, as I nod my head and smile.

Coddled in the sheets, he's sleeping besides snoring lightly, turned the other way. I watch the shows on NDTV GOODTiMES, designers throwing tantrums, bridezillas in the making, friends and family cheering the gorgeous couple as the destination wedding comes to its end on the beaches of Bali, or cooking organic, vegan meals, a dash of French mustard, a sprinkle of freshly ground cayenne pepper, or power yoga sessions on the beach and in the courtyards of traditional houses in Kerala, the elite of our nation glowing and abundant in their health, with all their wealth.

Enough. Or there's no end to this. I press the button, the TV blinks off.

---

This was my life now and I could scarcely believe it – even though my father's worried face still told me he sensed something was amiss, even though his retreats to the prayer room that increased every day annoyed me further, even though thoughts of my mother floating somewhere in Bombay far away from everyone . . . all kept me tethered to the real world.

But at least now I save bank aunty's number on my phone. Now I pick up her calls on the first ring instead of avoiding them for days. And to bank aunty's shrill voice inquiring after the status of my instalments, at least now I arrange secret meetings with her, transferring white money bit by bit, converted from my seedy cash earnings. At least now I was slowly less and less in debt, though of course I had to invent a part-time work-from-home job to explain the accruing loan repayments. Content writing in a tech startup, I tell my father, same as I have told bank aunty, and even make a fake contract to show him, forging logos and signatures.

And then one day I get a WhatsApp message as I leave some five-star hotel or the other. The bull-cartel man, Russian, Ukrainian, Georgian, who really knew. The mysterious pied piper who unwittingly led me into this strange, make-believe world.

He says he is coming to town and wants to see me. I become excited almost immediately, but at the same time I also don't want to see him and wonder if I should ignore his message. After all, I don't want him to know this is what

I have become, that I have walked openly into his very prophecy, a glamour whore, using my body when I have such a bright mind full of potential to do a hundred things or more.

But here I was, leaving a client's five-star nest, making plans to visit a few more as the week progressed, making forty thousand rupees or more per week in hard, safe cash, more money than I had ever dreamed of, responsibly earning my keep for the loan, keeping the family hearth burning with Amazon goodies and fine Italian cookies in place of Good Day biscuits, chocolate bars made of real cocoa sweetened with date syrup instead of refined white sugar.

But there is no point hiding anything, I realise, he would know anyway, captain of his hidden, nameless monopoly of an industry. I might as well see him. And so that evening, telling my father and grandfather I am visiting another friend who needs an accomplice to go menu testing for her engagement party, I go to see him in any one of those hushed self-same hotels in the heart of Lutyens I know so well by now.

I knock twice, discreetly. He opens the door, gives me a curt and professional side hug and says, well well, you look well. And then almost immediately he says, so there's somebody I'd like you to meet.

---

The first meeting at first, then the next, then another two weeks later. Nothing unusual, nothing too different, much the same as the others. That same partially bored vibe, the sex much like the others. Wanting to finish quickly. I wonder why he – all of them – bothers if he just wants to finish, doesn't even seem like he enjoyed it.

Like an addiction they need to keep up. Such drudgery. The fucking and then the quiet, going to the window for a smoke, coming back to bed, falling asleep almost the next instant, off to meetings the next morning on the dot at 8 a.m.

But he leaves me money. He leaves me more than I can ever dream of. Almost double, sometimes more than what the others leave. I can't believe it. Is this what he normally gives girls? In a crisp, white envelope by the bedside table, every single time, so it's the first thing I see when I wake. Thick notes filling up the envelopes. I wake up, count the notes one by one very carefully and, pleased with myself, begin my day with a jolt in my step, applying lip gloss after my bath, whistling in my head all the way to the breakfast buffet in the hotel, fluffy American-style buttermilk pancakes in Smoke House DELI.

I am intrigued. Why leave so much if all this is such a bore? Why do it at all?

And as I sit there chomping down my pancakes, drinking my freshly squeezed orange juice I realise that there is something about him I cannot quite pin down, put my finger on. As though this boredom that he wears is just an act and inside he desires me with all his easy money. He desires me but doesn't want to and so conceals it from himself, but reveals it to me by throwing all this cash at me. Unlike the others, whom I never think about the minute I leave the room the next morning, he leaves me with a dull thud of wanting – of needing.

I needed to know everything about him, needed to tear open that mask. And so I googled him on my phone through the intermittent signal in the elevator on the way up to my apartment the next day. And that's when I realised who he was – one of the top three builders in Delhi, with diversified interests in telecom and retail. Media investigations cited his market share, his personal wealth, speculated over his connections with municipal authority figureheads, politicians, IAS officers across the chain of command, other real estate tycoons and businessmen. I couldn't believe how long it took me to figure out who he is. All I had to do was a Google search, and there he was, splashed all over the internet.

And as I scoured his company website as I reached my room, I saw Casablanca listed as one of the top key projects. Casablanca Phase A, where I lived, but Phase B, C, D, all the way to F, currently under development too, although under-construction apartments in all these blocks were already up for sale. I couldn't believe I didn't know this.

And then there was the shopping mall, one of India's largest, three massive convention centres, more land acquired for schools, hospitals, to meet the needs of residents across all the phases of Casablanca. And this was just in sector Delta, Greater Noida. There were other projects in Dwarka and in the north, beyond Rohini and Shalimar Bagh, all dotting the periphery of the city.

I blink. I can't believe who he is, where I have just been, what I have become. I look outside the window, at all that is his, back at my phone at all that is his. Thrilled at this easy proximity to power, fallen like a bolt right into my lap.

And although I didn't know what to do with this knowledge, for rarely if ever did we speak, I knew I had to keep this going with him, this thing, whatever it was, whatever shape or form it took.

And then one night he comes back to bed after a smoke, very quiet as usual. He turns over, as always, and just as I am about to sleep mumbles something. I don't know whether he's talking to himself in his sleep, after all I barely know him, so I keep shut, pretend to be asleep.

He clears his throat and says I just don't know what to do, this time very clearly, turning around, lying on his back, looking at the ceiling. I just don't fucking know you know, a crack in his voice. Pleading for a response from the world.

I swallow my saliva down my painful throat, dried with his cigarette from earlier this evening, very much wanting to say something.

About what? I ask finally, after the silence has gone on too long.

He turns to me, as I turn to him, and I can see the whites of his eyes, red veins branching from the corners.

This morning he tried it again. In the school bathroom of all places. They found him bleeding there, passed out in the cubicle. The principal called us and we rushed. Last month it was his friend's place. Apparently he carries a blade with him in his backpack.

I keep my eyes fixed on his, the shiny whites, the darts again.

I don't understand where I have gone wrong, he says flatly, what I have been doing wrong, voice cracking some more, breathless.

We've given him everything. I work like a dog, like a slave for him, only him. That's why I'm building all this – these apartments, these malls. That's why I struggle all day, risking all these crores, giving bribes, getting bribes. Doesn't he realise how stressful it is for me? Does he think I want to do this? That this is some kind of career choice I have made? That I enjoy this?

A few seconds of awkward silence.

I'm not sure what to say, if I should say anything at all at this point.

Your son? I ask foolishly.

He shakes his head, sighs and says he's just so blinded by his own pain. And then scoffs, typical teenager.

And then, without another word, no more explanation, he gets up, stands upright and goes to the window for another smoke. Slow, deliberate, ruminatively looking out the window at the few passing cars. I keep my eyes peeled on his back. After he is done he lopes back to bed, covers himself with the sheet, looks at me and then turns around on his side.

And just as I am about to turn the other way to sleep, he suddenly grabs me, heaves himself on top of me, and before I know it he is already inside. Fucking me hard, in and out, as though crashing himself, banging his arms and torso, bruising his head over and over against a wall holding all the world's pain, all its chaos, as I cry with pain, with pleasure, as he slams his hands over my mouth, as he sinks inside me, biting my neck, chewing on my skin, spending himself inside me, writhing like an animal as it ends, making love to me with so much loathing for the world, for himself.

After that night, he reveals himself to me, bit by erratic bit, even though I never ask. Because I never ask, don't probe like with the others on their investments and grand financial agendas.

I just listen, nod. He needs me, it is clear to me, much more than he realises.

It begins as always with no drama. Meeting, greeting, a peck on the cheek, dinner, coffee, wine as though brokering a deal. On to the act.

But bang in the middle he stops, pushes me away. Lies back on the bed.

I'm tired of everything, he says to me one night.

Then he tells me about his father, his son. How he is becoming a disappointment to his father, no matter all this money, this soaring ambition, these glittering cities he is building. How his son disappoints him so much in turn, like karma, he can't stand the sight of him these days, skulking all over the house, hunched over his laptop at odd hours of the night.

Why, I ask, not sure if I am asking about the disappointment of the father or the son, but he tells me of both anyway.

Of his father's chemical processing company he's almost entirely liquidated. His father built it in the sixties, back when building any business was so difficult, you needed permits and licences for every small thing. But his father put in a lot of work and it had gained prestige over time. Nothing remains of it today except on paper. He sold it off, and with this fresh investment moved into real estate. He knew this was where the big league was, he enjoyed the glamour of it. He wanted to make his mark in a real, tangible way.

But he didn't realise when he was setting it up that he would have to spend his days not being a builder but doing what he has never really liked. Perhaps this is what it meant to 'be a builder', he says, appeasing this MLA's son here, that bureaucrat there, police commissioners, deputy commissioners, JCPs all day. In a way he has it lucky because he just had to step into his father's shoes, his father had already forged some of these connections over the decades, through his extended family, through his relentless potential to network at every wedding, every Diwali card party. Nights at the bar with this one important, that one freshly elected, it was all carefully strategised.

And at some point, he realised, his father was doing it not necessarily to further contracts, not necessarily for the work, but was networking for its own sake. Networking for networking's sake, a weird kind of high.

But the truth is, he doesn't really like it, it feels dirty in ways he can't fully understand. In his heart he's always been a loner, he knows this. But this way of living is necessary, for this is how things work here. How else will the land come to him so easily, how else will he get what he needs – cement and steel, metal and, crucially, labour – at such subsidised rates. And how else will he make his revenues too, because so many of those investing in his apartment complexes are those granting him these subsidies in the first place – for themselves, for their extended families, a cousin here, an uncle there, for their networks in turn, to park all their cash.

Win-win for everybody.

Except that he's tired of it lately.

He can't explain it, can't understand why he feels like this these days, but he's become weary of this constant appeasement, this deal here and that deal there, this constant mental ticker inside his brain calculating his profit margin, how he is secretly screwing the other party over. This need to keep your guard up all the time because if you don't there's always someone else – a politician, a bureaucrat, another builder – to fuck you over.

But recently he's stopped caring, refusing deals with the people that matter. He's been losing favour with the politicians who have been complaining to his father, and his father to him. It's unbelievable, he says, here I am building an empire worth a thousand crore rupees and I'm still answerable to my father.

And then adds, almost as an afterthought, but that's how it should be.

I blink into the night by way of response. I can't understand his world.

But my son doesn't get any of this, he continues, almost without pause, and I realise that he's in a monologue. I am just the listening prop, although a necessary one.

True, he's only fourteen, but at fourteen I was so focused, studying hard, going for my engineering entrance test classes to get into IIT without fail thrice a week, even though I never wanted to go to IIT, although I did sit for the entrances and clear the exam. But I did it just to prove to myself I could. To prove to the old man I could do whatever I set my mind to. That I wouldn't be dependent on him.

I knew I was going to follow in my dad's business at twenty, and that's what I did, didn't question it. But look at him, sitting on his phone all day. I barely see him these days in fact. Almost never talk to him, have no idea what he does after school, if he even attends his classes. I don't know who his friends are, although he doesn't seem to have many.

Have you tried talking to him, I ask, thinking of the most obvious thing to say, pausing him in his tracks.

He looks at me, faces the ceiling again and says you know, it hurts me so much to see him like this, so wrapped up in himself. He was so happy just a few years ago, playing basketball after school every day. So when I eventually went to talk to him last night, although I hadn't decided what to say, I saw his earphones plugged deep inside his ears. And so I just left him playing Grand Theft Auto or whatever.

Obviously, he's tried to kill himself twice now, so he must be depressed. There's something so wrong with that boy.

But he doesn't talk to me, locks himself up in the room, and I don't know what to do.

Just adding to my stress, he says, clicking his tongue, shaking his head.

Silence then, as I take in all this.

It's stressful as it is, you know, he says, a few nights later. Half of it is the problem of so much cash – all the cash I need to spend, and that's fine, but what do I do with all this cash that I get? The way I'm going, all the offshore accounts, all the property and gold blocks and funds and investment schemes in the world will not be able to contain it. I have advisers dealing with all this of course, but I too have to always think about it. So I always need to make more, and the more I make the more I need to figure out where and how to keep it.

Then there is the incessant pressure, the acquisitions. I don't want to, but we have to push people off the land you know – farmers, just regular workers, we have to forge false cases, we have to pay off the cops, the lawyers. I don't want to do it this way, but there's no other way of doing it. There's no other way to function. I don't like this violence, but what can I do?

I'm not sure if he expects me to answer, but there is nothing really that I can say, so I keep shut.

And these investments, he says. Just crores upon crores upon crores – I can't differentiate between ten and fifty and hundred any more. I've suddenly become so pliant, so weak these past few months, I've begun to agree to invest anywhere, buy all of it, blankly agree with my advisers too, when they warn me not to.

The thing is, I've stopped caring ever since this happened with my son for the second time. What's the point of it all if I can't even save my own son? Nowadays I just feel like all these apartment complexes and malls are building themselves.

One week later he tells me about the meditation retreat he has returned from the previous night. A little outside Shimla, and his wife insisted on taking him there. Beautiful place, in the lap of snow mountains. He meditated as best as he could but it hasn't helped. Nothing helps except for these Nichiren chants every morning, it's the only thing that keeps him grounded. And then last night, she told him that her guru has advised a havan in the house this Saturday morning with him and his son to cleanse the air, and he doesn't quite know how he feels about it.

She gave him a silver ring with the number 7 engraved on it, also from her guru, and so he wears it just because you don't want to argue.

I say OK, and then he's off again, as though that was all that he needed by way of a listener.

He barely knows his wife these days, he says. He doesn't like who she has become. Everyone at home eats dinner at different times, whenever they want, depending on their schedules. Life is carrying on in its motions, his wife happy and chatty at family functions, his son opening up at dinner parties with his own friends, uncles giving him a sly drink behind his back, his family happy outside the house, like in the billboards advertising his apartment complexes. But back home, stony silence again and he can't figure out what he has done wrong, and they never tell. The only people he really talks openly to in some way are his servants, his cook and driver who have been with the family for thirty years, whom he trusts with his life. And a few of his employees, some of the top management staff. He loves them more than his family, it's true.

How did this happen?

And this moment I want to tell him about my mother, my father, my family, and ask him if he knew what happened to my family too, but he continues, doesn't let me speak –

My parents were frugal, he says. I was born into a rich family, one of the richest in Haryana, but growing up I didn't realise it. We never threw money away, like how people do these days. My wife, she's using this family money to invest in an online fashion shop, but she's just doing it because all her friends are doing the same thing. I don't even think she's interested in fashion. It's bound to fail. And once it fails, she'll start something in interior designing or something. How many of these fashion and design retail startups are there anyway? And my son, I have no idea how much pocket money she gives him every week. I wasn't brought up like that – maids trudging up the stairs to his room with platefuls of mutton kebabs ordered from outside – talking so rudely to me and his mother, if at all. What is he so upset about, he lives like a fucking prince! I wasn't brought up like that. And I hate to see him being brought up this way.

Three days later, he tells me, and he will tell me again, that these days, right in the middle of meetings with development authorities, with investors from the US, with his marketing team, eating dinner alone in the massage chair, at the club, he has begun obsessing again – fantasising as he did about three years ago right after his mother died about walking out one day from his office, his home, wherever it didn't matter, just walking, walking and walking till he reaches the mountains or the ocean. Living out the rest of his days walking across the world, begging for alms. It's what keeps him going, this image of himself in robes and dirty nails and matted locks. Flinging the cash that constantly erupts at his feet to the wind, to the countryside, to the outstretched hands of millions. This, this image of himself and his daily Nichiren meditation keep him going. His meditation is the only time of the day or night he can afford to stop worrying – about the company, about his investments, how his marriage is dissolving, about his son who has become a stranger.

He says all this to no one but me, he tells me. There's no one else I can say this to.

He doesn't want this life any more, it disgusts him, wears him out – the cycle of excess, of anxiety. He wants out. He has tried gurus galore – his wife's and his own, his mother's, his father's. They've given him rings and metal bands and sacred red threads to tie around his wrist. Advised him to add letters to his name, change the layout of his house to face the east. But nothing works, only a complete cutting off, a hacking off, he knows, is what is needed. It's all or nothing. The more he goes in to work every day, the more money he makes, the more he fantasises about throwing it all away.

One day, I will simply disappear, he says after a pause.

I look at him and wonder how far gone he is inside his head. He seems like a well-functioning property developer, at the top of his game, but clearly inside he is barely managing to hold it together for his next meeting. I wonder if he needs help, a psychiatrist, medication to calm his head, a therapist he can talk to. But I know better than to suggest all this after I did one time and he stopped mid-sentence, turned to me, clutched at me and told me he only needed me, no damn psychiatrist. And so I stroke his head and kiss him tenderly, offer him my body that is a receptacle for his worries, my body, my listening, my tenderness that opens him up, like a catalyst that gets him talking.

And the more I listen, the more he talks, the less lonely he becomes, the more comfortable I am with him. The fatter the white envelopes, the crisper the notes.

---

And now.

A month and two weeks since that night.

Bowling with him in this blue alley again, on top of the mall. High above the land he has leased to private corporations, adjacent to a plot he has just bribed his way up the maze of DDA officers to acquire, on which he will build townships guaranteeing first-class lifestyles to the millions that seek it, or that seek returns on investments from the booming Delhi property market which he is a chief player in, as I only too well know now.

I know all this, not because he tells me anything, he barely talks business with me, but because I Google him the minute I leave him. And I Google the brigadier too, fat man. But there's much less about him on the internet. A private Facebook page with a blurred photo. A vague investment portfolio. Nothing else. He is probably an arms dealer, or a contractor like much of the retired army, I think.

But now, in this bowling alley, we're alone except for the waiter in a clownish apron serving popcorn and Coke at the counter and, should we want them, Punjabi samosas. Wherever he goes people hush, make way, sort of bow. Electro-funk plays softly and in another time, a month or two prior, we would have danced to it, right here, he getting turned on by the ease with which I sway, turning me on too with his undistracted attention.

But now only this silence.

Now we watch each other's backs. Vigilant for any stray phrase or word. Strictly sticking to small talk – where shall we go tonight? The mall? The bowling alley? The penthouse?

Earlier tonight when we met, he took a necklace, dangled it in front of me slowly, watched as my eyes trailed along the locket right to left to right. I smiled back sweetly, the monologue still playing in my head – to give my testimony to the cops tomorrow or not – will I, won't I, should I, shouldn't I, with every turn of the pendulum. How foolish I was for so long, playing the ingenue and then falling for my own act, following him around like a trained kitten, not knowing the first thing.

Those first few heady weeks he told me so much about himself. A monologue like a man deranged, as though he was waiting for me his whole life so he could begin to know himself. I thought I knew him at that time, that he had opened up something secret of himself to me.

And then that Friday night that changed everything.

The night that made me question my mind. Did I do too much cocaine? Piled myself with too much booze? I questioned and questioned myself, but no. It was all too clear – the Nepali boy slumped on the toilet seat. I lifted his drooping head, slit eyes wide open. I stifled a scream and dropped him as he slumped back, and I ran back down the stairs, knowing I could still save him.

But I didn't dare.

I ran and hid outside. Then back to the sofa, back to my rightful place at this party of builders and heads of industry – steel works, mining, manufacturing – these politicians, back to my corner of the brigadier's mansion.

Sitting on that sofa, numb to all but these snatches of conversation. They're speaking of a new retrospective in Lado Sarai, in a brand-new studio whose basement has been converted into a gallery for experimental mixed-media installations. The lines are clean, someone says, but the asymmetrical depth was entirely lost on me, says another, bending down to do another line off the coffee table.

I look at them. I have no idea what they're on about.

I shut my eyes, rest my head on the sofa. The butterfly patch is spreading on the ceiling, dripping off his neck from the toilet above us. And this stench that fills the room, his cries – how can they not hear, see?

I look up.

But when I open my eyes, the blood, that stench, disappear, but his moaning rings on, and when I look around I see they're all looking down at me with blank eyes, and by the time I realise it is me, that I am moaning, I am screaming and not the Nepali upstairs, I am carried away by him or them or some of them together and something is forced down my throat and I am locked inside the bedroom on the ground floor, some distance from the lounge where everyone continues to party.

And now, as he sits beside me in this bowling alley and clinks his whisky and Coke with mine, I'm not sure what he knows. Does he know that I saw them, not just the boy in the bathroom but in the small aangan behind, he and the fat man whispering outside the water tank. And then in the morning dark, he caught a shadow watching before I ran back to the bed, to where he had had me knocked out.

I think of the bull-cartel man who may or may not be Russian. I think of telling him, the morning after, what I saw when he drove me home and I pretended to be asleep in the car. After all, he was the one that brought him to me, me to him. He is the only one I can tell, if there was any telling to do. And then I laugh to myself in my head at my naiveté. I barely know the bull-cartel man after all, and who knows how he was connected in all this?

It was best to shut up.

And after that night he shuts up too, as though that night didn't happen, or at least as though nothing strange happened that night, as though it wasn't obvious that both of us knew some poor children had been murdered in that house and we were both very much involved.

Nothing through these six weeks – just the chase, the mind games, the fucking like a chore. And taking a cue from him I realise the best thing to do, for now at least, is to follow his lead and pretend like nothing happened.

And it's only now that I realise that there is so much I don't know about him. So much I thought I knew, but can never know. Whether he is tired of his life and still wants to escape it all, or whether it remains an escapist fantasy. He comes inside me, and I take all of him in, but we know nothing of each other. Tense silence. Checking himself these days before he speaks about his spoiled son, his beautiful wife. Shutting up just in time.

I return again and again to the websites about him bookmarked on my browser – his company website, his personal website, news articles, interviews. Rereading about his vast market share, his speculated personal and business wealth, his close ties with anyone and everyone important, his offshore accounts in the Bahamas, his shell companies in Singapore. And I realise what I am set up against were I to open my mouth.

After that night I don't see other men any more. I deactivate my account from the sex sites, even though he has never told me to, doesn't seem to care about what I do away from him. I come to see him in these strange places, in this blue bowling alley on a Tuesday night, so empty it almost feels private, and then I realise it is.

Although I itch to ask him who, what, why – always at the tip of my tongue – some better sense, a kick in the shins, some grounded sense of self-preservation prevails, and I stop.

And so we don't talk of that night, the black hole that swallows conversation, and talk less and less as time passes. He doesn't tell me any more about his family – of the disappointments passing through the bloodline from father to son. Of his fantasies of running and leaving it all behind. We don't tell each other how lonely we are, separately and together. But still we meet, an addiction we are too feeble to kick, a bad habit too old. And so we still meet on these stone-silent dates, driving each other wild, further up the wall of isolation.

And now.

I watch him bend, each finger in each hole as he drops the ball and I watch it roll and smash into all ten pins. He turns around and walks back and I know it is my turn next.

So I lift my glass of whisky and Coke, finish it with one neat swig. Get up and pick up the ball with a sudden levity that only a keen sense of drunkenness can bring. Conscious again of the electro-funk playing in the background. But then there is a buzzing, like a bee from behind, and surprised, I turn and watch him, the dead weight of owls on his eyes chanting the Lotus Sutra. I turn and drop the ball, it smashes into all pins but two.

Old Man. Sick Man. Dead Man.

I watch the ball disappear into a netherworld of blue balls to rest among all his secrets – his crores in fraud, his sophisticated tax-evasion schemes, his sweet-talking the politicians, his scamming the public of their hard-earned money. He was tired of it all not long ago, but now it seems all that has disappeared.

I look at the alley and think of how I lifted her dead body, along with him and the brigadier, throwing her in the pit. His eyes bored into the side of my face in the car the next morning, perhaps wondering why I helped when there was no need.

And then I think of something else I hadn't considered before – if I did that, what else did I do that night? Smother her? Cut her open? An accomplice to her murder, or a murderer too, like you, like the fat man?

And that's when I realise that we're in this together, whatever happens, and this is something I cannot escape.

---

Long days and longer nights in tense limbo, barely breathing. We meet, we barely talk. We fuck, we drink, I obsess over that night, but nothing happens.

Paying back my loan from the money I made from clients, from him, bit by bit to bank aunty, but nothing else. Telling my worried father I would take care of it, not to get involved. I was an adult now, I could manage, I had savings from my Sainsbury's days. Also that I had had another job babysitting for an Austrian couple thrice a week in England. He is suspicious at first, probes me. But the lies fall out so convincingly I almost believe them myself. They were in the same town as the university Daddy, but at the other end, just twenty minutes away. The parents both working, the father in banking, the mother in the marketing division of a publishing company, and I heard of this job through my classmate Nila who had worked with them earlier but wanted to focus on her assignments now. That's all

Daddy. That's it. A three-year-old son, who loved drawing dinosaurs, that's all.

David, I add, his name was David, even though he never asked.

And then he asks me how my content writing job with Suntech is going. Shit, I think. Shit. Shit.

Amazing, I say, appraisals are in a few months. Isn't there an office you have to go to, he asks. No, no Daddy, I say, it's a work-from-home model. And when he looks at me searchingly I say it's a new-age thing, and he shrugs his shoulders and for a while at least seems sort of convinced.

He shuts the door of my room again and I shut my laptop, breathe. I would have to be more careful, to keep careful track of all the lies.

But at least partially, I am relieved. And life goes on much the same as before. Not getting a job, not getting on. Waiting, watching, waiting.

Meanwhile the scaffolding mounts, labourers climb higher, concrete grazes the sky. During the day he is signing the papers that are making all this happen, hiring lawyers and crushing the claims of activists, consulting the best accountants at dinner parties and lobbies of hotels in the nerve centre of the city, or in the satellite townships of Gurgaon and Noida, over the finest scotch with Yanni in the background, not a trace of corpse stench. The deal closed over hard cash in a suitcase with clasps that reflect the solid palms of the men that exchange it.

Hating this life perhaps, as he once told me, but making it happen nonetheless.

And me? I can do nothing but wait. To see where this goes. To let the situation run its course.

And so I walk a lot these days, up and down my apartment as they sleep in the dead of night after I come home from our dates. Get up with a strange zealous vigour that emerges from the bone up, surprising even myself, and walk. Silently, with the fluffy slippers on – from my bedroom to the bathroom to the alcove and back; from the crowded puja room to the kitchen to the balcony of neglected plants and back.

And earlier in the day, round and round the apartment complex, to the gym, an auto and long metro ride away, Jor Bagh Park from my childhood, another metro ride to Connaught Place, the stuff of Sunday childhood dreams, round and round.

And also, and a lot, in the nearby malls. I tell my dad I need to go to the cafe to work, and walk.

I walk a lot, walk in the malls these days, these giant, looming malls that dot the edge of the city, scattered all over the outer suburbs, the ones he may or may not own.

With nowhere to go, and nothing to do, I walk like a ghost in the malls these days. Waltz through sliding panels, through the revolving doors. Pat down at security looking jaded for the checker, impatient as I grab my bag, as though I have friends or colleagues to meet, appointments to keep.

I slide past the canvas strips of security, out into the icy blast.

I know the layout like the back of my hand now. I was here just yesterday, and know I will be here tomorrow, but still I pause to take in everything as if crash landing on another planet. To the left there's a new promotion offer today, yesterday's Alto replaced by a pale-gold Honda City, festooned with the same giant red ribbon. To the right ladies-who-brunch are getting free makeovers, or skin consultations, or blow-dries. It must be Women's Wicked Wednesday, I realise, and confirm with my Google Calendar.

On these mid-week afternoons, the malls done up for the season of festivals are swollen with boredom, awaiting the weekend rush.

Across the mall, silhouettes with bags slung across shoulders laugh to each other as a subdued saxophone plays. I stare at the flexes that fall five floors down, displaying models of every race and colour in flowy, asymmetrical clothing, curling around each other, pouting in shades of neon lipstick. And the screen changing every second, models sashaying down the streets of New York, or Milan or Paris, some urbane promenade in the Mediterranean or the Caribbean, some real or imagined global city outside of this world, this time and place, they are laughing now but gracefully, having fun, staring seductively at the camera, hiding the secrets of their luck and success.

I watch all this, and watch the others, watch them watch all this – retail piling on itself, rising through the glass panels to the cloudless Delhi sky. The mall reflects this light, a white haven of possibilities. A chance to forget the world outside. A chance to forget the Nepali boy whose throat was slit in the bathroom, the small girl I threw into the pit with him, dead I thought, but could she still have been alive? Those two then, but how many before, how many after?

Stop it, I yell inside my head, STOP! I push the click and reel away, lock up the rapidly flicking pictures deep inside my head somewhere, throw away the keys.

Now walk determinedly to Nike, Adidas, Puma, trying on the latest sneakers, back to Levi's now pulling on new hip-fitting jeans, so soft to the touch, the T-shirts made from organic cotton with bold quotes – Netflix N Chill, There is No Planet B, Keep Calm and Coffee On, Hustlin' Hard.

Now to the cosmetics section. I stand before a wall of wellness products – a shampoo for every texture, a face wash for every blemish, squinting my eyes to read the ingredients on every bottle or tube or container. The tiny salesgirls in tight black shirts and pants with dripping lips and shimmering teal eyelids swoop like vultures. They look up at me, give me advice for my skin, point to a cream, a lotion, a moisturiser-toner for the day routine, after-toner for the night routine. Feel through the dry hair, click their tongues in unison and shove four bottles in my face.

I look down at a full bucket of fried chicken wings under my nose. Look down at the coffee creamer under my nose, the donuts with rainbow sparkles, the cookies with unicorns and wonder if the Nepali was beaten somewhere else first and then dragged to the bathroom? What were they expecting, leaving him comatose on the toilet like that? I wonder what happened to her body after we threw her in the pit. Was she burnt? Was Nepali the morning after we left? Does anything remain – an organ, a joint, a stray and tiny ear bone?

It's all a blur, thick fog masks that night and I don't remember anything properly after I was knocked stiff in the room. I only clearly remember the Nepali slumped in the bathroom, the muffled scream of a young girl. There could or could not have been a fire. At the end, I was next to her body on the ground in the backyard of the house, carrying her with them, throwing her like a soiled sanitary napkin into the pit, turning around, feeling nothing.

I shake my head, close my eyes, blank out my brain. I take a moment.

Then open my eyes and wonder what the hell I should do with myself.

Suddenly the children's train wails its arrival with a panda, a lion and a bear popping out of each bogie. And beside them sit the children – delighted, scared, some waving to their parents who take photos on their phones as the train goes around the mall, the passengers getting on and off, on and off as the train chimes – Hush my darling, don't fear my darling the lion sleeps tonight . . .

And I hum to myself even as the train chugs to the end of the mall, don't fear my darling, don't fear, because nothing can happen, you're safe with him, you're in it together, he's too big to be taken down, as I push against the click and reel that crouches in the grass waiting to pounce, as I spend the rest of the day gliding up and down the mezzanine floors, as I sit in Cookie Jar or McCafe, blow bubbles into the chocolate shake, jab at the ice with the straw, chew at its plastic end for hours, telling myself not to fear because the lion sleeps tonight.

But the noises – all noises, a mother calling her son into the coffee shop, the ping of a card machine, a child screaming – have become louder. I jump at passing headlights on my way to the mall, I jump at the shrill whistle of the security guard. I look at life all around that somebody, somewhere monitors on a screen.

I glance at my vibrating phone. The list of reminders drops down – the apps that need updating, the mobile bill that needs to be paid, new cashback offers from MakeMyTrip and Google Pay and Swiggy, my Paytm balance too low. Newsletters from organisations I signed up for but never cared about, new posts piling in my inbox, the tweets, someone has tagged me again in an unknown album on Facebook, the notifications ringing alarm bells off the hook.

I get up. Ride the escalators up and down, watch my inverted self in the mirror above, on the polished panels on either side – misaligned, the head and torso prised a degree apart, my pale face ballooning. A deer caught in the headlights. The kajal smudged and ugly. Frizzled knots of hair framing the face.

And walking past the rows of mannequins like stoic mutants – bald, emaciated, draped in flowing haute couture, devoid of features, still managing to look distressed with noses up in the air, staring vacantly with hollows melted into their faces for eyes, like the kaftan-draped women from that night discussing the retrospective in the Lado Sarai basement in art shows in New York or Berlin they saw a month earlier. The women of his world. Featureless, inscrutable. I stop in front of one and reach my hand out to touch her face.

And then the shop attendant jumps to life, as if from nowhere, and says, may I help you Madam?

I walk on.

The future is a white wall that stares me in the face in the apartment, where my mind wanders wild, then jumps to the film reels of that night – the Nepali I know for sure by now, and of course the girl. But who really is the fat man, the brigadier? Who is he, I had wondered as I saw him catch me peeping through the curtain and I ran back to the bed. How does he know him? What is this connection between them? Are they just friends? Do they have some kind of a business connection?

Inevitably, this happens.

So I avoid home like the plague.

Instead, I escape to Starbucks or Costa Coffee in these malls, to order a mocha chip iced coffee and a turmeric latte. Here I open my laptop and spend hours browsing through the LinkedIn profiles of old school and college mates, the business schools they've gone on to graduate from, the host of impressive skills they have gained, the courses they have successfully accomplished – SEO optimisation, resource mobility planning, data visualisation. Careers building data-driven actionable insights, building resilient supply chain management and consumer strategy frameworks. I see the multinationals they've gone on to join, recommendations from superiors, glowing feedback from peers. Browse through the extra-curricular activities they are interested in, the causes they care about and volunteer for, the hobbies they still manage to fit into busy schedules – gymming, swimming, Zumba, yoga – try to prise these passions for myself.

And then I Google these companies that my friends belong to, which are their new families, and on the websites of these companies watch rousing videos of new global synergies spun out of thin air, of the power of human capital, of the inherent, underlying goodness of the human resource, the renewable energy channels championed by their companies, the sustainable growth models and corporate social responsibility programmes educating the girl child, the Christmas eve workshops with the children from the basti.

Children as poor as the girl, as the Nepali.

Stop.

I rush to browse through my LinkedIn connects, and their connects, and their connects – a battalion of human resources that thrives in a fast-paced, results-oriented environment.

I learn of offices moving to co-working, co-sharing spaces, where the innovators, the entrepreneurs, those who dare to dream, tap on keyboards all day and meet like-minded dreamers such as themselves through the worldwide networks that these co-working spaces provide them.

I learn of work that seems just so much fun.

And then I google the current share price, market value, of these companies, to keep abreast of, to feel engaged with the world, to make myself seem intelligent on weekend outings with my friends. Read about their production line, their five hundred or more stock-keeping units. Note the sudden mergers, acquisitions, the shocking devaluations, the renegade companies that have broken away, the takeovers predicted. The names of the CEOs, the directors, new executives, I note them all.

And after all this, I browse through my friends' Facebook profiles as I slurp the last of my coffee, straight to their photo albums and tap the right arrow quickly, quickly, so all I see is a blur of photos of the Eiffel Tower or Tower Bridge or the Empire State Building, the cooler ones in exotic secret beach getaways, in Peru or the African savannah.

A blur of fun 'n' games, a blur of smiles. Cheeky tongues lashing out at cameras, vaguely being able to make out the countries they are visiting, deftly avoiding the weddings and honeymoons and birthday parties, the anniversaries and graduation ceremonies from reputed foreign universities that whirr past the corner of my eye. And then I do this for friends of friends, and then for their friends.

Suddenly a sensitive YouTube advertisement on overcoming anxiety pops up, as if from nowhere, fills up the screen, jolting up the volume. I mute my laptop embarrassingly and glance over my shoulder.

But no, there is nobody there, only a couple taking photos of their cake, from the right, the left, with the cream on top, with and without the complimentary cookie, rearranging the spoon, uploading it, swooping down on the comments that begin to trail in. #foodporn

An update from my Instagram account, their dessert now on my screen, the couple must be orbiting me at some distance in my Instagram universe.

But when the corporates arrive for their power meetings between 11 a.m. and 12 noon, I hurriedly put away all this Instagram business. Now I put on my spectacles, set my mouth into a firm line, back ramrod straight. I open PowerPoint or Excel and swiftly type away at imagined presentations and account sheets and governance decks, the clacking a source of comfort, edging me on as I type up lines of half-remembered poetry from school into the small grey boxes – When the Mind is without Fear and the Head is held High . . .

I ask the waiter for another cup of coffee.

I skid up the escalators to the stores selling Samsung and Apple gadgets, hear out the barrage of details about the latest model – the choicest fruit waiting to be plucked – shining on white columns, spotlit by overhanging strobes. Same conversation as that night I realise, as the salesmen tell me about its impressive data capacity, the lightning internet speed and the warranty periods. I nod my head. And the laptops – which model the most lightweight, better than the last one out three months ago, sleeker, most customer-friendly, auto-loaded with the best browsers, apps, the most efficient operating systems.

Then I say thank you very much and leave abruptly.

The world feels a large, infinitely large, quick place, the people set in their ambitions, marching ahead with certainty to fulfil well-analysed dreams; and me, a step askew, with my head in the clouds. Bewildered, thinking vague half-thoughts through half-words and phrases that lead one to the other, leaving nothing, leaving only this schizophrenic trail.

Armed with a foreign degree but not having learnt the first lessons of life, the most basic ones everyone needs to know to survive.

And now this all-too-powerful net I have caught myself in. This click and reel that follows through the day, even into these neon afternoons in the mall. These images of me burying a small girl in the backyard, leaving the Nepali for dead drooping on the toilet, they will never go away. Uncertain of a future, of my next move – to come clean to him and finally ask him what the hell happened that night, or not? To threaten to finally go to the cops? To actually go to the cops? To leave an anonymous tip with the media? To post a message – something cryptic even – on my Facebook wall? To tell my father, my mother, hell even my grandfather who wouldn't understand anyway.

Or not?

But I do nothing.

Instead I sit in these malls, in these cafes, anchored by dread that beats like a low drum, makes my body a heavy thing, collapses the muscles, caves in my knees.

I tell myself to shut up, shut up, shut my mind to blankness. Then open my eyes and name the things that surround me – a decaffeinated frappuccino with hazelnut syrup, with extra whipped cream, two free all-American chocolate-chip cookies. A spoon, three tissue papers, a table mat. A world of familiar logos.

I walk around the malls slouched, fatigued, angry at myself, at my own crippling indecision. Angry that I go see him every other night, despite everything, failing the promises I make to myself, every morning.

I walk around telling no one of anything, holding on harder to the pieces of my mind slowly drifting apart.

It scares me, this business of living, this business of life.

---

And these days, after my routine glidings through the mall, I take the airport metro – back and forth – home to airport to home. I sit like a queen, a jet-setter, a global, cosmopolitan business-class traveller, and imagine myself to be in transit mid-air, circa AD 2095 or 3000.

The commentators on the airport line speak better English than those in the regular metro, and stepping from there to the airport line is transporting oneself from the great big heaving Indian market to a luxury mall that could be anywhere in the world.

On these metro rides, I lean against the glass panels with the map of the underground etched like a constellation with yellow and purple and red stars as I connect the dots, transform into an intergalactic explorer.

When we ascend to the city, the blurred outlines of labourers with their bright yellow helmets whizz past. On bridges and highways under construction, a sea of labourers flat on the tarmac of to-be-built roads. Heaving and sweaty, hungry and bored, their wives carrying wet cement on top of their heads, their children playing cricket barefoot on the highway. When I see them I avoid looking at them altogether, catching only their bright helmets and headless torsos.

They could be any of the nameless, faceless army of the Nepalis, or the little girl who screamed before she was finished, before we threw her in the makeshift pit – fathers, mothers, uncles, aunts, brothers and sisters, neighbours of the boy slumped on the toilet, the girl.

Any number of the million migrant labourers who make their way to the city, hungry for shavings of dry crumbs brushed off the table, a chance to eke out some kind of living. Someone that night – the brigadier, him, someone else, one or two or three of the others – ended the lives of their children that night.

But why? I wonder again and again, more than wondering who else was involved that night, more than wondering where the murder weapon was hidden, if there even was one. More than wondering what happened to the Nepali.

More than all this I ask – why? He who has everything, why would he need to kill such dirt-poor children?

More than all this I turn to myself and ask – why did you help them? More than anything, I turn to myself and ask – why did you not feel anything in that moment, how could you not feel anything, no guilt, no terror, no fear as you cleaned your nails of the dirt that lay on top of the dead girl under the earth, behind the brigadier's mansion.

---

And on my nightly walk in the empty subterranean garage of the building trying to fit in a little exercise, one day I spot him. He's partly hidden by the trail of SUVs, in the dull blue-white light of this place, but I can still see the top of his head. I've seen him before, the thin boy with the khaki green All-Star sneakers, walking his husky around the colony, on the phone in the elevator, smoking on the terrace of the apartment block opposite ours.

But there's a strange incandescence in his face tonight. I hear him talk to someone, but when he sees me he stops abruptly and I see there's nobody with him. I walk on ahead, feigning nonchalance, and at some distance hear him mumbling again, but what exactly I can't quite make out.

The next night, creeping behind the pillar, he suddenly turns around and says so, do you want to join us?

---

Sitting in front of the now-working television with my father, a little stoned, in the middle of the 9 o'clock news on NDTV, I burst out laughing. He looks at me quizzically. They're doing such a bad job! I say.

Who?

I stay silent for some time and he looks at me a little concerned, then back to the news.

But a few minutes later, I can't bear it – let's watch something real – I grab the remote from him, switch to BBC, then to CNN, Udaya TV, ATV Bangla, turn increasingly hysterical with every flick of the channel.

Then stop laughing abruptly.

I get up, walk very slowly to the TV, peer down, close to the universe of buzzing pixels, closer till the end of my nose touches the screen. And on the other side of this 36-inch flat screen, finally, I begin to see.

I go to the balcony, slide the French windows back, look up at the sky, and from the other side of the sky the truth beams down. I look at the highest floor of the tower opposite, at the cranes perched on top. Look up further and see him peer down from the other end of the sky, just a flip of a coin away.

I return to my wide-eyed father and announce, remote waving in my hand – it's one big corporate scam!

I rush to my grandfather, groggy and full of medication, and say – it's just a corporate scam!

The men look at me, and I look at them, and then my father says it's late now, let him sleep.

I catch a glimpse of the male nurse before I go to my room, a look of concern clouding his face, toying with the possibility that this much isolation must surely be turning this young one quite mad.

Later that night, after the 9 o'clock news and the late-late radio show, after Shahbanoo has been laid to rest, the men fast asleep, the male nurse's smoke long finished, I hear their hushed voices from my seventeenth-floor apartment. As always, I put on my hoodie, wear my white sneakers, zip myself up, hands in pockets, close the door softly behind. Follow the hushed trail of voices to the far end of the underground parking lot.

They're standing in a tight circle, in the yellow slot marked 1502, in the shadow behind the cars. Torches shining below each face, mouths moving swiftly.

First come the latest government scams, Ambani and Mallya and Birla, match-fixing, IT raids of the rich and famous. I creep quietly into the circle, they make space for me, without glancing up.

He points his torch at each of us. Beware, he says, your Apple devices are now open. We take our phones and iPads, our iPods, out from our pockets in unison. Look, he says, and we stare back at the CIA, or the FBI, RAW, the IB, Mossad, the ISI, the KGB undercover as the CIA on the other end.

They've implanted malware – a shrill woman's voice – it's on the latest WikiLeaks cables, classified CIA documents leaked.

Don't be stupid, says another, it's really the Freemasons, it's always them. They effectively own the world's military-industrial complex, Google, the NASDAQ, the president, and the president after next. They essentially own your ass. Look at the back of the dollar bill, think of what the chakra on the Indian flag really means. And besides, 9/11 was always an inside job. And of course, all the world's politicians and businessmen and movie stars and pop stars, all the world's ruling elite are part of one big child sex trafficking ring, worshipping the devil every night, raping and then killing children, and then finally drinking their blood.

I listen to this and my blood chills. What did they know about that night? Did they know I was there? That I threw her in the pit? That I left the Nepali for dead?

And besides, everyone really knows the royal family of England belongs to a long lineage of lizards, she continues, and I breathe easy.

We stare at the dank floor in solemnity. We must hack into the Grand Lodge in Washington, says another. The hacking groups meet every Tuesday after midnight on the third floor of the Ministry of External Affairs in Chanakyapuri, another spectral mouth.

It's the Illuminati! I pitch in, the drones are now infiltrating humanity's bloodstream through micro weapons of biochemical warfare they have unleashed on the public. We must wear our anti-tracking devices at all times! Then the man in the corner – genetic engineering is underway on an unprecedented scale, right here as we speak!

Sit, says the leader. We sit.

The world is overrun by power-sucking pigs, he says below his breath. Think nanny state. Think non-taxable think tanks. Think military-industrial complex. Think revolving door. Think leaking of classified data to the media.

We listen to him, amazed. He puts on Assange's interview on YouTube for the next hour. WikiLeaks must publish or be damned!

We hoot in applause. The stray dogs bark wild.

I download Telegram as they demand, suddenly freed by encryption. Add friends, vague acquaintances, my ignorant father, yes, clueless mother too, distant cousins, upload links to educate the world to be wary, vigilant, alert to propaganda of all kinds.

Death to the White House!

Bitcoin the harbinger of a New World Order!

World Bank = World Terrorist!

Creative Commons RulZ!

The leader stands up. He says the era of organic life shaped by natural selection has passed. A new era of life shaped by intelligent design descends.

Tomorrow, he says. The birds are beginning to chirp. I stand up with the others, turn off my torch, stuff it in my jacket pocket. Silence, and then somebody coughs. I realise all their eyes are on me. Right, I say. Right. Then turn around and walk home, the smiles of my white-faced anonymous peers frozen on my back. And when I turn to wave goodbye, I see that they have all already vanished, all except the boy with the green All-Star sneakers watching me, face half hidden under his hoodie, which partially covers his T-shirt that says, 'You can never get enough of what you don't need,' lit by the white glare of his phone, black holes in place of eyes.

And following these nights of revelation, slowly, very slowly, in those self-same malls, under the magnified glass eyes of the building librarian, by the empty jacuzzi, in my white room under the razai, beside my accomplished friends celebrating their brand-new wealth and personal successes, amongst these men of my household drifting through their autumn lives, I come to realise my own place in the grand scheme of things.

---

In between all this – the malls and the metro hurtling into the future – in between dreams, they come again, the pictures sure as day. Click, click, click, one body, two, God knows how many more. Him digging in the courtyard with the brigadier, me throwing her in, a child's hushed cry, it sticks to the back of my eyes, scratched into the retina, won't go away.

I wake up with a start.

My heart jumps out of my mouth to the ceiling.

Seven a.m. and the sun as sharp as noon. Buildings stand whitewashed and erect outside. Through the skeleton of the building that faces my window I catch other skeletons further away, a puzzle that never fits.

I am here, I tell myself. I am safe.

But I am the perpetrator, I remember. The bad guy. And as every day, the realisation sinks in that he and I are still suspended between truths. That today too I have to carry on as though nothing has happened. But by now I know how to put the pictures from that night away and face the day. From the bed, I look up at the shadow of my head hiding beneath the covers.

Then brush my teeth and get out of the room.

In the living room, my father, the assembler of small things, is assembling a broken model of a rocket, as he used to every Sunday morning, and now does every other day.

Aastha TV is on. A beatific woman in a white sari sits in an evergreen forest and discusses how the mind can transcend its present circumstances to become one with the universe. My grandfather sits on the sofa, watching this with a blank face. His nurse feeds him daliya. He is doing a good job, this male nurse, but my grandfather's trembling is making it difficult and the food dribbles down his bib.

I go to the kitchen to get my breakfast. My father is leaning against the counter, clicking his tongue in frustration. Morning, I say. My father looks up at me, says hello and goes back to his phone. Sup, I say.

And then he says, I'm trying to find this OTP but don't know whether it's in . . . I cut him off, how difficult could this be? Do I really need to show him how to do this every single time? I grab his phone. I mumble 6721295 quickly and then log it into the bank app and give it back to him. It's all done now, I say, as he looks up at me a little bewildered.

And as I leave the kitchen with my full bowl of daliya and milk, he mumbles to my back, thanks, and then adds, almost an afterthought, you know, there's no harm in just talking to him once in a while. Ask a few questions, ask about his life, his past. Just make some conversation na?

I chew the insides of my mouth. So today, instead of eating my breakfast in my room I decide to sit with my grandfather.

His eyes are glued to the screen, but he opens his mouth when the male nurse heaps the food in. Why do you like this programme? I ask, unsure how to break the ice. Hmmmm, he says, as he glances at me, then back at the screen.

After a few moments I decide to take the plunge. Who is she? I ask, looking at him squarely in the face, who on earth do you talk about all the time? Will you just please tell me?

He looks at me confused.

Shahbanoo, I say softly.

He looks at me for a few seconds. Then his face lights up, as though he remembered his granddaughter is alive and well, of excellent physical and mental health, and sits in front of him, even cares for him. He holds my head in his hand and says, stay with me here my beauty, we will build a life in this city of Delhi, become my wife, I will take care of you . . .

I look back at the electric-blue cataract that fogs his eyes. Wait for my brain to tell me the right thing to say, the right thing to do for once. Think of anything that will comfort this old, delusional man.

What would he do, if he knew what I had done, it strikes me for the first time so many weeks after that night. What would my father do? How would they feel if they knew I was sleeping with rich men for money and helped them bury a small, poor servant girl in the backyard of a rich man's house? That I left another for dead on the toilet of the bedroom, when he could have still been saved.

Suddenly the male nurse says that's it, open your mouth again . . . aaaaaa . . .

I watch my grandfather drool white mash down his chin on his blown-up blue baby's bib. Watch him make such an effort with every bite, painfully swallow every mouthful.

I feel a rush of love I cannot bear. I cannot watch him any more. I leave the room with my bowl of half-eaten daliya as my father quietly shakes his head to himself.

---

In my room, I position my phone carefully, put on the reel and get into perfect expression for the Dubsmash and TikTok video. I upload it on my page, wait for the comments to trail in, checking every two minutes. I call the

Vodafone helpline, over and over again – I'm Dreaming, Every Day. The World is Our Playground . . . and then cut the call just as the kindly, enthusiastic automated woman begins, as the bored customer support executive begins, Hello welcome to Vodafone thank you for giving us your precious time . . .

I follow the Twitter accounts of celebrities – film stars, designers, musicians, journalists. Follow their fans' accounts too, seeking validation for my 280-character, bite-sized philosophical musings. And when a tweet, a page, a video, a meme is spreading – becoming viral, faster and faster, I retweet, retag, repost urgently, immediately, dropping meals, half-conversations at the table, dropping everything else. This buzz must never stop. I keep my phone by my side all the time, checking for updates, taking watchful note of each painfully slow like to my post, the comments that never seem to trail in.

I reach out to old friends and random acquaintances I couldn't care less about on WhatsApp, Snapchat, Voxer – Hello, howz you? Exchanging deep thoughts for a few minutes, philosophical truisms, and then, it was so lovely catching up with you after so long, brb, ttyl, gtg. Kbye.

I spend the days pole-vaulting through pop-ups and advertisements and websites. You deserve to make money from browsing, screams an ad linking to a YouTube comment that says I used to be a drug addict, now I sit at my computer making money with clicks and buttons, as a Facebook pop-up claims to hire Indians for ₹15,792 a day to work from home. The internet knows me better than I know myself, I realise, popping up clickbait I wanted but didn't know I wanted.

Then I change the moniker of my Twitter account.

Dysfunctional/Chaos Seeker/Femi-nAzi.

I change the moniker of my Instagram account.

Wanderer/Soul Seeker/Humanist.

Suddenly I look up and it's already 1.35 p.m. Three hours and twenty-two minutes have passed doing this, doing absolutely nothing. Once again I realise I am wasting my wasted days further, losing myself in the deep wilderness of the internet.

---

At night I dream dreams more real than these days of my waking life. They pass through my body like a spectre. Just before sleep they come crashing in breathless succession – gifs and memes rolling around in my head, the incessant scroll from my Insta and Facebook feeds feeding into, nonsensically referencing one another; selfies, close-up images of plants and cats and landscapes, half-notes played, shifting one to the next every nanosecond, all crashing into the bottomless reserve of YouTube videos mixing with lines from a stray WhatsApp forward and messages from friends of friends, a long-lost aunty.

Or dreams of the future – so far ahead – a thousand millennia from now, when technology and our bodies have merged, are one thing and there is mass digitisation of consciousness, a unified social brain tapping into the internet of the future, which is one giant nervous system. Sensors float gently up and down bloodstreams, chips connecting our individual brains to pools of mass consciousness – a resource hub, governed by no person, no body, not even a singular machine or a machine cluster. This resource hub gathers and organises all thought – stray or essential, vague or crucial – to eject leaner efficiencies. Human-androids cannot yearn or desire here, and so there are no altercations, no arguments, no violence. Artificial intelligence has made life infinitely cleaner, better. Everything occurs in a manner fated by the machines, ruled by nobody.

But I am dragged out of these peaceable dreamworlds of the future by a fish hook that pierces through the lips, ripping flesh to yank me from behind my navel, dragging me across dimensions. I let out a low gasp and bolt awake.

No, not again, not again, I sigh, even as they begin to bombard me – click, click, click, the pictures again, hushed, children, digging, the dirt poor. Money, watches on swarthy arms, glittering chiffon monotone shawls. Blue-sky eye shadow. Dark bronze hair tint. Art shows, art talk – retrospectives, travelling exhibits, farmhouses that glow like space stations on Mars. Like giants inside their mansions at night, when they stepped into the sunlight they were mouse-men, all.

Back to the Nepali still slumped on the toilet seat, blood dripping on the freshly waxed floor.

Stop it, stop, I catch myself screaming out loud.

Silence. The dead of night.

A pause, and then the weight of my reality drops on me like a construction slab from a crane, and I turn with a crash to the window, letting out a cry of regret, hoping my father does not knock at the door to ask if I am all right, again.

I look at the clock overhead – 3.27 a.m.

It's in moments like these, charged by a fear so ancient, so innate, so real, but one I cannot articulate to myself, one that I cannot even understand, that I realise how alone I have made myself in this world. Cutting ties with everyone, even my own father, my mother.

Standing in the middle of a bridge burning at both ends.

Lying in bed, I hear the drill boring through the night. Instinctively I get up, go to the window, look down at the JCB ploughing into the ground and wonder why he is working at this unearthly hour, when all men ought to be in repose, why he is so furiously building these cities of the future.

---

Well into summer now, still in my new home, high up in the tower.

Many months since I saw what I did. Though less often, they come to me still, the click and reel. And along with it the knowing that I helped them cover their tracks. Chronic, low-lying guilt about feeling nothing but numb about all this.

We meet at night still, but less often, once in two weeks at first, then once a month. When we meet, we fuck in strange places. We now have a pad – a penthouse in one of his buildings. We talk in snatches, dangling conversations that never round up. We avoid much eye contact.

Much of the same life still, in exasperating, but essential, limbo.

Still nothing in the media yet, even the small-time internet sleuths seem interested in more exciting news – the girlfriend murdered and cut into thirty pieces by her live-in partner. Stored in a fridge, her head bashed in, reserved for the freezer. Routine crashes killing the sleeping poor across the boulevards of this city.

Well into summer, the heat wave that lasts the century. The sun, small and white, a star dying into itself. It bores through the sclera of the sky, an inside-out eye, onto this city and its accursed inhabitants. My father turns the AC on, then off, then on and off again through the day to save his pension money as coal carriages chug faster to feed more ACs like ours, in apartments like ours, with people working in office complexes and business parks like the ones I should be in.

I watch the news anchors and their panellists debate the country's transition to electric mobility, the country's policy paralysis in its transition to green and clean energy. The crop burning, the endless pit of fuel consumption, the million cars on the road. I watch the youth around the world march for their right to a future.

I watch this for a while, and when he turns off the AC for the third time in an hour, I leave as the newscaster announces that the CM has activated the Graded Response Action Plan and primary schools are to be shut because of the intense heat and the high levels of pollution.

This summer, Delhi is a desert town. Cowboys in Jaguars and Porsches roam the streets. Cycle-walas and auto-bhaiyyas disappear. I drive past the poor, comatose beneath the yellowing dried leaves of sheesham trees, lined on traffic islands. These streets littered with corpses covered in white cloth, too incapacitated to move.

I step out of the apartment to the car, the city squelches out every drop of moisture within.

Highway cafes, my new discovery. I drive straight to the parking lot of a spanking-new Dunkin Donuts next to the petrol pump along the highway, discovered just a few days ago. I wear my sunglasses tight to block this white day, looking and feeling svelte, cool, removed from myself, a cut-out from a fashion magazine, boredom plastered on my face. These sunglasses that betray eyeballs unhinged, white-cushioned Nike Air sneakers tapping.

I walk in and take my rightful place in the corner by the large glass window, park myself in the armchair beneath the blazing AC.

These days I go to these highway coffee shops, Dunkin Donuts, Cafe Coffee Day, Barista. I alternate, never the same coffee shop in succession. I collect freebie toys with the sandwiches-of-the-day, which I discard in my dustbin, to later find my father has put them in the showcase set, alongside the old family pictures at the Taj Mahal, India Gate, from another life.

Sitting in these cafes, I fill in feedback forms with earnestness, making up double personalities, triple, fleshing out would-be-me's with other names and lives. I tell the marketing interns the secrets after my own heart. Tell them I am working on an environment sustainability project, or with a women's rights group, setting up micro-credit loans for BPL women to safeguard themselves against drunk and violent husbands, fathers and mothers turning a deaf ear. Making myself credible, productive, on the healthy side of the good fight. And if the four lines allotted for the contest question are not enough to evoke my shining example, and if the paper runs out, I write on napkins, back and front, staple it all and leave it on the table for the manager to pass on to its rightful cubicle.

I come here for the free Wi-Fi, this safety zone, where people chat across the table, typing to keep time to the music, always upbeat – American pop stars crooning of bad romances or the electronica that never stops, smooth, like the coffee freshly grinding in the machines and the waiters sliding across polished granite.

I come here to overhear conversations among bright workers of the gig economy – freelance graphic artists, UI/UX developers, singers and videographers exchanging shop talk about new platforms where they can acquire more gigs. I come to hear of fintech startups popping out of the cyber-hubs of Gurgaon, of entrepreneurs discussing seed-capital instalments with investors for their tech-based agri-solution enterprises.

Because everything feels possible here, because everything here is the opposite of sitting in my room with the door shut as I browse the internet for hours pretending to be working on a deck for Suntech Ventures but am really fighting the click and reel, I come here.

I come to escape the chronic lethargy of prolonged afternoons with the old men of my home.

So I sit here reading endearing messages on the styrofoam cups as I whirl them round, reading, rereading clever riddles, silly jokes, facts about how the donut was discovered as an accident in a bakery in some Midwest American town a long time ago. How donuts first had no holes, they were just fat blobs made of sugar, refined flour and the sweat of American enterprise.

All-American enterprises, wayside cafes and friendly neighbourhood juke joints, teenage watering holes of suburbia that now dot our metros, sugar and caffeine instant in the blood, feet tapping, heads buzzing, the beat always on, work that never ceases, life that never dies, the stock market always on in some part of the world.

These are days that roll into each other, days that melt into one another.

The metronome of cappuccino machines, fingers tapping on keypads, the electronica now a combined soundtrack in my mind which keeps me moving, keeps me running faster than the treadmill, keeps me one step ahead of this world conjuring its underpasses and overpasses, its highways and freeways.

And out here, just two tables away they are forging a new startup – personal care products for the man, a line of face creams for new mothers, healthy ready-to-eat breakfasts for couples on the go – chalking out potential investors, listing deliverables, laying out distribution channels, discussing marketing plans. Innovation, Ideation, Incubation – the new models of the growth engine.

And me, I just watch all this. Not doing one productive thing, sprawled on the leather couch all day, a cool customer sipping at her cappuccino, ears perked at the conversations.

I glance out the floor-to-ceiling windows. A line of cement mixers lie parked on the kerb-side in their endless churning. Tarmac glitters and then cools outside as afternoons turn to dusk, fire bolts by mid-morning. The screeching of motorcars on the F1 track from a few miles beyond, over the drone of vehicles driving out of the city. Speed rushing out of my ears, out through my head, accelerating with every car.

And outside the billboard advertises a new toothpaste with diamond crystals, the sun sparkles off the edge of a canine inside deep red lips. Cattle amble under the billboard chewing cud, as though all of time was made for cud to be chewed, the herders strolling behind, whistling, swinging lathis on their humps, the women in a shock of pink or magenta sashaying along with a bony child on their hips.

I look up at the TV, which plays the news on mute so as to not disturb the latest pop hit. Mountains blaze in the far north of the city, and as I do a double take I realise they are mountains of garbage. This afternoon the sun has struck the landfill that houses all the city's garbage. Methane rises and the fire has spread, the tower burning, the poor who sort through the rubbish choking, fire engines rushing to the site. I am amazed, can't quite believe the images on the screen are real. I look around but no one seems bothered, the cafe buzz is still on.

And then they call out my name – mocha cappuccino for Ms A – in a characteristic singsong, and I put my best game face on. I pick up my coffee and chat a little with the server at the counter. I ask him about his phone, it's the iPhone 11, he tells me, rolling his eyes, shows me how quick the internet speed is, and then goes on to tell me the iPhone 13 is already out, seems surprised I don't know. As I turn around with my tray of the single mocha cappuccino, I wonder how he can afford a phone more than double his monthly salary, or perhaps he pays EMI.

All day I sit here, tapping my fingers on my cheeks, tapping my sneakers to the beat, waiting for a doomsday prophecy – any, some – to happen, strike down on the world, for the world to be struck by a meteorite, an ice storm, a snow blast, an endless summer, a sudden overflowing of the clogged Yamuna. Nuclear fallouts, I beseech the universe, comet strikes, the return of the dinosaurs that trample on cities, shattering earthquakes, military coups from friendly neighbours, the newly elected government gone wild, alien attacks, and finally, I wait for the sun to swallow the earth.

But it never comes. Nothing ever happens.

---

Dusk now, and it is time to leave.

Sitting at the rear with my back to the highway, facing the dried fields beyond. Smoking gently, sipping it.

Twilight in the suburbs of Delhi, but the heat remains, it doesn't go away and I feel it, inside and all around, in the metal cranes perched on top of the apartment blocks, trapped in the labourers' helmets as they descend, inside their heads, sweat clinging to scalp, sticking to the back of their necks even as they air them in the breezeless night.

The heat, it radiates from the cheap, fake diamond glinting on the nose of the only woman labourer in the group.

The heat, it remains in soldering starbursts that come and go, on and off, in empty frames of rooms in buildings scattered all across that will make homes one day, to house the people that eke out of Mother India.

Sweat itching on the scalp, clutching at the roots.

From the spaces in between, the labourers' dinner smells – hing, ajwain, kadi patta frying, and after the night meal the cheap ganja, mixed with rat poison, with crushed twigs, with bird shit, with anything at all. Elsewhere the farmers gather the surplus or spoilt crop of wheat with their sickles and set it alight. The crop burns, the fire grows, the land dotted with funeral pyres, a site of construction and charred remains.

I stay here. I stay till the last trails of smoke from the black ground have gathered in the sky, till the night has spread like a bruise. Till the labouring men have shut their eyes on their cots, clutching mobile phones that play Bhojpuri music, raunchy and mournful, to their bony chests.

A suckling bitch with an army of pups gives out a low whine. She closes her eyes and rests as the mongrels encircle her. I watch as one of the dogs leaves his pack, trots towards a mirage shimmering at some distance, leaving a trail of spit as he walks.

I look back. Pulled by the bright pink of the bougainvillaea as a fence around the garage of this highway cafe. I get up, feel a papery petal between my fingers. Dry as dust, it crushes with my tender touch. Suddenly, from somewhere beyond, the sharp, stricken cries of a peacock in heat, then another, and another, a cacophony of peacocks and peahens seeking salvation from the night as the day drains into the open brush of keekar and shock of peach kareel.

I breathe deeply, pluck a bougainvillaea, tuck it behind my ear, turn to leave.

Shadows lengthen the scrubland, people return to their abodes, smoke and mirrors from the skirt of a wandering banjaaran.

As I drive home, I see a perfect crimson sun skirt the horizon behind the tower of garbage in the distance, in the far north of the city. It self-combusts, jutting smoke into this city's smogged sky.

This city, where everything has always already been lost, seven kingdoms, seven civilisations built, and then destroyed. Has the time for the next come? Has the ruination of this, its last, begun?

---

They give me a hard and unexpected confidence, these outings to the cafes in the malls, the highway cafes by the petrol pumps. So much so that I've begun to meet my old friends from school again, whom I haven't been in touch with for years.

A – u coming? When I see the message on our WhatsApp group my immediate reaction is to say no. I type to tell them I have a family function, a professional commitment, but as I am typing I realise I actually do want to go. To get away for a few hours from conjuring mind games, from the click and reel, from apocalyptic fantasies.

From my questions mushrooming compulsively in my mind, even after all these months – who is the fat man, the brigadier really? What is his connection to him? Who was scratching whose back that night? From my own thoughts growing wild. If he killed them, how many more before? How many in the future? Am I just his passing phase, soon to be a statistic? It leaves me with such fear, this thought, such a strange thrill.

And refusing to pursue this line of thought, I wear my black leather jacket despite the heat of the evening, put on the burgundy lipstick stolen from my mother a long time ago, set out.

I rush to the brewery of the DLF Emporio Mall where we have decided to meet. As I enter, I realise I am the last to arrive, and embarrassed, I park myself on the empty chair, nod to the rest. I look around the table at them, genuinely happy to see them in the flesh so long after latching on to their social media avatars through the years.

My friends, all here, all so full of life.

I lean over to my left and overhear a conversation about new jobs, new phones. On my right, talk is of new husbands and wives. To my immediate left and right, everyone already engaged, everyone already nicely tipsy. And taking a big chug of beer, I overhear the guys at the far end talk about the latest investments of a real estate firm. And I realise it's his company they are talking about. They are arguing over the stake he has procured in a competing real estate firm – 45 per cent, no, 50 per cent, I'm telling you it's 45. Fifty-five per cent, I correct them from across the table, knowing this not from what he told me, because he never spoke of such things to me, even back when I was meeting him regularly, and it has been three and a half weeks since I have last met him, I realise in that moment. Not from him directly but from an article I read in ET I had bookmarked on my browser, as I bookmarked everything about him.

Immediately a hush takes over the table as someone sniggers and they look at me, and not quite say are you like living under a rock or something?

I decide to keep my mouth shut for the rest of the evening. Later, a little drunk, as I hide my shame in the glare of my screen, I want to yell at them that I am sleeping with, am the mistress of, the CEO of the company whose stakeholding they were arguing over so passionately just half an hour ago, as though it was their own. I want to slam my drink on the table and tell them that though I may appear a bit dishevelled, a bit lost, I am closer to, more proximate to power than they could ever be. Real power. That they may know how much stake he owns in this new firm, but I know him like they never could. I know his anguish, how sick he is in the head. We share a murder, I want to yell out. A dark secret.

But thankfully I bite my tongue in time, continue drinking.

A little later, I go out for a smoke. From the balcony I look at them chattering away.

Here I am, a mouse amongst those of shining CVs on LinkedIn, those leaving trails of laugh-out-loud emojis, hugging emojis, a trail of 'love youz' on Insta and Facebook. Their posts accumulating thumbs-ups with ferocity, ever popular on social media, rich and getting richer in the real world.

Then my friend waves at me, beckons me to join, and I smile and mouth 'two minutes' as I go back to my phone. As I aimlessly browse the internet, I wonder if someone somewhere who is putting it all together is very close by, putting together my frenzied attempts at sliding into the DMs of celebrities, my Google searches on how to be happy? How to be sane? My Quora questions: What to do if you feel you might be losing your mind? My Quora replies to the like-minded, c'est la vie! – weaving it all together, building the road maps, laying out the paths I am marching along happily, dumbly, at this very moment. I rush to History on my phone, my heart in my mouth, and click 'Delete all'.

I crush out the cigarette, go back in and sit down. Fix my mouth with a smile. Laugh loudly at jokes I don't understand. Raise a toast to our future with the rest of my generation.

Someone says my equity is my life insurance, and I nod to no one in particular.

My friends, returnees from the best universities of the world, returnees from a year teaching English in Vietnam or China or in the rural heartlands of our country, from backpacking Euro-trips, from courses in business administration and marketing, from unpaid internships in Mumbai. Joining the sea of the workforce – financial analysts, market research consultants, entrepreneurs investing in primary education on the side. My friends, who went abroad to study wishing to return, who went to gain international exposure, soft skills to plough into this country, sow into the economy, raise high the rightful flag of our GDP, the millennial returnees.

My friends investing their inherited wealth in silken boutiques that retail quality, homespun, home-grown fabric, in cake companies that produce bespoke cupcakes as tiny as thumbnails slathered with buttercream flourish, in spas for the rich in Khan Market and Aurobindo Market offering mud baths, Swedish massages with lemon grass oil.

Rich friends from rich families with no loans to pay off, although I had partially paid off mine, I reassure myself.

Rich friends with rent money from houses their parents and grandparents owned all over the city. Rent money trailing into their bank accounts every month. They didn't have to work, but worked anyway and loved their jobs, were good at them.

They don't want to go to Ganga Dhaba and A2B at Green Park Market any more – our old haunts. They want to go to the European restaurants playing jaunty French music. To the fancy bars that overlook the city. And at these dinners and lunches, they talk of their visits to other European restaurants and bars across the city, the best desserts, the buffet brunches in the hotels, the places offering good, and over-hyped, food, the ones with terrible ambience or tasteful décor. All the places I could never afford. Sugar-free. Gluten-free. Vegan. Organic. Farm-to-table. Menus with the details and histories of every dish, the gardens they've been grown in, the ethical farming standards, the name of the farmer who has grown the wheat for our lavash.

We make plans for the next weekend.

I go back to the apartment complex, sit on my haunches and dip my hands into the lukewarm jacuzzi that gushes for nobody. Put my head into the mouths of the penguin bins that wail in silence, pluck at the astroturf outside the squash court.

I go to the partially built gymnasium overlooking the highway beyond. The workers with their heads wrapped in white cloth look at me suspiciously, the contractor on his phone yells at them to continue. I step on the treadmill and press the start button through the plastic packaging. Surprised it works, I begin to walk, increasing the speed, then faster, till I am jogging so fast I cannot think.

Or I go to the building mandir, white-marbled and newly polished, just beside the children's park. Watch the young priest perform the aarti, then enter barefoot as he leaves. I stand in front of the gods – Krishna and Radha, staring back with vacant eyes, bejewelled and drowning in shawls of red tinsel, thick garlands of marigolds. Puppets in a Rajasthani play, children's dolls. They do nothing for me, these overdressed, over-made-up statues mean nothing to me. I turn around and clang the bell loudly as I exit, wanting to shake these gods out of their smiling stupor.

In the empty underground parking lot, with the stray dogs snapping at my heels, I race against myself. Up and down all afternoon, from our old Maruti Swift at one end, smack against the wall at the other.

And sometimes, in the noon-day sun, I squeeze myself into the children's swings in the park and kick furiously against the perfora. The swing creaks, that wrench behind the belly, and higher now, higher, my Nike Air-cushioned sneakers block out the windows of the towers all around that rise like cardboard cut-outs.

The swinging shuts out the listless stares of the building beauty parlour ladies, the building gym instructors, the building lifeguards.

The swinging shuts out the incessant babble in my head. It shuts out my friends discussing their wedding venues, the surprisingly high returns on their mutual fund investments, on their newly purchased stocks. It shuts out me, just a glamour whore, as he said I would become, my first real full-time job, now a kept woman of a real estate tycoon, a child murderer. An accomplice to murderers.

It shuts him out too, growing distant as the days pass, him picking me up and throwing me on the bed, forcing something down my throat that night. Stony silence all these days after. It shuts out the Nepali and the girl, it shuts out the stench that only I smelled, the blood from the toilet through the ceiling that only I saw.

It shuts out the glitter-eyed rich, talking biennales and film festivals and literature festivals from his world, those I had nothing in common with, had nothing to say to.

It shuts out the hundred questions in my head when I am with him, the hundred more he leaves me with.

It shuts out the live wire on which I now stand, gazing at the future floating at the far end of the earth somewhere.

---

And abandoning that fourth round around the building, I stroll outside the apartment complex. Make sure the earphones are dug in, knowing this evening will only be possible with them. And on Spotify, put on the music – hallucinatory, discordant, unsettling – beats like table tennis through my brain, a tick in each ear. 'Secret' by Trent Reznor and Atticus Ross, the soundtrack of *Gone Girl* on repeat – the beats like static, like a failing heart in an ECG test, like the aliens have finally descended, like a CIA agent hides just behind that corner.

Like a very rich man and his very rich friend have come together to kill very poor kids, for no permissibly known reason but for the pleasure it gives them. Like discovering that I am capable of burying a murdered child for no permissibly known reason either.

I stop in my tracks, plug the earphones deeper, bring myself to the present. Then cross one side of the mega-highway. Walk along the divider. Sit down between the billboards advertising other apartment complexes, just like my own. I roll a little joint, and as I take the first drag, then another, stare down at my hands that escape their outlines as the sun, aglow, leaks pink. I watch the junkies at the side of the highway laughing, at the traffic on either side, smile at the disembodied heads that turn to look back, the shriek of a driver, the frown of a woman riding pillion.

I get up, stroll across the divider, taking photographs and videos of the traffic in quick succession.

After dinner I go to my room, watch the videos of the traffic, put on the fastest EDM I can find – 2,000 beats per second, more. Pause, drag back to the beginning. This time speed up – 1.25x, 2x, 2.5x, shutter-speed full, time-lapse mode on, the traffic zipping now, the junkies junking now like puppets in hyperspace. I laugh out loud, feel my pulse race, my feet twitch.

Pause, play, repeat.

Pause, play, repeat.

I watch the cars zip across the highway to the beat of the synth, the sporadic red, white and blue that trails faster than light as the windows of the apartment complexes blink on and off and the few people at the zebra crossing scurry like ghost rats.

And the sun, it disappears very quickly into the underworld.

This could be Guangzhou or Seoul, or London, I think excitedly – the nerve centre of the new world order. This could be the beating heart of Tokyo. As I speed up the videos still, an alien thrill bolts up my spine. I watch these videos at full speed and think of the whole world as nothing but a collection of points that are great and small cities, each city a community of corporations, each corporation a community of co-workers, each pulsing, each alive.

I play the video again.

This could be a scene from AD 4000, when humanity has conquered Mars, or Jupiter, or a planet yet unknown in the Andromeda Galaxy, having long burnt Earth and all of civilisation with it. When humanity is no longer bones and marrow, cells and DNA, but part android, our hearts and thoughts, desires and fears connected through some progenitor of the blockchain, and all life is instantaneous and transparent.

Out here, watching these frenzied videos after all day spent roaming the part-empty malls, the highway cafes, it's possible to believe all that I have been reading, all the cafe chatter from the university town of my past life, the stray chatter from Starbucks this afternoon – that AI will take over the world, that automation will replace the inefficiency of living, breathing labour, that data is the new oil, that those who control data control the world. That an army of faceless, nameless, shapeless algorithms living in a nether world are hacking their way through the fibrous muscles, through the tendons like fortresses, through the blood vessels and synapses, pulsing straight through the folds of the brain, around the DNA spirals, to capture the A-C-T-G codes that make up who and what we are – all the way to the ocean of our subconscious.

That the machines really know us, better than we know ourselves.

And the cloud is no longer just 'up there' in the machines, it's around us, inside us. We are always, already embedded inside the cloud.

I open the door of my room.

Glimpse at my father and grandfather making small talk at the dining table, the male nurse sitting on the floor breaking his paratha. I watch them and it occurs to me that they, like me, are nothing more than highly tangled clusters of biochemical sensors – all their achievements, all their failures, their dreams and desires and all that they have left behind and could or did not become reduced to codes mined by the powers that be. That the algorithms, even right now, even as I watch them paralysed by this dark truth, sitting in the shadows, are making their way into them, and they do not even know it.

And I wonder if they and I are fodder for the social media companies, our most shameful secrets resources for the tech giants, isn't the rest of the country, too?

The next evening, a few hours to sunset, I drive to the urban ghetto near the apartment complex. The village in the city, as I would later think of it. The one that supplies all the maids, the drivers, the handymen, the plumbers, the electricians, the ward boys, the ayahs, the day boys, the male nurses and Ramu kakas of our apartment complex and ones just like ours all over our sector. As I drive there, I think of telling him to add this to his massive billboards – twenty-five minutes from the international airport, fifteen minutes from the best-class international school, one minute from an urban slum that supplies all the essential low-skilled help you cannot live without.

One turn off the highway and I arrive with a bang in Bharat, just off the kerb of India. Swerving, breaking, honking, turning, switching, cursing.

Cross of wires above rusted, leaning poles, women carrying dazed babies hooded under red pallus, sitting listlessly on blue tanks stored with water lined on end, gathering mosquitoes, schoolgirls giggling at each other as they pass my car.

Up ahead an open, fallow field beside which a trail of men hangs out, sitting on their haunches, leaning against discarded cars. I park near here, because it's the only piece of open road I can find.

I look around me.

Stuck, the garbage by the rails. Stuck, black boars gorging off piles of plastic, aluminium containers of dal, composting tomatoes and sludge falling out from a half-broken public toilet. Stuck, long lines of two-rupee shampoo sachets, plastic sticks of white chocolate, jars piled high with ladoos that nobody eats, oil from kachori vats on the ground. Honking, scooters moving jagged, hustle, young men thin as rails doing what it takes to survive their birth. Stuck, these women, suffocating this country with their fertility, these men with their virility. Stuck, the scheme entitlements that do not come, the benefits from India that choke up, get dropped by the wayside, disappear before they can reach Bharat. Stuck, people, people everywhere, sitting listlessly, waiting around for a better job, a better house, a better MLA, a better water connection. For electricity that does not trip for several hours in the day. For English education for their children that can take them out of here.

Stuck, stuck, stuck.

Stuck in Bharat, chasing any line one can find to India.

Stuck, the tiny screaming girl, as small as a sparrow. How old must she have been? Seven? Eight? Nepali, maybe twelve or thirteen? Following their parents from Jhabua, from Chitrakoot, from Mandua, from who knows where he came from in Nepal? Stuck in this brutal megalopolis, forced all day to make chai, make khaana, wash bartans, do jhaadu, wash cars in the farmhouse of yet another Delhi billionaire. Faceless, nameless migrant house help.

Dropped here by some uncle, a father, running away from home where it wasn't possible to stay any more.

At 3 a.m. last night, I woke up sweating, the click and reel flitting across my mind. Fed up, I decided on another approach. Instead of pushing it away, I decided to calm myself and try to remember instead. I tried to develop some logic, some chronology to that night, expecting to hit the wall of brain fog.

But this time, Muniya's bright face flashed before me. Her slightly tapering eyes, her half smile. I was surprised at how easily I remembered if I just halted the racing thoughts for a moment. And then I realised, the child whose body I held, who I threw in the pit with them, had to be Muniya.

And then Muniya again. Muniya struggles to carry a fair, chubby toddler in a thick pink jacket, the granddaughter of the brigadier, he tells me, as we wave out to her mother who walks ahead of them in the mall, an ice queen in Gucci dark glasses tinged with purple crystals.

Muniya there, and Muniya who also served me peach iced tea when we had gone to visit the brigadier three or four weeks before that night. Muniya! Chotti madam ko refreshments de do, his daughter had yelled shrilly, used to this charade of young women her father's companions ushered in every now and again, I guessed then.

Muniya there, and earlier that night too, always in the background. Of course she was not the only one, there were at least half a dozen staff, but she was there when the others left for the night so she probably lived there? She was also the smallest. She could have been anything, belonged to any category, any demographic of swollen statistics that sought to explain why a seven-year-old lived alone in Delhi.

Muniya. Orphan? Trafficking victim? Runaway?

Now murder victim. Dead. Buried. Lost to the world.

How did I know the scream was Muniya's? I had seen her the same night, another flashing memory – sitting on the steel stool in the kitchen on her phone, dangling her legs, too wrapped up to care about the party outside. The only staff in the house that night besides the Nepali and another man with a thin moustache who I am sure left soon after.

I hadn't looked at her face when we buried her.

Muniya was stuck, like the Nepali, who possibly wasn't even the Nepali, who could have been Assamese or Manipuri, I never found out. And after Muniya served me iced tea, after glimpsing Muniya cutting onions, chopping chicken and later on her phone in the kitchen, I saw the Nepali at the far end of the driveway cleaning his owner's gold Jaguar, another morning, some days earlier, before she had given me iced tea. I don't remember much else about him because I of course paid no attention. I was just the racy girlfriend, the high-class hooker, the flashy, glittering arm candy, and I had no business inquiring after the well-being of servants.

I didn't care of course, until now.

They were stuck, Muniya and the Nepali, like the rest of this ghetto, and now they are gone. The Nepali too, I am sure of it, because even though I didn't step inside that house again, I knew the moment I saw him that he would be dead by the morning. And Muniya? Muniya I took care of myself.

Boom boom.

Boom boom boom.

Suddenly the EDM speeds up again.

Electric pulses through the nerves. I bob my head to these beats and look outside, at Bharat again. Bharat – outside and all around the window. Full of Muniyas, the Nepalis, who would remain in some sort of service to me and the likes of me – dusting my car, serving me refreshments – but whom I would never really know, who would remain for me always in Bharat, and always remain for me just a Muniya, a Nepali. All one and the same. A mass of the poor. All invisible, till they are killed at my doorstep.

And I am part of the killing, the hiding.

---

In the highway cafe.

Sitting on the toilet, listening to the teenage girls gossip ferociously about the boy on the armchair outside. His sexual exploits with an Arna, with some Meesha, his two-timing on the side.

Dull pain in my abdomen for two weeks now. Missed periods which come with clockwork regularity, my body telling me I can depend on it, even if life falls to shit.

But not any more. I look down at my stomach, wondering who lies inside. I caress it, knock on the door at the navel. Then, forcing all thoughts out, I take out the pregnancy kit and the drops of urine saved from the morning in an empty glass bottle I found at the back of the kitchen shelf.

One drop, two, three, like a lab researcher in the sample well.

Holding it upright. Waiting. Back to listening about the bastard, how he had three-timed the girl's friend from college two years ago. Another group of girls comes in, and these two leave. Fast-talk, talk so fast I can barely understand, nahin yaar, haan yaar, doors slam in and out, lip tint, rapid blinking under a thick brush of mascara. Hand dryer on and off, water gushing down the tap.

The five-minute wait that never ends. So clinical, this act of discovering life growing inside you. So straightforward, black or white, this or that. One line and you are still singular. Two, and forever double, forever changing everything.

Changing everything.

I blink my eyes, slowly, one . . . two.

The first thing I think, well, there's no need to be too surprised, this was expected, given we haven't been using protection lately.

Everything changes.

Outside, girls come and go. Some knock on my door, try to jam it open, click their tongues and use another toilet. Some croon to themselves. They come and go, come and go, these girls, and all leave with a flush, the smell of a soiled sanitary napkin.

I am unsure what to think, feel. Unsure how to act, whom to call, where I should go and what will become of me and this person growing inside. I lift my shirt and look down at my stomach, still surprisingly taut. OK, I think, OK. And then stand up with a sudden swoop.

It arrives as if from nowhere, this sense of self-preservation. A click in the brain, and that's all it takes to change the world. I chuck the test into the bin, don't let myself feel anything, tell myself I don't feel anything, anything at all. It wouldn't matter then, this way or that. Here or there, life or non-life.

And then I press the handle of the toilet down with a hard force and leave the cubicle, Game Face On.

---

*He's on top of me, naked like me. Watches as I turn to face him.*

*At first nothing. Then he gives me a playful smack on the side of my face.*

*I turn my head, then wait a few seconds. Face him straight back. He hesitates, then smiling, smacks playfully again and I am forced to turn my head to the right. Pause. Then turn back straight to face him. A playful smack, and a turn back of the head, a smack and turn, smack and turn, till I can sense him fuming, this fuming that heats him up, and I can feel his heat on top of me, first above my belly button and then all over as he drops himself on me, climbs on top, gathers my hair and bunches it behind as he bends down to suck a kiss out of me.*

*But instead, he spits in my open mouth, pulls the blindfold down, spits in my right eye, and knowing it's coming now – the left one and ties the blindfold back on.*

*Hurting me, knowing it, wanting to.*

*Then he gets up to go to the bathroom, has a long shower, gets dressed in his suit again – I can hear his cufflinks rattle – and before he leaves puts the AC on full blast, knowing how much I hate the cold.*

*He closes the door behind, calm and collected, happy that his trophy girlfriend is caged in his private suite, on the top floor of the hotel chain of which he is the largest shareholder.*

*But before he leaves the room he comes back to my side, climbs on top, whacks me across the face so hard I whimper like a puppy. He examines me for a few more seconds. Then goes out once again, for another drink on the rooftop bar to survey his property far and wide in the outer suburbs of Delhi.*

*And I am left with the hard sting, his phantom palm on my left, faintly bloodied cheek.*

# Two

*I lie in bed, there is nothing else I can do. I scream, counting four straight minutes on the clock that is electronic and so does not tick.*

*But no one comes.*

*I scream till I am hoarse, not caring if I am found out, naked and tied like this. If I have to finally admit to the cops, to my father and my mother, my friends, about how all this has come to be. If I have to tell them I am a hooker. That's how I met him. Don't care if I have to admit I left the Nepali dying on the toilet.*

*Muniya too. I will tell them everything.*

*He is a murderer, or at least an accomplice to one murder that night, this much I know for sure. I am an accomplice too, but he has never been like this with me before. He has distanced himself over these months, yes, but never this.*

*And after this hard slap I know he is a stranger to me, that I never really knew him.*

*And now I know that anything can happen. I have to get out, get out, out . . . I scream loudly. But no one comes.*

*I count to 438. But still no one.*

*I turn straight back and wonder how it has got to this, me lying defenceless, open to the world. Feeling so stupid about myself as the AC rattles on.*

*I am freezing. And broken. And there is nothing I can do about it. Nothing I can do about it now but think back to how it got to this.*

---

I shut the door of my room. Take off my clothes. Stand in front of the full-length mirror and look at myself.

The first few weeks I didn't feel anything, only vaguely aware that my body was undergoing some change inside, and life continued as always. But soon after, as faint as the two lines that appeared on the test, I began to feel something. My breasts now heavy to the touch.

A dead ache of a body.

I message him to tell him I am pregnant with his child, and as I am expecting he tells me I have to get on with my life. But later, when we plan to meet at the drive-in theatre inside the new mall, he ditches me, and ditches again when we plan to meet three nights later.

Two nights before the abortion. I wake up as usual from the click and reel – toilet, blood congealing, slumped boy. Lamborghinis, servants whispering, the smell of a body burning. Now mixed up with this parasite eating its way into me like Pac-Man.

Every night, for a month, this has been going on. I wake up, lift up my T-shirt and shout, what do you want with me? What? Then stuff my mouth with the pillow so no one hears.

Tonight I calm myself, but know I won't be able to sleep. And so I perform the only ritual I know to placate myself. To the mirror.

I put on the bathroom light and leave it slightly ajar. Then creep closer to the mirror on my cupboard and peer into it. Then open the cupboard to take my hairband to tie my hair back into a bun. As I open it, a sari falls from the shelf on top, all six yards of it, spreads on the floor.

I have never worn this sari, not worn a sari for so long in fact, not sure if I even remember how to. Instinctively, I inhale the sari and my dead grandmother's perfume – lily of the valley. I look back at myself in the mirror, and at that moment want so badly to play dress-up with myself, return to a childhood playing Miss World with the girls in whichever colony we were posted then, borrowing dupattas from our mothers to fashion makeshift saris. I go to my phone, put on old Hindi music.

I rummage through the shelves for a petticoat. Deep purple, it doesn't match the maroon of the sari but will do. A fitting blouse that is parrot green, again not matching, but I'm beginning to have fun now. Then the sari, tucking it in at one end, spinning myself around as I made my grandmother laugh as a child, and then the final flipping of the pallu behind the shoulder and the sari begins to take shape, frames the body.

I pin my pallu on my blouse firmly with sari pins I find in a box. Pin the pleats that fall like waves.

I look at myself in the mirror.

Something's missing. Instinctively, I reach out for the make-up box, trace kajal under my eyes. Find a maroon bindi by the side of the cupboard. I hold the tip of my pallu, around the back to cover my bare shoulders and open waist, then cover the top of my head with it. I join my hands and say 'namaste' into the mirror, hold the tip of my chin like a village bride, bend my head and smile coyly. Bend down to touch the feet of the elders. Then I cover my whole face with the pallu so no man can look upon me or I'd be forever cursed by all manner of demons.

I giggle at myself, at what am I doing, playing dress-up like this in the middle of the night.

Now closer to the mirror, looking, really looking at myself. Still something missing, so now lipstick, rose pink from the box clashing with the maroon sari, eyeliner, mascara, foundation, blusher. And then the jewellery – the elegant, muted bracelet my mother gave me, the heavier pieces passed down from my grandmother before she died.

All of her jewellery given to me in the hope of attending her only grandchild's wedding – gold earrings, pendants encrusted with diamond studs, a set of gold bangles, her own wedding chura, maang tikka. I wear them one by one, elegantly sliding, fastening, clasping and then, all at once, all together, all the sets of bangles, both the pendants along with the cheap ones, the junk jewellery from Chandni Chowk and Colaba I picked up as a teenager, a glittering mash on my face and fingers, jangling on my arms, dancing to the music, thrusting my hips, making exaggerated expressions like bashful heroines of yore.

Look back up at my face in the mirror again.

So finally, it has come to this. I see the whore that I really am, a whore to the gods of glamour, as the bull-cartel man prophesied.

I wipe the lipstick off with the back of my hand, sit back on the bed, feel like a fool.

---

Sitting on the bed, facing the mirror in the half-light of the bathroom.

My face a riot of pink and red. Sparkling with gold and fake diamonds. Sitting like this, I begin to sob softly so I don't wake them, but really I want to scream, take out these bangles and nose rings that poke at my skin, smash them against the wall, these earrings and tinsel that itch, remove these heavy sari pins.

And then I caress my stomach, wondering if she has seen any of this.

She. The first time I have thought of the parasite as a person, a girl. I look down at her, and then like yesterday hear the revving of motorbikes.

Every night they come from across Noida, from Delhi, to race each other on these wide highways that stretch to Lucknow in their sports cars. I go to my window to watch, knowing this will not end well. And I watch transfixed, even though this happens every night – boys doing wheelies, the crash of a bottle, some loud swearing, faint shots past midnight, and once more as always, the night ending in a foolish ruckus of men and their machines. Then the cops arrive, making a grand show of it, there is some shouting, money changes hands, more bottles of whisky.

I look at them and at the watchmen of my building who return to their cabins, sit outside on their haunches beside the plastic chairs to smoke their beedis and discuss the events of the night. These kids, their history, their family backgrounds – how many uncles in the police service, whose father is an assistant secretary to which minister – exchange notes on the extent of their networks . . . the gossip of men.

I look down at my stomach jutting out of the sari, look out the window. And then a fury rises in me – me, inside, spangled in jewels as the boys trash the freshly painted dividers on the open highway. Suddenly I feel a sharp need for this to be a girl inside.

I grip the window jaali. The night silent except for the sports cars and bikes as they screech away. And in this moment of quiet, I begin to think of my body differently, with tenderness. I think of it working hard, preparing itself, cleaning the house, painting the threshold, a little garnish on the sweets – a housewife before the festivities begin. Making and remaking – all of this for nothing, all to be laid waste.

And once more, I feel a fury of love for my daughter.

It's a girl, it has to be.

But now it is morning. Time to remove the blusher and mascara, to stop this game of dress-up, to take out the bangles, unpin the sari and dress in sober clothes. Time to wake up for the clinic.

But later, when I am laid out flat on the bed with its taut white sheet in the white light, the smell of antiseptic like clogged cotton balls up the nostrils, awaiting the anaesthesia that will take all this away, the nurse looks at me, asks me to get up. She takes me aside, makes sure the door is locked. Then sits me down and gives me a cup of tea. She tells me that there is no need for this, that I have miscarried already, a few days ago, possibly, she adds.

She clears her throat, looks me in the face and tells me that she is gone, that she has been gone all along.

The time three to two, baby-blue Krishna on the nurse's phone screensaver, three pens on the table. I dart my eyes back to her and nod. Then pick up my purse and leave the room, mumbling a thank you, although not quite sure why. I walk out to the waiting room where he is on his phone. He looks up at me and I nod. He looks a bit confused but I get out of the clinic, not caring who pays for this, if there is any need to pay at all, not caring if he knows or doesn't know what has happened. I hail down an auto, yellow and green like the summer leaves that rain down on the city. I sit at one end as he rushes out of the clinic and gets in, sitting at the other.

Chalo, I say irritated, to the auto driver, tell him to drop me at the nearest metro station. He looks at me searchingly, and when I don't turn to him goes back to his phone.

I shut my eyes and wonder where she went. Why she bothered to come at all if she was going to leave so soon, even though she was to leave anyway, I remind myself, we had fixed the date for her departure almost as soon as she arrived.

And when did she go, when? On one of those tinsel nights? On one of those nights I was dancing and singing to myself in the mirror?

I open my eyes. He's turned away from me now, looking out of the auto from his side. The auto-wala locks eyes with mine through the mirror, then darts his eyes towards him, taking in his suit, the clean cut of his sunglasses, knowing he is a big man and I clearly some kind of mistress. Sensing some delicious drama.

I look outside, force myself to think nothing, only observe the present from a distance. Observe and don't respond, as his guru told him, and he told me so many times. In times of stress, push all thoughts away.

Don't jump to conclusions, don't get caught up in emotions, don't think.

And so I only observe. Watch the tarmac speed past, listen to the sounds of the city – the blare of the honks, the cry of a child; a young boy clutches the wrist of a girl trying to cross the road, she cries out, they laugh. I am watching, not thinking, just watching, watching the city streets, and then watching me watch the clot of blood that stains my underwear on one of those sparkling nights that I had dismissed offhandedly.

She was already gone.

She. Her. It was a girl. It had to be.

We reach the traffic junction. A flock of hijras gathers outside, thrusting me out of my thoughts. They place their palms on my head, gather their fingers to my chin and say O gudiya rani, O fair, beautiful one, and call their friends to fuss over me, as though I were a blushing bride.

They are heckling him now, teasing us, his age, my youth. He clicks his tongue in irritation and pulls out his wallet, hands out a thousand rupees each, brushes them off. They erupt in joy, grab the notes and twirl them above my head, tuck them into their blouses and say may you be blessed with a thousand sons.

---

I saunter among the graves of granite, pale powder blue, long and thin, flat and square, each raised tombstone marking an anonymous life below.

In the courtyard of the whitewashed tomb of Hazrat Chirag Dilli, far away from the suburbs where I live, is a field of unmarked graves. I come here these days, all the way from the far end of the city, through a metro ride, a switch at Rajiv Chowk junction, an auto. Come here every day to sit in the lattice shadow under the arches, lift my face to the sun glinting through leaves of khirni trees that line the courtyard which the neighbouring children play wild amongst, do their homework, chase a black cat.

In the name of the compassionate, the merciful, the beneficent . . . whispers an old man with a white beard in prayer, bending before a small grave. I come to watch these battered graves, mourners that scatter rose petals on tombs as the crows croak through these eternally stretched afternoons.

I cover my head. Lower the dupatta to hide my face, glide through this world of gauze and shimmer, watch it through a prism of the brightest blue, a shock of fuchsia.

I swat at flies. I doze in and out of this heat, this stifling, pounding grief.

For whole months I go like this, a whole summer come and gone. And then the rain comes – a howling dust storm at first as the children leap in joy, and then the shower that washes away the cheap blue paint of the tombstones, and the grass grows tall and spills out of the graves, weeds and dead insects swept aside, the khadim rolls up his bedding and stuffs it into a niche in the wall.

But how still the smallest grave remains, the only child amongst the dead.

I sit here by her grave. Watch moss collect in the puddle of her tomb, the leaves that float, grainy droppings dissipating in the rain, a few petals blown from another's grave. I look at my pale face reflected in the muddy water, the elbows and knees, the hip bones that jut out like an adolescent's, the punched-out hollow of a stomach.

This body that roams fallow and ready to burst in this city.

I hold myself tight. I rock myself to sleep at night.

---

And I'll mourn for you, I will, from the crack of light on the ceiling, the morning bell ringing in circles from the puja room, the agarbatti sanctifying this world for a day.

I mourn for you little one. Clutching a pillow, suffocating a passing sigh. Peeping into a passing pram, tousling the sun-bleached hair of a wayward beggar, pinching a cheek, kicking back a football, a moment too long at the children's park, standing beneath aisles of Cerelac, of nappies, of crayons, a dash of Johnson's baby powder, blinking dots of kajal on cheeks, on foreheads, on chins, to ward off the deceiving spirits.

Beti Bachao, Beti Padhao painted white on the doors of every school across this immense country, as legions of schoolgirls in blue and white uniforms, in red ribbons letting loose their plaits of freedom, emerge through the rusted gates after yet another day of school, giggling behind covered mouths, full of fresh secrets.

A-Meena, Superseena, Big Boys, Lazy Girls STATUE! they play, aam churi chappan churi, machli jal ki raani hai. Girls hopping to langdi all over the land. Whirling chunnis – yellow and green, blue and pink – that slap each other through whirling fugdis, bangles that jangle and fall to the floor, dupattas come undone, shrieks of laughter.

And in the park near my house one day, a gaggle of girls sings and plays –

See, see my playmate, come down and play with me
We will be friends forever more, more, more!

I watch them. Watch them God-promise they will meet each other tomorrow in the playground, after school and homework and tuitions.

I watch them and I mourn for you.

---

I tell of you to my grandfather, in constant tremor these days, floating in his personal faraway. In the afternoons, when he and the male nurse are asleep, the fan creaking circles, I sit beside him on his bed. I make up a name, a school, activities, friends, clothing, hobbies. I speak. Speak of you faster and faster as he looks at me with his deep sockets for eyes, smiling absently, and then puts on his FM radio for it's time again for Saregama Classic Gold.

The male nurse looks on curiously.

Holding a passing child in the metro, in a bus, in a queue, passed to me casually as the mother fishes in her purse for loose change and grabs her child back when the fare is paid, and I keep my hands busy by brushing a hair, twiddling my fingers, tapping against the steel rail with the one-rupee coin. Mourning in silence, you of no name, you on my lips at the breakfast table with my father, almost telling him about you as I chomp through cornflakes before reason takes over and you are safely locked inside me again.

And I'll mourn for you, through everything that must follow, as the future comes rushing headlong, through new loves gained and lost, under strange new skies in far continents, through fresh grief and giddy joy, parents and friends and lovers sick, ageing and gone, new children and lives to build, you'll haunt me the rest of my life.

I'll mourn for you little one, lost before you could even become, now and for always, up until the very end, until this very life is taken away and I am gone too, like you.

---

And Muniya? The dark refrain in my head, again and again through all this mourning, all through the day, all night.

Muniya is dead too, I respond flatly.

Who mourns for Muniya?

Do they even know she's dead? Who is they? Is there even a they?

One dead inside you, one dead of you. One you helped die. One you helped kill. Threw her into the pit like a soiled sanitary napkin. She was probably dug up and cut up, or dug up and burned the next day.

And you did nothing about it. Didn't give yourself in. Didn't try to find out if she had family. Didn't confront him, didn't confront the brigadier, didn't tell a soul.

Why?

I ask myself this, again and again, repeating this interrogation, but feel less and less for her even as I do. The more I repeat it, the less I feel.

And although I keep checking the internet for any article, any blog, revealing what happened that strange night, as I have been every day, then every other day all these months, these days I feel less scared about it. Less guilty about what I did to Muniya, what I did not do for the Nepali. Less of a connection to either of them. Less sure if all I saw and experienced was even real. These days I care less and less for Muniya, for the Nepali, less and less for any number of the other dirt-poor children of the neighbourhood they may have raped, butchered, left for dead.

I worry less and less about what he thinks I know, of what I do know, of what I don't know. Of him finding out, not finding out, what I do or do not know.

I don't wish to know anything more.

I care nothing for our mind games, that once kept me so on edge.

Who he may or may not have killed, why he killed or did not kill them. What new corporate park he is now building, and where. How many families he has kicked out for this through means violent or not, how weak the construction of their rehabilitation housing at the other end of the city. How many hundred crores he seeks investment for, or is being questioned by the ED in regards to. Where he hides his money offshore, using which ingeniously designed shell operation, how he manipulates and falsifies his stock prices, perhaps on the advice of his old friend the bull-cartel man.

I don't care for any of this any more.

I am dried, hollow, nothing inside.

Worn by all this mourning, but cannot stop, not yet, not till it's further worn, crumbled, one with the ground.

---

In the carnival of the coloured chamber, under sheets of tasselled red and gold and green lies the pir. Inside the enclosure the men chat, pray and sing his praises, pour rose petals on the tomb which scatter across the floor.

Here, the scent of the woman fills the air. But the woman never enters. She cannot. Locked outside the enclosure, she knots the sacred dhaaga tight. There she sits on her knees, clutching the marble jaali, mouthing urgent prayers. Another sits whispering broken sentences to herself, palms open to the sky.

Round and round the enclosure of the saint I go with the others, the men that enter and leave, pay their homage and see to the business of the dargah – the distribution of food, the allotment of funds, mic testing for the evening qawwali. But the women remain, facing men who block their view of The Beloved One. If they enter inside, the all-seeing dead will see through to their nakedness and they will be eternally punished for possessing breasts and beautiful bodies, for possessing men, for leading even the benighted pir to a fall from grace.

And so the woman must wait at the threshold, as women do, as women have done, for aeons gone and aeons still to come.

But deeper still in the complex lies the Shehzadai – mistress of her age, eternal almsgiver. Princess Jahanara, deeply beloved daughter of the emperor. In this cloistered zenana strewn with dusty carpets and broken chairs, women let loose their own possessions. In the far corner, a young woman unfurls her wet hair to shake off a preying djinn. Another sits cradling a dead child in her lap, swats flies around his grey mouth. And when they come to take her away, she gets up and looks around vacantly, still holds the corpse. A blind old pockmarked woman sings to herself, hijab billowing in the breeze, blue cataracts glinting in the sun.

And so in the autumn of our love, as embers burn to ash and I must leave my unborn to eternal rest, I dress my head with a scarf and visit this shrine of women grievers. Talk to them, gossip, listen. Listen to stories of dutiful daughters and wayward sons, of caring husbands, of terrorising lovers. I make tea, distribute halwa, scoop khichdi into bowls for the stream of needy that pours in. Place my palm on the marble tomb of the fakeera that sprouts a single neem plant that grows higher and higher to the purple patch of Delhi sky.

---

And men are everywhere, everywhere, twenty thousand men bow in the courtyard of the Jama Masjid as the azaan beams to the pink sky, a crown of pigeons takes flight, an army of pandits declaring their staunch piety to all from mandirs across the city. And men are bulging into the women's compartment in the metro, craning their necks, standing on tiptoes to look inside. And men are on the roads – driving autos, cabs, cycle-rickshaws and Lamborghinis, whistling and hooting, smacking cards on the grass in the lull of taash-filled afternoons. Lying on the streets, in a drunken heap. On motorbikes, humming an old tune as I try to cross the street, a stray pinch on the thigh, a graze of my nipple, turning over his shoulder to look at me like a lovesick puppy as he drives past. Men on the covers of *Forbes* magazine, lining up in the corridors of power in the capital – Krishi Bhawan, Sena Bhawan, Sanchar Bhawan – controlling the reins of the city.

But scattered amongst the monuments and tombs of the lives and times of the great and powerful of this city are those of women – an empress, a wet nurse, a whore.

Randi ki Masjid. I go to her to share my grief, to hear her own, to know we are akin. I go to the masjid of the nautch girl too ambitious for her time. Mubarak General Begum, thirteenth and favourite lover–wife of a British general gone native, once dancing to his hookah smile. I go here to the far north of the city, to the shrine caked with red earth, with loudspeakers blaring prayers from pious men. But here too a woman must stay out, so I wait outside as the men kneel to pray at the feet of the whore, doomed in her rising power.

A time of retreating showers.

I climb the stone slabs gingerly, edging green with moss and decay, sharp rock jutting out, and watch people traipse up and down to the glory of Humayun and his entourage, turn to the warrior Isa Khan's enclosure, saunter to the far end – the venerable barber's resting place. But I stay here, where only a stray bat wanders, on the star-shaped platform at the centre of which lies the cenotaph of Bu Halima – naked, exposed, without a tomb to enclose her. And on my knees, I trace the outline of all that remains of this woman from a distant land whom no one remembers, to whose breasts the emperor once clung.

A gust of wind, the pale grass shivers, ashen leaves lift to the sky. A sudden afternoon storm. She lifts her niqab and whispers a secret in my ear – dust is always the destiny of all.

Roshanara Bagh – in the pleasure gardens fountains spring out of the pavilion, couples steal kisses, girls blush and boys croon, birds leave bright plumage in flight, squirrels dash in and out of sight. I curb a passing memory at the throat and in my tightened chest as I wander further through the gates of this earthly paradise.

Outside, marching in solidarity, the city is boiling, men and women, children and the old, all castes and races shout at India Gate, spilling across to Raisina. A young girl jumps on a combatant, claws his arms, another bites his shoulder and is finally shaken free. Ten girls chain themselves to the wheels of a car screaming for justice. A young man rises from the spray of a water cannon, pushes a soldier to the ground.

A river of flames around India Gate all night, every night.

Protests erupt around the country as Nirbhaya – the One Without Fear – is martyred for the motherland. Men grow defensive and wary. Real men don't rape resounds through gallis and mohallas, women are set ablaze. The whole city, the whole country, now conscious that it has bitten itself raw, that it is at its very core – a primordial moment of its history.

Hamara Inam, Mahila Samman in tri-coloured brushstrokes at the back of an auto. I hail him down, get inside warily. There's a morcha for Nirbhaya bitiya at Jantar Mantar tonight, aren't you going? I'm taking my daughter and my son too, he says proudly.

We're signing a petition and putting it up on Facebook tonight, three young girls in the metro, I'll email the draft to you soon. A boy pushes through the crowd as the train stops at Rajiv Chowk, cuts conversations and cries above the voices – rapists should be hanged till death! Urges us all to join the vigil at Pragati Maidan on Friday night, flings pamphlets and is out of the coach as the doors ping shut.

She has become the city's daughter, India's own. Claimed by everyone, everyone fighting for a stake of her. Details of that night on the bus – on the internet, the TV stations dissecting it all – inflame the city. Where she studied, what movie she was going to watch, which bus she was on, who her boyfriend was, the route the bus was taking. How many times she was penetrated, by which of the six gang rapists, the iron rod that bore in from behind, a frenzied hand that thrust inside and pulled out something pulpous, something wet – her intestines that seemed to have no end. Fear. Kicked off the bus into a ditch by the side of the highway, because she was dead anyway and there was no real pleasure in raping a corpse. Not really. But wait, kicked her half-dead face again, kicked, kicked till she had no eye or mouth or nose, tore her hair out, bit her breast, for a woman running loose with a man in the circus of the night in a city like this did not deserve her womanly blessings.

All these details and more to feed the anger, the protests, demands for corrective litigation – women's tribunals, women security personnel on the streets, a militia of women to drive our taxis and autos. The Indian media, the foreign stations, swoop down, broadcast reports across the world. On these nights Delhi becomes the eye of the storm, the cynosure of the whole world.

The city runs riot with its ancient wrath, out on the streets every seething repression runs wild.

And it is only much later that we will care to think of her as a girl, an ordinary girl with an ordinary life, studying medicine, just out on a date after college. And it is only much later that we will be able to call her by her name – Jyoti Singh – know her face, the medical college she went to, the dreams she had, the last movie she saw, a fleeting romance of youth . . . give her back to herself.

And it is only when the rapist stares at us through the camera and says aloud what is known anyway, the oft-repeated dictum of the modern, moral-less girl in a bar, in a disco, drinking and dancing and enjoying her life and showing no qualms about it, a girl out at night on the streets with a boy who is someone other than her husband or brother or jijaji or cousin, a girl who dares to have interests beyond her husband and house, who dares to study and harbour ambitions to make something of her life. Then he blinks, eyes on the interviewer, the camera still as a lake in winter. She earned her rape, he says plainly. She was asking for it. No decent girl would dare to do such things, he continues, and therefore no decent girl would ever be raped.

After all, a jewel more precious than a diamond, if thrown to the streets, will naturally be ravaged by the dogs.

And it is only when this happens that the city sinks deeper into its own void, the city bitten too raw. For what these deranged rapists were saying was surely not all that unfamiliar. It's what, after all, the nation has been saying to its daughters all these years – we must protect our women against the temptations of the West, inching closer all the time. Punish those who succumb, who yield to these modern ways – dancing and bars and movie date nights, parents who allow their girls to roam around half naked at night. Horrific, yes, what happened to the girl, but which half-decent girl roams around the city at night like this?

And so the wife-beaters, the dowry reapers, the abusers, the psychological torturers, the eve-teasers. But not just them, the aunties and uncles, the mamajis and mamijis, the kakas and kakis, the appas and appis, the neighbourhoods and communities across the country peer into the rapists' eyes and see something beyond lust – a thirst for war. See retribution, public punishment, for these modern women who have transgressed so beyond the pale of what our India is.

And when they go to bed that night, they are both surprised and comforted by this same battle cry that rings faint at first but slowly louder in their own ears. They realise that they possess values similar to that of the rapist they must so publicly abhor.

And although embarrassed, they tell themselves . . . because, after all, a jewel more precious than a diamond, if thrown to the streets, will naturally be ravaged by the dogs, and then turn to the side, hug their pillows, and only then does sleep arrive.

Wake up India, she's dead! scream the headlines the next morning. The case fast-tracked in the courts, the accused thrown into prison, the jury ensuring the livid nation the perpetrators will be handed capital punishment.

And so the rapists are hanged in the prison gallows and their ageing parents weep for their sons and for themselves for they will have no son to set their pyres alight and set their souls free from this wretched cycle of life, of death, that just never seems to end.

And it is only later, much later, when the media leaves Nirbhaya to eternal rest, for there is really nothing more to say, and after all at least here justice has been served . . . It is only when the media gets back to routine eve-teasing and sex crimes from elsewhere in the country, when the everyday theatre of tragedy presents itself again to the public, each TV panellist lobbying her or his own case, each arguing in favour of its own constituency of broken women . . . only then does the fury of the city congeal, remain corrosive in the gut.

It is only then, much, much later, when the attention shifts from Nirbhaya and disperses to the routine crimes against women and girls across this giant nation, does this, our city, go back to its routine city life, a state of perpetual weariness.

My father, my grandfather, his male nurse and I, we watch the 9 o'clock news, reading the tickers as they flash past, raining down tragedy after tragedy, watch the screaming matches of the panel of experts – wide-eyed, in silence, in our apartment on the seventeenth floor in the far orbit of the city. Sweating on the sofa's plastic covers, thighs sticking as we get up to serve ourselves another chapati, another helping of dal from the kitchen counter.

Through all this, I dare not think of Muniya, of the Nepali, but still I check the internet, still relieved the media, the city, is too consumed with Nirbhaya to be concerned with a few poor children, murdered many months ago.

---

From a hidden chamber in the old city, I hear the clamour outside. Before me lies the only woman to have ruled the kingdom and its capital. Wrapped in a man's robe and turban, cunning lining her brow, Razia Sultana – dispenser of justice, of war-like talent, with admirable attributes fit for a king. She faces the windows of the neighbouring toilets and the back-alley drains choking with vegetable scraps, mutton bones and shit – sludge that reflects the swollen moon tonight. I place my face on the mound of her grave and stay here, in the stench of this refuge, in the hallowed burial place of the woman who ruled Delhi seven centuries ago.

In the hush of the mornings I walk into Purana Qila, not visited since a school outing. I walk on the path flanked by stately bulbous palms, up the slabs of sandstone, all the way to the pointed terraces. From Humayun's Gate, I watch the black smoke rise to low clouds, the shrill cry of trains that criss-cross the land, the saffron flags that rise from Bhairon Mandir. Listen to the bhajans and bells that ring the morning aarti.

It's a special prayer for Nirbhaya's soul, the priest intones.

Then down towards the masjid. I walk up the stairs to the jharokhas – dank, forgotten, misused by lovers and crack addicts. Here, I lean out through the window into the drench of pale sunshine.

I stay here, watching the jade algae pool below, waiting till the crows huddle on the spindle branches, till the watchman whistles to leave, the group of boys that pumps up the volume and pretends not to hear. I stay as the inky evening spills into this enclosure, where the ladies-in-waiting watched through the centuries the processions of courtiers and their wares and their cavalry, the elephants and jewels, the emperor bowing to breathe in a rose. From where they observed the murder of kings, the internecine politics, the cycle of dynasties through the purdah.

I draw back the curtain and wait as the city burns, hear the howl that resounds through the night.

---

At the back of the jeep sit five girls, heads wrapped tight in colourful dupattas, a jeep full of butterfly dacoits, eyes flashing red to the song of the siren. The loot from this evening's farmhouse raid. The woman constable stares vacantly, she judges them in silence. But she has nothing to say to them, and neither do the men cops driving out in front, on this their daily beat. Suddenly one of the girls jumps out, rolls on the street like a broken rubber doll. I brake in shock, barely missing her head, then swerve around and pass the cries in the jeep, drive headlong into the night.

On the way home I see a group of young university students putting up a street play. In white kurtas and blue jeans, red dupattas tied in knots around their waists. They are sloganeering about dowry, female infanticide, acid attacks, marriage to cows, dogs and peepul trees, child marriage – the scourge of the Indian woman. A rape every ten minutes. Palms as fisticuffs, voices in chorus, young boys' too, a drumbeat, a stomping march that circles on – nahin chalegi, nahin chalegi! I park along the footpath and watch them from my car, unwilling to step beyond the chassis into the city outside.

And careening into the shrill protest cries, zipping through spaces in between, comes the squeal of a little girl, head poking through the sunroof of her car, Minnie Mouse headbanded, arms open to the rush of the wind, in all embrace of the wounded city night.

---

Driving around the city. Light and aglow. Bright yellow hives of amaltas scatter on me as I glance up to take in their wonder. Like a bride granting a wayward blessing to one in waiting, they shower on me all the goodness of the world. And blessed to be the one, I drive around with yellow blossoms in my hair and a heart hardened over time.

Nothing lasts, I tell myself. Nothing remains, nothing is constant – not governments, not the colour of the sky, not the pristine highway, not the cityscape, not nature's rolling on, not grief, not even love.

Nothing is meant to.

And I let the pieces of myself fall to the grounds of the city, across its streets and fields and waysides, as I exist above and beyond it, even as I continue with ordinary life, with this wandering across the city, with home and eating and drinking.

Meanwhile, the world moves on. Indian startups are bought by giant tech firms for several hundred crores, Chinese and Japanese investments pour in. Industrial parks mushroom, high-speed trains zoom in and out of the city, new power generation units, a new highway, new automobile manufacturing units are built in the neighbourhood. New airports, malls and shopping complexes everywhere. And you sit and mope for lost love, I tell myself, head shaking.

But the truth is, I too did not want to move on. I wanted to hold on to the past, to lost time that sifts so swiftly through the fingers. I did not want to welcome happiness and light just yet, I was not ready. Still too in thrall to my grief.

No, not today, please not today.

I see them all the time at the Jai Prakash Narayan Apex Trauma Centre signal that leads to the rush of MG Road, now blocked because of the month-long Nirbhaya protests. But now, today, I don't want them here.

The signal turns red, the cars stop. I brace myself.

The girls are at the signal as usual. Haseena, Shafeeqa, sitting and gossiping, inhaling lungfuls from a bottle of acetone. I remember their names from the times I have stopped at this signal before and I heard them call each other out. A dark blue bottle of Camel Gum pokes out from the pocket of one of the young boys sitting cross-legged on the divider. A baby crawls backwards behind me, its bottom caked in dry shit. Not an adult in sight.

Not today, I sigh to myself and then roll up my windows before they swoop like baby vultures.

And then, aey Muniya, Muniya, shrieks one of the small ones out front I haven't seen before. Yeh didi ko le lo.

I freeze. Muniya?

And then careen around to see a small girl, five maybe, or six, narrow down on my car, now plastered against the tinted window. She looks at me absently for a second, then turns around to look at the other honking cars, at her friend who begs at some other window in that same nasal sing-song characteristic of all beggar children begging at the windows of cars, of trains, outside malls and inside markets across the country.

Muniya yes, but not my Muniya, I realise with relief.

She is dead, remember.

My Muniya?

Your?

Muniya?

Hello didi, how you are, she drones, half smiling with that same listless, bored look as the others. Performing a routine act like school – loads forced to sing 'Jana Gana Mana' every morning at assembly. Sassy too, almost annoyed with her circumstances, looking for some excitement.

I look at her squashed face.

And then knocking, baring her teeth, whining hello didi, beautiful didi, sundar didi, repeating verbatim the dictum of her compatriots.

I press the button, the window lowers and she juts her hand into my face. Although I've never seen her before here, I know this hand, this dazed face, know this child too well. I want to shove her away from me.

Instead I open the door. Get out, kneel and look her straight in the eye.

What are you doing? Why aren't you in school? Trying to sound angry . . .

She whines some more.

Then a little louder – what the fuck are you doing? Where the fuck is your mother?

She stops whining, giggles.

Very slowly now, why the fuck are you smiling? Hasti kyun hai?

She giggles louder now, harder and louder.

Instinctively, I hold her small face in my hand. Then brush a stray hair aside tenderly, caress her cheek. Finally she stops laughing like a child deranged, a little hesitant now, and looks at me quizzically.

Then I slap her clean across the face. Harder than I intended.

Immediately she yells out, are you crazy? She's gone mad!

I grab her, hold her smallness to me very tight. Hush her screaming and crush her malnourished skeletal body to mine, press her face against my chest, pushing it deeper, pushing, the wet snot and spit through my T-shirt, the cheap intoxicating fumes as she screams. And in that moment, all I want is to finish her off, snuff out this wasted little life once and for all, clamp down on the misery that is her future – crack, charas, brown sugar, prostitution, poverty, spilling children out on this very divider, dead or barely alive, on other dividers across this city, this country. The slums bulldozed again to build stadiums, slums bulldozed to ensure a visiting dignitary from the first world that India really is shining, slums bulldozed to ensure the middle class exactly the same. A million, ten million in queue for their rations, a million more waiting, what is left for her but rape and rape again – the teeming poor and their poorer cousins from our million villages that arrive in this city every day, rapping on car windows, half-wiping windshields with dirty cloths and then slobbering on the windows, leaving their spit and palm prints as the cars speed past.

I want to just do her a bloody favour and end it, once and for all. End this poverty that festers all around, festers inside.

And then I remember him and the fat man, the brigadier who dragged her body from behind the water tank. And then I remember what someone had done to the Nepali dead on the toilet. I remember turning around and lifting her up, throwing her into the pit with them even though no one asked me to.

Doing dead Muniya a favour.

But suddenly she smacks my cheek and I look down at her, bawling, fisting at me now, smacking me wherever she can.

Leave me, chudail. Chod randi, chod. By now the other kids have run over, they're screaming, kicking, hitting me wherever they can – all over my hands, my thighs, jumping to reach my face, the cars behind honking, drivers poking heads out.

I look down at little Muniya, in shock a minute ago, now roused and in a frenzy. I prise her from my body. Sorry, I say quietly, under my breath. Sorry, sorry, sorry to the shrieking mob of kids.

The signal will change soon, soon it'll all be over, I think, I have to do something now.

I push them all away, these little leeches, and swing open the car door, reach out to the glove box, fish inside for the Happy Meal doll he gave me a lifetime ago on one of our date nights. Long, blonde ponytail that reaches her waist, gaping lashes that leave her in perpetual shock. I place it in Muniya's palm, tighten her fist around it.

Sorry baby sorry, I say still, and then promise me you'll study, promise me you'll become a doctor or teacher or social worker, an air hostess, promise you'll . . .

She looks at me, suddenly quiet, searching, confused, her eyes flicking on mine, right to left to right. Didi, she says suddenly, will you come for my happy new year party? I live just over there in Nizamuddin, will you? Will you? Will you bring chocolate cake for me from Khan Market, woh bada icing waala? She points in the distance.

I look towards Khan Market, then look up. The full noon sun bores above, splitting the bleached sky.

And then Delhi blares its horns. The other kids fight for the doll, tap my hand for biscuits, ice cream, chocolate, samosa, morphine, something oozing sugar, something fast and thrilling, anything really, anything at all. The backwards-crawling baby crawls down the divider. Someone – Shafeeqa – runs back to grab him.

I look at the silver Honda right ahead, the giant highway pillars behind, the cars whizzing opposite. Sure, I say, I'll come to your party, and pat her head. Then, as the signal turns quickly push her away, back into my car, shut the door. But before starting the engine, turn to watch the angry cars honking, the drivers shouting behind, get out of the way, what's the matter with you? Some of us have places to go. Horns that blare through the brain. I muster a look of intense revulsion. Nod my head in accusation. It's all over for this city, all over for all you people now. And when they start to bump at the trunk I know it's time to leave.

I slip into ignition.

Coast along, turn to make a right. In the rear-view mirror, Muniya and her gape-eyed doll are already gone, back to her happy new year party dreaming of chocolate cake from Khan Market. Back to her life laid waste. Gone, swooped up by the other beggars, the cars, the city.

Muniya is gone, I tell myself, as I drive along the road numb, not knowing where I am going, why. Lost and losing myself inside the maze of this megalopolis.

Muniya is gone, I say again, cut up into a few dozen pieces by now probably, scattered all over the grounds of the compound of the house, the dry, dense forest just behind.

Your daughter is gone. Down the dank drains of the newly installed toilet, dead before she was even born.

He is gone, I realise with a heavy finality, disappeared back into his world of art auctions, of bespoke couture, of phantom wealth, of crony capital and child murderers, as the lice-picking women on the footpath opposite – Muniya's sister? Shafeeqa's aunt? Someone's mother? – watch the oncoming traffic stop at the signal and strut their way in methodical, practised formation to rap at our rolled-up windows, dividing themselves among the ranks.

---

And when I stop to consider how it all unravelled, I see it was in these days of December 2012 and the days that followed after, when I was so wrapped up in myself post the failed abortion, numbed by the city's violence.

Numbed and sinking, I didn't notice how quickly he drifted away, as quietly as he had arrived – a click of a door, a turn of the head, a tap of an app and there he was, sitting on that plush leather chair by the window that first night, watching me with a blank face. And just like that, now he was gone.

He is gone.

The day of the failed abortion, I stepped out of the auto and into the metro station, not looking back, nothing to say to him. And since then, I have messaged him – SMS, WhatsApp, even Facebook Messenger – once, twice, called the mobile number he used only for me, even his landline once, over these months.

Initially he responded, but just hello, how are you, are you looking for a job these days? Just these perfunctory, casual messages once a week, then once in two weeks, less and less as time passed. And when I responded, nothing back, till I messaged again, two days later. I held on to the hope that he would call, message, just something, but as the weeks passed I had to finally admit to myself he wanted nothing more to do with me.

Just like that, he has dropped me from his world, erasing that Friday night – Muniya, the Nepali – erasing our affair, erasing the child we could never have, throwing me back into distant orbit all the way home to Greater Noida, where I belonged.

Everything changed after that night, but the less he messages me, the less he responds, the less I see him, the more I miss him. With a hard force. Her too, never known. I miss them.

And so to mourn for her, to not miss him, I walk these days. In the winter smog, I walk all over this city, non-stop, up-tempo, outpacing the jumbling thoughts in my head.

Take the metro to the central Delhi of my childhood in Jor Bagh, my youth, blossoming into a woman – the faded pink symmetry of low blocks that lead one to the other, a childhood spent scratching out the eyes of politicians with black ballpoint pens, delicate foliage of the overhanging khair trees in endless afternoons of lukka-chuppi, of kabaddi and hopscotch, the stupor of summer holidays.

The night guards in cabins, the shrill whistle and lathi-tapping of the watchman on his rounds, the white Mother Dairy packets falling in the mud, mango dollies after school.

Nothing changes here. Nothing ever will.

I walk in central Delhi now, through carbon and fog that settle low in the lungs, make the amorphous dread something real. I walk and walk and reach IHC, IIC, IGSS, Paryavaran Bhawan. I meet a government building with one thousand windows, snaking corridors of paan stains, offices and cabins in cupboards that lead to more such cabins, with paper files wrapped in twine gnawed by rats.

I meet a dead end.

I walk. Roam around the beautiful expanse of Lodhi Gardens, forgetting the metropolis that belongs to this century just outside. In the foreground, Sheesh Gumbad in decay with black doorways that lead to nowhere. Crows perch on the spindling branches of a lone tree that has shed all its leaves to brace itself for winter.

I take a photo of this on my phone.

This city, this wrenching beauty of this city. Breeding dark fantasies. Everyone feels it. Everyone secretly unsettled. A haunted house of a city. History's necropolis, masquerading as a metropolis. Ten thousand bodies hidden beneath the earth. One small body, on top of all the bodies of history, beside the towering water tank at the edge of the compound in the brigadier's farmhouse in Noida. The other young body from the toilet, at the other end of the compound? In someone else's compound? In the forest beyond?

Where? Where?

Where where where?

Night sets in as I turn to leave. This desolation, these silences, those dead before my eyes, what do they say to each other in whispers as I pass by?

I walk further. Stop at a rampart slick with dew that glows gold, the moat that surrounds. I pick up a stone, hurl it against this wall of the city. It hits the wall and falls to the ground.

I pick up and hurl another stone.

I peep through the chinks in the gravel mortar, pick up a twig and scratch at the crevices, pull at the weeds, dig through with my fingernails. The dogs wake up, snap at me, spitting saliva on my ankles. A watchman appears from somewhere, shrills his whistle. Haanji? Kya Chahiye? Madamji? Hello?

But before he can say anything else, I am already gone.

I walk in the Delhi of my childhood and I met a bastion here, a crumbling wall there, a citadel. I turn and go back and meet another citadel, a fortress, a great and glorious tomb.

I walk along and reach a roundabout that splits out – Janpath Road, Akbar Road, Motilal Nehru Marg. I take any one of the roads. I reach another roundabout. I go round and round the junctions and boulevards of this city, a labyrinth stuck in the mind.

Tick-tock, clip-clop. The next night and I wear my high-heeled shoes. I walk over drunk men, poor men, poor drunk men slouched over the street, half expecting an arm to grab the flesh of my calf, pull me down. I walk along the inner circle of Connaught Place, cutting through drunk teenagers falling out of My Bar Headquarters a whirr of men loitering in the shadows, opening their mouths to say something, smacking their stinking booze-addled lips. Then a nasal voice from behind – side-please-baby-side-side – a hijra in tight jeans and a swishing ponytail makes her way like a hurricane through the Saturday night crowd as the men hoot and snigger. I weave in and out through the inner circle and outer circle, a carousel of red and blue disco, winding into the sleazy heart of the city.

I am hungry for you I say to myself inside my head underneath my breath, hooded beneath my black coat, my stomach a tight knot, palms clammy but ripping out the thin cloth inside the coat pockets as I walk feverishly across these city streets, these city nights.

It rings hollow into the night, my hunger.

But I am so hungry.

So I go to his house. Enter the enclaves that flank India Gate and beyond, past the mansions of the richest, the power brokers – the politicians, industrialists, bankers, real estate moguls, media tycoons. One happy joint family controlling the largest share of the country's economy, feeding off the fat of the land. So silent, these mansions, so hidden one would think they were all dead inside.

There's a high gate at the entrance crowned with rings of barbed wire. But I know a way in from behind he had showed me himself when we spent an afternoon inside when the rest of the family was out. I scamper in, safely out of view of the watchman in the cabin glued to his mobile out front by the gate, the other colony guards smoking outside, tapping their lathis. Inside, the orderly and the butler, the cook and his retinue, and all their wives and children, are getting dinner ready, laying the table, washing the dishes before piling them with food. I creep along the alley behind. A half-starved cat eyes me, licks the lid of the garbage bin.

I sit against the ivy thatch wall outside and wait.

The walls are thick, the windows with cut-glass fences so no one can pry. I can hear nothing. I sit and wait. Think of him on the armchair by the dining table, waiting for his wife, approaching his son and seeing he is still deep-eared with his earphones, leaving him. And then I think instead of a more realistic situation, given how swiftly he has distanced himself from me – him sitting with his wife watching TV, pushing a stray hair aside, laughing with his son as they sit down to dinner. I make up such blissful domestic scenes in my head, to mull over later, to toss over at night on the long way back home. To drive myself wild.

I wait for something to happen, anything at all. But nothing does.

I hear him say something, coming! Or No! . . . and then he's gone.

I want to scream to him that his daughter is dead, even though he knows this. That the mother of his dead daughter, his mistress, his whatever he wants to call me, still stalks him like this every other evening under his backyard, around his office, lurking around the club. Why or for what, towards what end she knows not. Coming undone in the chill of the city, as the city itself lances its recent, all-too-public wounds.

And I want to scream to him finally, that I remember everything about that night. Him carrying me to the room, giving me something till I was out. Him digging, wrapping, covering with the brigadier. Not speaking about it the next day, relieved I didn't bring it up, not the next morning when he dropped me at my apartment, not the day after that, or the next.

Not even the weeks, whole months after he got me pregnant and dropped me out of his life almost overnight. I didn't bring it up for months, and even though I don't know much, I saw everything.

And now I will scream from the middle of this, the wealthiest piece of real estate of our country, that you killed some very, very poor children. And yes, even that I helped you throw her in the pit.

I need to scream all this. I really will. Scream.

I look at the high walls all around. The neighbours housing MLAs, judges of the Supreme Court. Housing members of Parliament, policy experts, heads of reserve forces, of think tanks, of special task forces forged during emergencies, all sitting heavy. Housing more recently investment advisers, hedge fund moguls stocking their digital wealth on the other side of the world.

And then I realise how foolish I am, how ignorant of the ways of the world, of the consequences that this screaming could bring. This revealing everything all at once to anyone who would listen. How naive and how young.

But it doesn't leave me, this need to scream. To do something. Do something, I need to do something . . .

Palms in my pocket, I clasp at the lighter. Take it out, click it on and off. An arsonist's rage flickers in the black of my eyes. It rises in me, the threat of something mad, a little off the rails they'd say, and it draws very close. Then erupts, and before the questions creep in I light the tip of an ivy leaf from the thicket on the wall. Watch enthralled as the fire spreads to another, and another, then another.

But the leaves crush to dust and scatter with the breeze, just as I crouch to blow the fire out, beginning to panic.

I calm myself down with a nervous smoke, sipping as quietly as I can. Stamp out the butt, twisting it around with the heel of my shoe till only the stub remains. I leave his house, the backyard, the front yard, his glorious colony, am back on the crazed highway, scampering like a mouse with my heart in my mouth.

I am hungry for him, hungry for his wealth and my revulsion to it. Hungry for his indifference to his daughter. How casually he tossed Muniya. So hungry for her to end and I helped him with it. And how he slit the Nepali by the throat, probably. How he and the brigadier and who knows who else paid off worried parents maybe. Hushed up the media? Bought over the courts? Hungry for how easily he has brushed it all aside and moved on. How he ignores all of this with me, has never spoken of it for so long, as though not speaking will make it go away.

And then it did.

Hungry for him, for this city. Hungry for the brutal wealth and casual poverty of this city that I roam through wild day and night, for my perverse need to destroy it all, wipe it out in a giant blaze. Destroy myself with it. To chase it to its lair, the breeding ground of violence, right back to the cave from where it all began.

And when the next bug-eyed lech comes my way, smiling, singing, whistling, I grab him, scratch him, plunge my nails into his face, gouge his eyes out, his mouth, anywhere I can, anywhere at all, bite and kick and scream, I clench my teeth and hiss and snarl, feeling myself to be feral, a wild thing, wholly free.

And then I run because my life depends on it.

I walk these aching streets of Delhi, missing him, missing her. Pining for them. Hating him, hating him for pining for him, for craving him. Craving for nights like these with him. Walking to forget, to stop this missing, this loathing, this parasitic need. I hum into the echoless night to fend off the thoughts, this city.

I walk in the dead night, hot and flushed in the fog, biting parched lips, chilled but for these feet that won't stop walking. So lost, and always in heat.

Hungry and always in need, always this want between the legs.

I walk the streets of the city. I walk and walk and come home to a wet panty every night. A cold sweat of desire and desperation and easy despair, driven deeper, driven to embarrassment by the knowledge of its own insignificance.

---

And one night, a night like any other, I am walking under a grove in Jor Bagh, facing the ethereal glow of Safdarjung Tomb. Just walking, consumed with the dreaded knowledge that it ended long ago, the finality of her death that is the only real end. Walking, not even thinking, taking one step, then the next, then another, a man grabs me by my waist, covers my mouth and drags me to the side of the road. Shut up damn slut, chup saali chup, he whispers tenderly into my ear through gritted teeth as I open my mouth to scream.

He unbuttons my coat with ease, lifts my T-shirt, holds on to my waist, digs his nails in. Then kneads softly first, slowly, feeling his way through, feeling his way up and then suddenly faster, furious now, shaking me up, rattling me.

Still shaking, he unzips frantically, jams his cock into my waist through his half-open jeans and rubs against me, up and down pushing, pulling, clutching at my elbow, looking at me as though I am diseased, looking at his cock as though it is diseased, spitting at the side as he is about to come.

And then quietly, almost as uneventfully as he arrived, he sighs, let's go. Zips himself up, throws me dismissively into the dark shrub by the pavement, mutters his disappointment and walks off into the night, as though he is tired of this constant confrontation – his bickering wife, his ailing mother, tired of these women screaming in the streets since the rape of that Nirbhaya. Tired of the relentlessness of his own throbbing body and wishes more than anything, simply for a good night's rest.

---

A boy puckers his mouth at me, or croons an item song, or tells me I am his baby doll.

I stop cowing down. I look at him, and him and him too, these kids – fourteen, fifteen, with spiked, gelled hair, smoking lazily in the noonday sun, these layabouts lolling about eternally in the parks, on the parapets, listening to Punjabi rap and hip hop about rokda and kudis and Lamborghinis on full volume on their smartphones, loping in the streets, loitering like all of the city is made for them to loiter in. I say to them, shut the fuck up motherfucking asshole, this is why Delhi is the rape capital of the universe. I know I am screeching, that my voice is grating, and so I stop mid-sentence, turn abruptly and walk away as fast as I can, as I hear the kids roar and give each other high-fives, imitating my shrill chiding.

How to drive the fear of life into them?

---

And after dinner one day, my father taps my shoulder, and when I turn he gives me a Kinder Joy chocolate egg, For Girls! it says on top in bright pink. When I open the egg to see inside, a handwritten note in his broken writing – Daughter equals ten sons. Happy Daughter's Day! he says. Actually I think it was yesterday but anyway . . .

I look up at him. My eyes well, I look down quickly, blink fast. Open this side, he says.

I open the second layer inside the egg, peel it off.

It's a ladybug I think, he says.

I look up at my father again, would you like to assemble it?

My father, the eternal assembler of small things.

He smiles, takes it from me. Assembles it skilfully in a minute.

Here, he says, for you.

And before I leave to go out that night, he says wait a minute. Goes to his room, hands me a bottle of pepper spray, and says don't forget to take it every time you go out. As though it were that simple.

I don't tell him this, but take the pepper spray anyway, keep it inside the safety zip of my handbag.

I walk the streets of the city, one hand in my pocket, the other slid into the pouch of my handbag, feeling the rounded cap of the pepper spray, gripping the wooden hilt, slipping with sweat, gripping again as I stare back at every man, woman, child that looks at me, at every wounded, rabid dog, at the monkeys shrieking overhead, the parakeets and barbets screeching as though the world is about to end. At every car that whizzes past, all the city's citizens packed tight in the metro.

Walking, again. A few days after the man-grabbing incident. The same street, opposite Lodhi Gardens, because I must. Because it is mine too, to walk on. Dark, cold, hazy yellow light in patches through leaves. I hear him behind me, footsteps making time with my own, his shadow dipping in and out of mine, longer, heftier. Walking faster, faster, skipping now, obvious that I am trying to escape when suddenly –

I turn around and point a knife to slice his pupil.

Frozen like this, he and I, with the tip of the knife pointing straight into his eye, ready to slice through his retina, his hands mid-air holding a paper. Frozen like this, he and I, and I see the reflection of my own impassive face in his enlarged pupil.

His eyelashes flicker on the pointed edge of the knife. He swallows as the dry, broken branches scratch at my throat.

Sister! He screams suddenly and drops at my feet, shaking violently, his head on my shoes, both his hands on my shoes, simpering, sobbing, snivelling on my shoe, leaving a trail of spit saying sister, sorry sister, sorry, sorry, sorry!

And then I read the bold black letters from the paper he is holding, a pamphlet announcing a seminar on women empowerment in the Delhi University hall next Thursday evening.

Everywhere, every corner, by the turn of every road, behind every building, from all four, all five streets that lead out from every junction, at every roundabout, I seek hostility in the city, search for it everywhere I look. I seek it, and when I find it at every turn – on every street, at every junction, in the passing looks of every stranger, every beggar, every man or woman, wealthy, poor, every child – I become further hostile, hate the city further with every bone in my body.

And taking an Uber home one day, I cross my legs tight, then the other way, pull my skirt down, pinch my top up higher, tugging and pulling as I stare out the window into the black nothing, the eyes of the driver darting up and down from my body to the road ahead through the mirror.

I keep my eyes peeled outside, ignoring the driver, ignoring my father's frantic messages to come back home immediately, come now, as the driver zips through the toll booth and there is a sudden gunshot and wheels screeching and two men in white shawls fly off on a bike and someone screams aey madar and there's a man on the ground – the scrawny toll booth attendant on the ground, dark blood oozing from his head, and the driver turns around as we zoom past, looks at me in the eye and says ab aap hi batao, yeh kalyug nahin toh kya hai?

And it dawns on me, the idea enters my mind when I'm in the middle of ordinary life that perhaps I was not all that important to him after all. Certainly not as important as he was to me. These things, I realise – needing, wanting, loving a person – must be measured, else they lose meaning. And then I go on to realise that perhaps I was just another young girl, like so many other young girls that had floated in and out of his life. And the hurt that emerges from this realisation is not from the imbalance in the scales of importance but the glaring obviousness of it.

From the fact that it took me this long to see the truth of it, so plain now, so simple.

And I think to myself that if closure is what is needed, it needs to be now, a forced closure sure, but closure nonetheless, a closure that the girl from the other side of the mirror, who looks and sounds exactly like me, tells me is what is needed, and because I don't question her, because I think of myself as her, I acquiesce.

---

*You have snatched away all trace of me.*
*With one glance of your enchanting eyes.*

I am standing at the edge of the hall leaning against the wall, holding my almost empty glass of wine at his twenty-fifth wedding anniversary party that I go to uninvited, in the banquet hall of the best five-star hotel in the heart of the city.

I despise him for leaving me, I fear him for the sake of Muniya, for the Nepali. I have learnt all I could from this life lesson. But for closure, I need to go, I tell myself, telling my dad it was a friend's parent's anniversary.

From here I can see her perfectly.

Bathed in blue light, she's centre stage and dancing kathak as the musicians and singers play and sing this song of devotion from ten centuries ago. Dressed in a shimmering silver gauze anarkali, so light on her feet, a natural swan despite her age and everything she must have endured as his wife.

So this is how I am to meet her then, she resplendent at her party, surrounded by loved ones and friends and confidants, me in the shadows, simpering in self-pity. I can't see him, he's sitting right ahead, and of course he's entranced by her tonight.

I look around me. There must be more than two thousand people here, and I know not a soul, although I know of them, about them. Champagne and chandeliers in glistening reflection. A hall of mirrors, this evening, the kind I only read about in the pages of *Delhi Times*, in the high-society and women's magazines I glance through as I sit in the waiting room of the dentist's office, the beauty parlour.

Somehow I escape the hawk eyes of the events lady at the entrance manning the invite list. Scampered in mumbling that I was some politician or the other's niece.

I don't know a soul here, but I know this evening well – full of the painted faces of politicians and their sycophants, top-ranking bureaucrats, commissioners, corporators, media moguls, barons of big business – coal mining, aircraft, steel – and their wives. A room full of contractors, ex-army men-turned-arms dealers. They talk big, dropping names over who came over for lunch yesterday, the other pretending not to sound surprised.

Then the dance ends, the audience claps. He climbs up to the stage, makes a show of his shyness, gives her a peck on the cheek as they walk down the stage together. He holds the small of her waist, tucking a stray hair behind her ear.

The music changes, another lovelorn ghazal.

I look around. An old lady with massive black sunglasses sits alone in the far corner of the hall. All the tables occupied except this one, even though there are six empty chairs around her. I sit beside her and immediately she takes off, and I now know why.

But I tolerate her whining about the traffic, the pollution, the youth of this city that just like to flash their cars and money, no class left at all, as I drink glass after glass of red wine from the tender flutes, lifted with panache from the bowing server, and make idle conversation with her, agree with everything she says.

In between all this, from a distance, I keep my eyes on them. Always they walk hand in hand, her whispering to him, this power couple so used to being in the spotlight. His son is there too, mingling with the guests. Must be fifteen now, I realise, his birthday just last week. He doesn't seem suicidal any more, at least not tonight. A little shy like his father, but not out of place. I watch them and watch them, but he never looks my way even once.

And before the night ends, when most of the guests have trickled out but me and the old lady still sitting tight, squeezing out our money's worth of the night, the lights on stage dim again and he walks up and places his wife on a chair in the centre, to the applause of the audience that remains. Then the music starts and he is singing an old song, a little out of tune but still catching the right notes. On his knees now and he sings to her, asking her if she is the full blaze of the moon, or is she the blazing sun. Declaring that whatever she may be, whatever form she takes, she is incomparable.

There he stands, firm and steadfast, in the tallest tower of his empire. Nothing has changed, even after all these months, everything is as it has always been. But it is also so obvious that nothing will change, how I could have thought otherwise. I think back to the moment nearly a month ago now, when I almost screamed from his backyard to the world that he was a murderer. How I almost burnt his house down. Now I see him sharing a drink with the cabinet secretary and thank God I didn't open my damn mouth.

And I also see how he longs for his wife. Once he told me they never speak, but here now it is clear they share something – love, but of a deeper kind, familiar, built slowly over the years, even if it stands on the falsehood that is the open secret of his philandering. Still, it's something I would never know. I listen to him sing a love song to his wife on their anniversary, and realise that it is her he needs to be with, not me.

And so, when the song ends and the banquet room erupts, I drop the napkin on the table and leave, a faint smile and goodbye to the old lady. For what was left, what was there to do but to make a quiet exit.

Past the hawk girl, pressing for the elevator.

But before he even taps my shoulder there is the slightest change of charge in the air and I know he is in the lobby right behind. And sure enough, when I turn he is bending down, brushing my hair aside, and with the hot whisky breath on the nape of my neck, his chin grazing my chandelier earrings, he says, slowly, almost slurring – thank you for not making a scene. And then he kisses my neck, making my hair stand on end.

Then turns. Walks away, and is gone.

Abrupt, as always, unfinished. Reminding me of my place in the scheme of things, of my real aukaat – my status – of the underlying, unspoken fulcrum around which the city operates.

He was happy I had not made a scene.

I watch him walk away from me, back to the arms of his wife, the open arms of the city. The poster boy of Delhi's real estate sector. Dropping luxury dreamscapes, brand-new futures on fallow farmland overnight.

The whirring click and reel that I haven't seen for so long – it suddenly returns with a hard force. Screaming, real or imagined, a hand that clamps shut a mouth. Children hushed in the house, blood on the Italian marble floor splotched with brown granite.

And as the arsonist's rage crawls on all fours inside me, as the click and reel spins in my head, I am thinking how I should finally just open my gob. Now, it had to be now. Just drop a hint, a passing remark, an anonymous call to the media, anything at all and they would all come for you – this carnivorous city of jackals. And as I am thinking all this, I see the brigadier saunter to the bar, turn and lean against the table as the bartender makes his drink and he looks around listlessly. Then suddenly he spots me staring at him from the lobby through the doorway, a tap on the back and he turns to get his drink then promptly turns again, raises his glass to me and then saunters off to meet the cabinet secretary, and they clink their glasses, raise them in unison.

---

On my way back, I take the metro to who knows where.

In my drunken haze I find myself through the lines – red, purple, blue, a slippery game whizzing through this subterranean world, delirious at its ease.

Suddenly I realise I am getting my period. Of course I am. On a whim, I step out of the metro, now at Green Park, take the escalator up. There is a stain on the back of my pants I know, a few shocked drops on the escalator, on the mezzanine as I reach the first floor. I stand in front of the balding uncle, feel the heat of his embarrassment from behind, turn around and give him a wide smile, baring all teeth.

Sitting on top of the toilet, watching the blood drip down my thighs. I ask a girl outside applying lipstick for an extra sanitary napkin, but she has none, looks at me as though I am so irresponsible for not being prepared. I shut the door.

I can feel the hormones pin-balling inside. It's my first period since she died inside me, even my body telling me to move on.

And then I think of him – of how easily he plays with me, how easily he fools the world. I want to hurt him and make a spectacle of it for all in the banquet room, for all those snivelling and bending over backwards for him. For those whom he, in turn, snivels and bends over for, to survive his life. All of them, the whole coterie, the whole system.

But now, I need to do something now. I look for answers, for signposts on the door ahead. Pinky, it says, and below Luvleen, Gudiya and three numbers scrawled, women propositioning women in this metro bathroom, I don't know why, nor in the least bit care to inquire after.

A cramp that squeezes. Blanking out, but wait, you're in a public toilet somewhere under the city.

Get a grip.

But I don't want to get up just yet. And then I see myself as he does, a mousy thing locking herself in this public utility toilet as the metros zip below, as the traffic zips above. A sewage rat, creeping like the one squealing just behind these tiles.

Gazing at the watery blood in the bowl.

Fuck you! I scream out in my head. Fuck! Fuck! Fuck you!

I close the lid of the toilet seat, put my head sideways on the cool top, with my ear to the toilet.

Madamji? The cleaner knocks on the door. Suddenly aware of my shoes sticking out through the door.

I quickly fold my legs back into the cubicle.

This, the lowest of low.

How did it come to this? When and how did I become like this?

---

I gather my nerves, and hold it in my pit, behind the navel.

This will stop, I say to myself. I will change.

I will morph into a sharp edge, grow claws and canines to bite into the flesh. I will take this frazzled nervous energy that wastes away into nothing and become something. Hard, essential, particular, cutting straight into the sinews of his heart.

It was time to get a grip and to get up. I flush. Stuff some toilet paper up my legs, pull up my stained panties. Wear my high heels again.

I step out of the cubicle, look at myself in the mirror.

I take out my armour against the city, my sword and shield. From my handbag the darkest cherry red lipstick, and slather it all over my lips, then smack them in the mirror, give myself air kisses, wear my shorts from my bag, tousle my hair for that out-of-bed look. Fit my trusty black leather jacket tight around me.

Put on my sunglasses, even at this dark hour.

I did come prepared after all, if only this.

I step out of the metro, hail down a rickshaw with all the swag this city calls forth, with all that it demands. Apply another round of lipstick.

And as I am ascending the escalator to the city a brawl breaks out. I turn around and see the guard of the men's toilet limp as fast as he can behind another man walking quickly away with a smile on his lips – pay your fucking entrance fee madarchod, he yells, pay up or pee in your pants and tell your mummy to clean up after.

Saturday night, Hauz Khas Village.

I zip in and out through the honking cars and traffic, the young and younger dressed to the hilt, full of drink and drugs. Such palpable excitement in the air in this long line of traffic that stretches from Aurobindo Market along the one-laned road.

I know this place well.

I walk up and then down the ramshackle two-laned street, waiting to see where the night will take me, and then the kids pass the fliers with the ladies night offers, with the one-on-one free margarita nights, free vodka shots nights.

I climb the half-broken winding stairs to the fourth floor, enter this party full of heaving bodies of the young and able and scuttle to the far corner of the bar. Pushed and pulled this way and that, guys screaming over each other to the bartender, a group of girls that must be attended to now! Twenty minutes later, I finally order my rum and Coke. He invites me to sit on the empty bar stool at the end of the table, gives me my two free margaritas.

Glitter in the sky, glitter in my eyes, shining just the way I like! croons Dua Lipa, releasing magic into the crowd. I watch them, tap to the beat taking all this in. Taking it all in and thinking to myself I am alone, they are in droves, he celebrating his long and successful marriage with his wife, glad I did not make a scene at his party, she dead before she was even born.

I needed to get very drunk very soon, if any of this was to make sense.

And so small sips at first, then very quickly bigger ones, then bigger as the party gets louder, DaBaby raps his way in and everyone gets drunker. I down my drink and then soon after, the free margaritas. Tap my feet, shake my shoulders, this beat just too addictive, too much too soon, then ask the bartender for the other free margarita, a vodka shot.

Still sitting but definitely drunk now, how and when this happened I cannot tell. A boy approaches me, then another, whispers something in my ear and then looks at me. I nod and then he shakes his head, and in the haze I see him leave. Next a man puts his arm around my waist, and I edge away as the bartender notices and starts to yell, so drunk now I push this man away from me with a hard force and he stumbles and falls on the people dancing and I get up and rush through the crowd towards the exit, still levitating.

But I've only just gotten drunk, barely even begun the night. So when I see that group of girls by the entrance, four or five gorgeous girls from the Northeast, in high ponytails and bronze makeup, shock of red on their lips and high black heels just partying this ladies night away with the girls . . .

You want me, I say to them – I want you baby, they say back.

My sugarboo, I'm levitating – we all laugh together with Dua Lipa.

And then the song changes, a Punjabi party song and the whole club goes wild. Dancing, eyes closed, high as a kite now, happiness that is all heavenly delight, happiness is having youth on my side, youth that is lost forever to him, I realise ecstatic, dizzy, vindicated. No matter his wealth, his power, his clout, capital, I will always have this over him. And spinning with this, I sing out loud with these girls, and when I open my eyes I see that a group of young boys has formed some kind of wall behind us, dancing but also ogling. They stare at us – me and this group of women out so freely enjoying ourselves, just us, no man to party with, no man to be escorted by, no man to protect us, no man to buy us drinks. It's a common sight these days, I want to yell at them, are you from some damn village, young women out on their own, spending their own money, happy to be just by and with themselves, 2013 for God's sake, what are you so surprised about? But the boys still can't believe it. I turn back to say this to the girls, to whisper how ridiculous men are, to roll my eyes high.

But then I suddenly need to puke, the dancing, all this drinking, my sudden period, all too much. I rush out of the club, not sure where the bathroom is, and as I ditch the lift and walk down the four floors two then three steps at a time, I think of his whisky breath on my neck and want to throw up again.

I find myself behind the basement of Smoke House DELI where the algal green reservoir borders the high wall. I find myself crouching in the dark, puking my guts out near the heap of garbage, with no one, no girlfriend, no boyfriend, to hold my ponytail back.

And once I am done and the world stops spinning, I light a cigarette in the mournful wash of orange light. Still in a drunken haze that mystically brought me here from the club whose name I cannot remember. And sitting here

I remember his whispering in my ear that makes my hair stand on end.

He was proud I did not make a scene.

It returns like a forest on fire, rage below the skin.

I look up. A sliver of the moon hangs low above the lake. I sit here on my haunches with the mongrels smelling each other between the legs, amongst the debris and filth, listening to pangs of pop Punjabi despair from the sheesha bar on the top floor, faint electronica from somewhere else, back to Dua Lipa again from where I came. The wife of the Gujjar landlord that owns this building and the next watches from the first floor, amused. Then she goes back, probably bored of this routine Saturday night debauchery, strange young people high out of their heads doing God knows what.

I look at the graffiti on the wall in front of me – a black-and-white portrait in honour of the founder of 'rock street', a thousand sprayed signatures to show that Azizi was here, Boom Shankar. And then my eyes drift to the far corner – a stunning lady in bright pink, bedecked in nose ring and bangles, peeps out of her ghoonghat giving boom-fists to all who meet her eyes. Justice, she says, we're coming to get it.

I smile, walk up to the wall to boom her fist.

Then turn around, take a deep drag and flick what is left of my cigarette at the dogs that fuck so desperately, so foolishly, fuck each other with no mercy at all in this dump, as though it was all so simple, just a matter of two bodies coming together in mechanical synchronicity. I look at them and throw my cigarette at them, kick to prise them apart, to cleave them asunder.

But the cigarette misses them, and they totter away and continue with their brainless fucking, paying me no mind.

I sigh, look back at the moon. Then walk out of this secret courtyard, a home for the neighbourhood junkies and street artists, those seeking a little respite from the party, a quick joint to calm the night, to let it hang a little loose. I walk through the small maze of HKV streets by the corner of Deer Park, leaving the eerie monuments by the water, the fortress walls shimmering dull gold.

I walk without thinking, deeper into the village along its muddied streets, the young and younger falling all over each other down the narrow staircases lit by fluorescent pink lights festooned like ribbons around passageways, these passages that lead to dark dungeons below, danker, darker vaults above.

By the slums at the very end where the village tails into the Hauz Khas Forest it comes out of nowhere, out of the garbage dump spilling into the pot-holed alley, the black boar and her babies nibbling through shit that spills out from the toilet.

Here there is controversy every day
In the name of religion you will get debate
If you speak the truth you will get slapped with Section 295
When you progress, you will get hate

I stop in my tracks, look this way and that.

The world is fucked, he's crooning in Punjabi from the dredges of the universe, the trouble keeps coming to you and the world derives a deep pleasure from it, sucks it all up.

The same tired refrain – the politicians are corrupt, only want your votes, then they forget all about you, the media is filled with fools sitting around gossiping like women. Here those who steal are social workers, here you'll get your character certificate on Facebook, Moosewala croons cynically.

I listen to this protest cry. Look up at the cross of thick wires blocking out the night sky. The flies by the open gutter. A black Alto crashes against the shikanji thela-wala, they jump out of their car, bang shut and scream, push the thela-wala against the wall, then back to the car before speeding off.

I sit still, watch the thela-wala crushed against the wall, half smiling, half bleeding as someone cries out and people rush to help, call friends from nearby.

It feels like God has given up when I read the newspaper in the morning, he sings.

I look back, still listening.

And it's necessary, I think, as I look at the boys loping out of the slum in their leather gear to the grunge that is the party outside, these boys with their waxed hair, their hands flailing, their mouths rapping end times to the smooth beat of this song. It's necessary – as I watch the white tourists pass by, high out of their minds, safe to their hostels by the side, the partygoers that gather about the late-night parathe-wala down the road, the chai-wala – it's necessary to arm yourself with a forced machismo wrapped tight around the heart. It's necessary to wrap it in this bravado, this exaggerated swag, to survive the melancholy of this night, this city.

The app on my phone pings – the last metro for the night will arrive in twenty minutes. I take a deep breath. Get up from my spot, look back at the half-constructed houses at the edge of Hauz Khas Village.

The boys still rapping with their hands in the air because every day here is war, and even at the top there are the vultures, leeches out to get you, never a moment of respite.

As I walk away, Moosewala is saying get up, my wrestler, my son, get up and keep telling the truth so the coming generations can learn something, as a hidden monument looms luminous in the forest beyond, as the azaan resounds to prayer over the shithole that is this world.

---

I walk the crescent along the Southern Ridge. I walk straight along the path, cutting through the moat to the lawn facing Rashtrapati Bhawan, the flag unfurled.

Fuck You, I shout. It dissipates into the vacuum of the night.

Fuck You, I say to the prime minister, to the cabinet minister, to the power elite, to the giant nation.

And Fuck You, I say, with my back to the President's mansion, walking past the street lamps, the huddled faces under shawls and monkey caps. The police vehicles, the media vehicles parked at the side, the beacons flashing red and blue. Past the hordes of protesters from Rajasthan and Bihar and Telangana and Jharkhand crouching for warmth, huddled under thick razais, stopping me in my tracks in languages I don't understand, from a hundred villages and districts and blocks, from regions and communities I have never heard of, are alien to me, from the forests and plains and heartlands of this giant nation I didn't know of, from castes and sub-castes with interlocking complexities and rivalries and secret alliances I never knew and will never know existed, bearing injustices and violence and instincts for survival I wouldn't believe, could never hope to understand.

At Jantar Mantar, a sea of protestors around the upturned red Samrat Yantra sundial. They sit under jute covers around makeshift fires and hold their placards and posters, sing songs and clap to the beat of the dhol as they gather in circles around the poet and activist among them. Here they protest against their eviction, the abysmal state of their rehabilitation housing, displacement by giant new dams, new factories, new mines, new corporations. New malls and universities and entertainment plazas. New industrial plants set up overnight on their land, leaching oil and chemical effluents into the river, the soil, the sea, the air.

They look around, trying to glean deeper meaning from these strange buildings – that odd half lotus in front by the gate through which they were all ushered in here by the police to protest to their heart's fullest content. But really, what are these things jutting out all around? Do they mean something?

They look around again, scratch their heads, ask each other what this yantra tantra is for. Jantar Mantar, say the leaders. They look around them bemused, till the absurdity of this place dawns on them, but more so of their search for answers, of their search for meaning. They laugh out loud and realise there is no meaning at all. None whatsoever. How stupid to even look for it. No meaning in these odd, globular half-circles of a building under which they now sit, no meaning in these relentless Dilli Chalo protest marches every year, and most of all no meaning in their own lives. Just a bizarre series of random orders to up and leave as the authorities from grand offices in grand buildings such as those all over this massive city tell them to one day, they simply have to leave – go back to where you came from, and if you can't go there go somewhere else, but it isn't our problem.

Flash and burn, that's it, that's all, no deeper story.

I watch them from a distance on these winter nights, stopping for a Mother Dairy ice cream sandwich from the cycle vendor, even in this chill.

I watch them as I bite into my ice cream sandwich.

Fuck You, they are saying too, in their own way, but I cannot hear it for they are saying it in a language, in a form I cannot understand, for reasons far outside the cloistered bubble of my being, wrapped tight as I am in my own self-pity.

A man stops me abruptly. Shows me a piece of paper that seems like a petition, mutters desperately in Marathi. I barely understand the strong dialect, from Satara maybe, or Ratnagiri. The man talks first, then urges the woman next to him, his wife probably. Ladies, he says to her and pushes her in front of me. Tai, she says, clearing her throat, aamchya zameen geli, with her hands joined now, aamchya ghar, aamche kheti, aamche mule, where do we go now? What do we do? Do you have money? We just need two hundred rupees to take us in an auto to AIIMS. Can you help us? Our daughter is paralysed, she needs to have a hip surgery in the hospital, we have sold our farm, my jewellery, taken loans. Please didi, please, she reaches out for my arm, now speaking rapidly in broken Hindi, her green glass bangles on my elbow. Do you know where the . . . I shake my head, drop the ice cream sandwich by the side of the road, shrug my shoulders and walk away without turning back even once, shirk off my bleeding heart that trails uselessly behind.

I stand against the compound wall some distance from the gates of Jantar Mantar, watching protestors gather inside – farmers, masons, artisans, tribals – protesting the usurpation of their land, their livelihoods, their homes. I shirk them, but as I watch them I realise I want to know them, want to know each one of them from lands and religions, cultures and languages so different they could make up a whole world. I want to know all their stories, every unfulfilled dream and all that they still hold on to. Why they have travelled for three days or more to Delhi, why they come here to protest year after year, what they are so angry about, how the state and corporations have cheated them again. How the police and courts have done nothing. I want to know them in all their complexity, attempt to understand their songs. Help them in any way I can, even just give her two hundred rupees.

I want to know them, but leaden heavy in my own grief, I have no room for another's, no capacity to extend my own, even though I want to so badly grieve their grief, join in their protest.

I watch their protest, shrug off the Maharashtrian family, then another from MP or UP, even a group from Andhra Pradesh that just wants to make idle talk, ask me about the bus service to take them to Inderlok Market. I shrug them all off and walk away as the cops whistle shrilly at them to leave, rough up some of the men, usher the women out now the time to protest is over. They stand up, gather their things and disperse, rendered dispossessed once again by the state, even from this, their site of protest.

And when it comes to me, my one-woman protest march against my vague and ambiguous cause – the apathy of a rich ex-lover, a miscarriage of love, poor murdered children, two at least, even my own guilt at throwing Muniya in the pit – the guards turn the other way and continue with their game of cards, their gossip, or just nod off.

This city, its vast vistas and vaster corridors of power, its expanse of lawns, all absorb my Fuck Yous, their Fuck Yous, says nothing back.

And every evening I come here I chastise myself. Look, I say to myself, look at all these people that have lives far worse than yours will ever be. You are protected by privilege, by money, by social connections, by your upper-middle-class networks. Nothing you do will ever compel you to protest in a city far from your own every year in the chill of winter. Look, just look, I say as I begin to walk again, there is neither a dam sitting on your land or your house, nor a company digging for minerals on the ground beneath which you stand. Look, you have joint FDs in the bank with your father, your mother, an internet connection, the English language at your easy disposal, a master's degree from England. There are millions of people all over this country desperate for a job, millions mangled, raped, handicapped, destitute, still cleaning shit from the clogged sewers for a living because they believe that is what they are destined to do, still avoiding trailing into the shadows of those above them on the caste ladder.

Look, just look, you can do anything you want, be anyone you want.

But this grief, it's still packed tight in the ribcage. It won't go away, even as I watch the protestors and shake my head in self-reproach, even as the grief now weighs in with guilt.

And they had joys, had happinesses, had lives whole, these protesters from all over the country, who were really full people, with complete human lives, I know this of course, of course I do, but I don't see this, can't understand it, blinkered as I am by my own grief.

And as I walk to the metro station I wonder when this grief will end. When will private grief give way to the larger, more important, more inclusive, more legitimate work of political grief? When? When?

When? When? When?

Will the two ever become one, will the river of private grief ever empty into the ocean of political grief, whose depths the river could never fathom, not in a million years of its emptying.

---

In my room, writing job applications now in all earnest, now that the hookering money is wearing thin and further prospects in this business seem bleak. Now that 45 per cent of the loan still has to be paid and bank aunty never forgets to remind me of this every three days or so.

Now that my father's patience is drying up and he spends all day tending to my grandfather who is fading fast, doesn't bother to talk much to me, doesn't care. Only food is on the table, I bought bananas for your breakfast, eat your rice now or it will get cold, oh it's the dhobi again at the door. Or, I am off to pay the property tax.

Now that there's nothing for me to do but to take up a job, make something of my life, do something real.

But still only mulling over the calls that come from the recruitment companies. Procrastinating, procrastinating, waiting, watching, waiting.

---

Back to the mall again, to the new high-end grocery store at the top of the mall. To Foodhall.

Standing in front of the wall of hair-care products – shampoos and conditioners, hair masks, hair gels for the morning, the night. Looking left, looking right, making sure no shop assistant lurks behind. Tapping the shampoo bottles one by one till I reach the most expensive one yet, the one with macadamia nut and aloe, the one with Himalayan spring water and black charcoal, the one with mythic oils from Morocco.

I reach for the shampoo on the highest shelf. Twirl it in my hand.

Suddenly it rips through me with sudden force – wanting to do something, to make it right. Wanting to make him turn around and look at me, really look as he walked away on his anniversary night after he told me he was glad I did not make a scene.

After being hardened inside me for so long, I want to finally give Haseena, Shafeeqa, their Muniya and mine a chance at life. The Nepali too. To give some kind of dignity to their protests. Wanting to do something real for them.

I look at these luxury hair-care products stacked to the ceiling and know what I have to do.

Quickly I tear open the plastic packaging and flip open the cover, squeeze out the shampoo along the length of the floor, on the other products on the shelves, in a frenzy now this way and that, all over the floor.

I can't quite believe what I have done.

But before I can think any more I move to the hand-wash section, the conditioner section, the hand moisturiser and leg moisturiser section to do just this – open bottles, close them, squeeze out the contents on the sanitised floor, on other luxury personal care product bottles before running out of the store, zipping past the cameras, giddy at the free night beyond.

And two days later I go back, taking a bottle of shampoo, putting it in the deodorant section, taking a deodorant, putting it in the shampoo section, soaps in the hair conditioner section, lemon face packs in the nail polish section, the body scrubs in the body lotion section, disrupting the placeholders and all things contained within in this posh haven that houses all and every product to sate every desire that man could ever dream of.

It's what I do these days.

And sometimes, at the end of the store, where I know no camera is fixed, I take these beautifully packaged bottles of personal care products, the blurbs to attract every customer so well thought through, written by bright marketing professionals with well-paid salaries. I take the choicest imported red cherries off the fruit shelf. I sometimes take the baklavas, the French braided breads, the hand-crafted artisanal chocolates and throw them on the floor, throw and then stamp on them, jump on them till the conditioners mix with the imported plums, the mayonnaise with the cheese, the finest splash of cherry red wine.

And sometimes I examine a bottle of dry wine from the crisp vineyards of Australia and then slip it into my coat pocket, one eye cocked on the camera. Then walk coolly outside the store, make no eye contact with anyone, and when the alarm rings I run as fast as I can, with one hand on the bottle all the way to the basement and drive straight home, drinking half the bottle of this stellar wine in my building parking lot.

I can't believe I'm never caught.

And nowadays I walk into coffee shops, cute little patisseries cool as a button, spend a hundred rupees, two hundred and fifty, on red-velvet cakes coated in cream cheese, death-by-chocolate brownies, a box of a dozen cupcakes or donuts, steaming cups of cappuccino or frappuccino with hearts as creamers, and pack them all up.

Then walk down the road, swinging the bag with one hand, chomping quickly, swallowing all at once, now rush to the side of the road, jab my finger in and retch out the rich maroon crumble. And when no one is looking, I tear the paper box into little strips, let them fly loose in the breeze. As I watch them, I imagine Muniya's happy days when she was a child, running beside a river, kicking at stones. The Nepali too, hiking in the mountains, watching mountains of crystal snow.

Increasingly now, going to the most expensive sections of Foodhall again and stealing gruyere cheese, caviar, organic eggs, slices of ham. I run out of the store, run out of the mall. I drop these fine products into the unsuspecting hands of the beggars. I push these fine wines, these all-new shampoo-and-conditioner combos that promise to smoothen every frizz, these night creams that moisturise every pore, these babka breads, these sourdough breads made of rye and millets, into the laps of the poor that lie against the gates of the mall, these junkies lying flat on the pavements.

They look at these things and look at me, turn them this way and that. I show them how to eat the caviar, with lemon, with bread, teach them the importance of the cleansing, toning, moisturising routine as some mall goers stop by to look at us, amused, confused.

I come home, from yet another day of bulimic bliss, another glorious day of shoplifting, a day of petty vandalism near the back row of the luxury store, a day of sly philanthropy. Righting wrongs, taking from the rich, distributing to the needy.

All in all feeling a tiny victory for Muniya, for the Nepali, even for myself.

But it isn't enough, I admit to myself eventually, not quite knowing what to do next. Just knowing this could never be enough.

---

And then one day, as I'm slipping another bottle of fine wine into my coat pocket, he spots me. The thin boy with the khaki green All-Star sneakers. The boy who walks his husky around our apartment complex.

He looks at me, gives me a smile and picks a bottle of wine, still looking, and pockets it into the flap of his hoodie.

I drive home, knowing he is trailing me in his car.

And when we reach the basement of our building, there's a group of them circled tight, torches flashing on faces from below. So Assange is still in prison they say, and then look at him and say where the fuck have you been tonight?

And so these days, I put on my hoodie and cover my face, wear my white sneakers, zip myself up, hands in pockets, close the door behind. Follow the hushed trail of voices to the far end of the underground parking lot.

He throws something at me. I catch it with one hand, turn it around – a can of black spray paint.

Come on, he says. Chop, chop.

---

And so freewheeling nights on the highway into the heart of Delhi. Popping out through the sunroof, the windows, spraying over ads on bus stops, shop fronts, road signage.

Climbing the vast billboards that line the highways. We form a chain to the top and spray all over ads for new phones, new cameras, new laptops, new watches and devices to monitor your calories, your heartbeat, your blood pressure.

Spraying property ads – a delicious pleasure. Black paint leaking across whitewashed walls, the sanitised floors, the three generations of a happy family, the sparkling teeth of the woman, the expensive glasses of the thirty-something father, the plump, fair children and their private international schools in Gurgaon where they learn French and German. Where they learn their table manners, their coding. We spray into their swimming pools, we spray their father's smooth rise to the top of his fintech company, the mother's new promotion as marketing director of her technology company, their grandfather's successful career in law, pocketing a wad of notes into the robe by the toilet of the third floor of the Supreme Court, one cloudy Tuesday afternoon.

And when we reach the billboards of his empire I climb up quickly shoulder upon shoulder before anyone else and spray every square inch till the billboard is one with the night.

Spraying across the billboard that is the billboard of my own apartment complex – Casablanca: A World Apart.

Paedo, I spray, even though I know it's probably not true. Philanderer. Playboy.

And then right above it for all to see – Child Murderer – as they cheer and I am relieved no one here knows the full truth.

In the car now and up and down Rajpath on speed. Beginning at India Gate, I poke my head, then torso out of the window. I press the nozzle of my spray can, let loose black paint into the air, scream into the night.

We zip past the ministries of home affairs, external affairs, defence on either side, spraying the road, the lawns, spraying black the air here too. We reach the grand Rashtrapati Bhawan. Past the secretariat building sitting stately and imposing, looking down on its misbehaving citizenry, its youth gone astray.

I jump out through the window, fit my balaclava tighter.

And so infiltrating this grand bastion of our nation, following the gang inside the Parliament building. They seem to know their way around here. Creeping like rats, grabbing the papers and files of the MLAs, tearing them up, throwing them loose in this massive hall. Running from room to room throwing down the ancient PCs on the floor. And then we hear them coming, the siren call outside, the dozen or more security teams, but we are ready, we are gone, and before they have even arrived. All they see are the dozen or more enemies of the state zipping past the security cameras, black ants scurrying past, like a smudge on the screen.

We are ready, we are gone.

We are legion, he says through the voice morpher, from inside the Guy Fawkes mask that beams down an unnerving smile on the millions watching us live on YouTube.

I'm watching him on my PC from the other end of the room, the refugee area of our building, housed between floors 13 and 14.

Citizens of India, he says. We are Anonymous.

And then the film takes over – protest marches of farmers and labourers, women and transgenders and Dalits all, as the background score rises to a crescendo. Then all music stops abruptly as a headless suit appears on screen, a Guy Fawkes face swivelling in place above, the spectre of cyber insurrection on every screen.

The battle is won, he continues, but the war is far from over. We are here to show this corrupt government that as citizens of this great nation, we shall not bow. This nation needs to unite again to be truly free. We are not calling for a rebellion, he goes on, neither do we want to overthrow the government, we just want a revolution.

Government of India, Expect Us.

A pause.

Then he shuts his laptop, takes off his mask, swivels his chair around and looks at me, smiling, his All-Star sneakers ticking to no clock.

Sitting in the glare of this room we have set up for our national hacking operation, stealing electricity from the building for the AC that blasts through day and night. Bringing down websites, social media accounts of the defence ministry, the ministries of external affairs, energy and power, mining and their various allied ministries. The arms dealers, global corporations – those with business interests and operations in mining, telecom, metal, heavy machinery, petrochemicals. The domestic conglomerates, all rotting from the inside. We time the fall of their websites like dominoes in cyberspace. And then we sit back on our swivel chairs, feet on top of the tables, hands behind our heads as we watch the black magic we have unleashed broadcast across every news channel, reporters and editors running helter-skelter between government representatives and party spokespersons and company headquarters, panels of cyber security experts, panels of screens beaming the crashed websites, all now displaying '403 Forbidden'.

I see this and I think, so this is it, this is how you bring down a system from the inside, unleash the worms that gorge through the intestines. And then, more an afterthought, for when is there time to think of anything but the present these days, I think, so this is how Muniya and the Nepali are avenged.

We do not forgive, we do not forget, says the headless suit on the screen, say the black holes for eyes, the Dali moustache wiggling in jest.

---

And one day, as I am taking rounds of my building preparing for the night to come, he arrives in style in a helicopter. It lands in the middle of the golf course adjacent to our building, and the men stop their game. Man Friday salaams, opens the door. He walks around, the men swarm. I look at them – sycophants, every one of them, hyenas appeasing the lord of the jungle. My father at the tail end with a golf club on his shoulder, trying to keep up with the others.

He has a chat, some nimbu paani, asks if everyone is all right, the pitch not too rough, the snacks at the bar OK, the drink top quality, any more suggestions? They say they are organising a tournament next Saturday and invite him, he says he'll ask his PA to check his schedule but yes, he'll definitely try to come. He shakes a few hands, a jolly pat on the back, and then he's off, back in the helicopter, just a two-minute ride to the head office.

He never looked at me once, didn't see me, or more likely ignored me glaring at him the whole time.

---

Crouching behind the bushes, silent but for these cars that fly through traffic signals to mow down the poor. Behind the high walls are the Lutyens mansions.

Mansions just like his.

Hooded and shielded inside our balaclavas, sticks in our hands, spray paints, our smartphones, with GPS off. She pops out from the other side of the wall, beckons us in.

We creep into the lawn, past the dining table, the inverters and heater stubbed with ash coal from a function earlier this night celebrating a recent promotion, a wedding cementing the impenetrable ties between the elite of this city further. Tasing the security guards and growling guard dogs in one swift sweep, leaving them incapacitated. We creep into the bedrooms, silent and invisible.

They're fast asleep, the men nursing fantasies of their next acquisition, the women lying in despair in their satin gowns, with arms that fall to the carpeted floors, losing themselves to drink or oblivion or frivolity, or all of the above.

And it's so easy, too easy, to slip into their vast bedrooms, to unhinge their walk-in wardrobes and unhook the bridal trousseaus, the designer sherwanis, to try on the latest Louboutins in front of the floor-to-ceiling mirrors, spritz the Chanel perfumes. It is too easy to unruffle the contours of their extravagance, to partake in it for ourselves.

We try on their gowns, retire on their plush sofas, plop on their massage chairs that overlook the lawns and a big jamun tree. In all earnestness, check out their art installations – bronze horses twelve-foot high, paintings with breathtaking belles from mythic times. The libraries with hardbound leather volumes on law, governance, every edition of the *Economist*. We see all this, we gather it all, we shift their places as we do in the high-end grocery stores, we spray on the sculptures, the exquisite art. We steal as much as we can carry, stepping over the tased security guards, now frothing at the mouth.

Crouching beside the fleet of luxury cars, flattening the tyres of the Mercedes S Class, the Bentley, the sleek

Lamborghini like a debauched princeling in the middle, luxury car-guards of his own either side. And for added flourish, we spray on the windshield, 'Tax the bloody rich', 'Proletarians have nothing to lose but their chains', 'The last capitalist we hang shall be the one who sold us the rope', or even 'Let the ruling classes tremble at a communistic revolution!', paint pigs in bowties sitting down to a dinner of butter chicken and mutton rogan josh.

And on the high walls outside their mansions we leave our signatures – A was here, we say, or Z, or M, and then run at high speed, giving ourselves fist bumps while clutching at the stolen loot – the ties, the Tahiliani underwear, the Marc Jacobs handbag, running all the way to our cars, dropping watches that cost more than the combined incomes of entire districts across this nation, of entire slums across this city.

Days of breaking into stores in Khan Market, into the boutique cupcake stores of my girlfriends, into their pop-up bohemian swimwear stores. Stealing cupcakes from the pretty window display done up with festoons and trinkets of the Eiffel Tower, artwork that scribbles 'Pa-ree!' or 'Voulez Vous' on the wall in pop.

Creeping over the walls of the golf course a stone's throw from Khan Market. We plop down to the other side and can barely believe we've made it inside. Eerie at night, the tombs at the edge of miles of manicured green, these tombs that gleam golden, beautiful Delhi backdrops to the tournaments, the functions, the parties and weddings. Armed with our cans we spray across the grass – a prophecy borrowed from an Urdu poet, his warning siren travelling through the epochs:

Wander not looking for worldly wealth; abandon the greed and avarice in man,

The pirate of death is on the prowl to loot your days and nights with the beat of a drum.

And one day, as we're running across Anand Vihar hunting for our next prey, I stop in my tracks, turn on my heels.

The glass gate, the watchman snoozing, the house behind we have no sight of hidden by the high walls.

The rest gather behind me, on their heels, ready to sprint. I turn back to look at them and say, not this one. Then walk ahead three houses down, beckon them in.

---

And through these days of giddy insurrection the news trickles in like a tap that needs tightening, slowly, though still always in the background.

My phone buzzes and the InShort app pops in a news story – dozens of children missing from a slum colony in Noida – with a generic photo of a slum. The slum about a kilometre away from the brigadier's house, I realise, checking on Google Maps. Dozens, I re-read to make sure it's real. Not just Muniya, not just the Nepali, there were others, at least ten more. And then the Insta and YouTube shorts pop up all at once about an hour later – FIRs finally lodged, a miscarriage of justice – another headline above a picture of a man and his wife, parents of a missing girl.

Later that evening, the ticker below DD News, below the key parliamentary report – Investigations proceed in the Noida missing children case.

That's it, that's all.

And then a TV report on DD again. A man sitting on a parapet talking to the reporter, a woman behind him ironing fanatically. Our daughter has been missing for more than a year he says, we have gone repeatedly to the police but have not been allowed to file FIRs. The cops tell us you keep breeding these kids and then you lose them and then come here to waste our time. If you can't take care of your kids, why have them. They talk to us like this, shout at us, and so we have to leave.

All we are saying is just file an FIR, just make an inquiry, she could be anywhere. Anything could have happened. We've looked and looked, even gone back to our village in MP. How could she have just disappeared?

The next clip – a circle of men, women showing pictures of their missing children to the camera, one lady says if a rich kid goes missing he is found in two days, and they won't even let us file an FIR!

A few days later, a few true crime blogs of local citizen city sleuths – Noida investigation of missing children leads to an unexpected twist. Children missing every few weeks from the neighbourhood of Karauni.

Read More. Coming Soon.

Coming soon.

I look up from my phone. Can't believe it, after all these months of nothing, me checking every day, then every other day, every week, but always thinking of that night, something is now happening.

I get up from my bed.

Go straight to the bathroom. Put on the flickering yellow bulb. Wash my hands, wash again, obsessively with the Dettol handwash from the basin, grab the Medimix soap from the dish in the shower. Dig out the dirt from under my nails.

I shut the door behind me.

Then stare at myself in the mirror.

It's all coming to a head now, I tell myself. Slowly, but it's all coming to a head. And I begin to feel it, a crackle of live wire in the air. All going to be out in the open soon. It will still take time of course till the mainstream media and prime time news pick it up, but eventually it will lead to the brigadier's house, and then to him.

And then, of course, to me.

Not wanting to think any further, I go to my backpack lying on the computer chair, grab the Lotus Biscoff, the stolen almond spread from Foodhall just last night. Dip my finger in, jab it into my mouth and lick it all up.

It's coming to a head, I tell myself, dipping my finger in again, it's coming to a head, it's all coming to a head, not quite sure what to feel, what to do, wondering how long till they come for me.

Wondering what the hell I should now do.

That night, waking up from bed, straight to the bathroom.

Muniya and the Nepali, I face them again in my mirror, after months. Months and months.

What did I know about them? Nothing, except that they were young and poor and dead.

I didn't know if they had family in Delhi, where they were from, why they came here.

What their dreams were, what they wanted to be when they grew up, nothing.

A hundred times I googled him, a hundred times the brigadier, but there was nothing about Muniya or the Nepali on the internet of course. Nothing about the house help, the servants of these rich men.

Why would there be?

So the next day, I drive to the slums near the brigadier's house, where most of the missing children are supposedly from. Like at the village near my apartment complex, I drive up and down the gallis. I want to get out of my car and ask someone if they know the brigadier, or Muniya, if she ever came here to play with any of the other children. If the Nepali ever came down to buy cigarettes. Just anything.

But there's no one to ask, I know no one.

So I drive home, anxious that something is going to happen soon, but not sure what to do about it.

---

*And now.*

*Cuffed, gagged, blinded – only the black of unknown light years ahead.*

*I rattle the handcuffs in a frenzy, foolishly, more and more desperate, till they cut into my wrists and I have to stop.*

*Calm down, I tell myself, calm, calm.*

*Then I remember his meditation, his guruji. I breathe deeply in and out, imitate his technique observed every morning. Nam-myoho-renge-kyo, nam-myoho-renge-kyo.*

*It seems to work, for now.*

*Calm now, somewhat. Finally.*

*Calm.*

*But wait. Wait. Wait a minute. What is this?*

*What is what?*

*This. What is this? What the hell am I doing here?*

*Nothing, you're just trapped.*

*Yes, but why am I here?*

*Because he invited you for drinks to his new hotel in Gurgaon, and like the fool that you are, you jumped at the opportunity to meet him after so long, and then of course he trapped you.*

*OK, but why now? And why on earth is he treating me like this? He was never romantic, or kind-hearted, certainly. Maybe he cared for me in general, wanted me to do well in life, but he wasn't ever too bothered, if I am being truly honest with myself. Whatever he was, he was never ever this. All these months that I have known him, he has at least always been civil.*

*But now hitting me like this? Spitting on my face? This calculated aloofness, this treating me like I am his possession?*

*Why is he behaving like this? I stop to consider then, for the first time, that night.*

*And only when I stop my panic and bother to think do I realise the absurdity of the situation – me here, now with him. Why now? Why did he call me to his hotel room now? After distancing himself from me, and then totally ignoring me for so long. Why choose to meet me now, why call me to his hotel after so many months, after the weeks of silence that followed that Friday night, after being so proud I did not make a scene at his grand anniversary party in front of his wife and son and the filthy aristocracy of this city. Why so long after she was dead inside, and he had sent me only one cold condolence message after that autorickshaw ride, as though she was someone else's, that he had no part in the making of her.*

*Just, I'm sorry.*

*So why here, why now?*

*And only then do I realise how paranoid he is. Of course, he is afraid I will open my mouth, say something to someone. Maybe even post something online.*

*He's tired of all these months of tense silence surrounding that one Friday night – clearly he wants to end this cat-and-mouse game. Now that it's all come to a head, pop-ups on the apps, even a few dailies picking up the story, one even published it in their online features section.*

*Features featuring the poor parents of the missing children – a dozen kids, they mention vaguely, but God knows how many more. Articles accompanied by zoomed-in faces, the write-ups focusing on their poverty, their injustice. The cops brushing off nosy reporters. Nothing still about the house, about the fat man – his friend the brigadier. But it's coming I'm sure. It's coming to a head.*

*Nothing yet of him either, nothing of me, but it's close behind, I'm sure of it.*

*He is feeling the heat now. So to keep my mouth shut, to make sure I don't open up to the cops, or send an anonymous tip to the media, or even post something on my social media – even something vague – he has brought me here to this room. Tying me to the bed and blinding me, teasing me first but soon scaring me through these games we played every night?*

*And like the lovesick fool I am, I walked right into his game.*

*So here I am now, duped, naked, cold as a corpse, cuffed, gagged. Blindfolded.*

*But, vulnerable to the bone although he leaves me, I see how scared he is of what I may do. And finally, I see that the chips are stacked on my side and that it is my turn to march the queen, and all her entourage, back to her rightful spot on the throne.*

# Three

*I spit out the gag with all the force I can muster, and much to my surprise, this time it slips out of my mouth easier than I expected. I gasp for air, then instinctively scream. Soft at first but then loud, louder, louder than I ever have, till my head is ringing and ears are ringing and my whole body is this scream from some place desperate inside, clinging to the rock face of my life, knowing this is all I have left, all I must do to survive.*

*Then, barely audible but sure enough, there's a knock on the door.*

*Hello?*

*Pause, and then a hello? Hello?*

*I can't believe it.*

*Quick I say, jaldi jaldi, come fast, screaming now, not caring any more.*

*In ten minutes it's all over and I cannot believe it. I am sitting in my clothes on the red, plush chair by the window, the gag and blindfold folded neatly on the table by the TV, the cuffs on top of these clothes, the key by its side. A perfect gift set.*

*The housekeeping staff was cautious, nervous, as he loosened the blindfold, but a few thousand rupees and I told him to get out, not to come back and thank you very much but I was absolutely fine and I would take care of it. Then I told him to run away before he got back, which could be any moment, and if he could destroy the CCTV footage from the passage outside this room, otherwise it would be very bad for him, and shoved some more notes into his hand.*

*As I grab my clothes he looks at me, not at my body but my face, bewildered, disgusted, scared, and then makes an abrupt U-turn and walks out with the notes bulging from the pocket of his beige pants. And in that moment I wondered whether this was the strangest, most terrifying night of his career. But I'd never know, because he left quickly and quietly, knowing very well whose room this was and therefore who I must be, most likely, in relation to.*

*Dangerous stuff, playing with fire, and so he disappeared as quickly as he came.*

---

On the road, finally after a night wrung with panic.

Morning now and I am atop sacks of grain and rice and potatoes, spread-eagled on the truck, waking up to the wind, swallowing the rush inside. Surrendered to the sky blue with light. My fingers dig deep through the grain as I throw it up to this sky, higher and higher, and nothing falls back on me, nothing rains down from this sky that accepts all offerings.

Dev Bhoomi – the abode of the gods.

And three days later, me, in the Himachal government bus, pushing it out of a giant pothole with the other passengers and jawans, grease and axle and the acrid smell of petrol as the bus finally emerges, screaming with a mad joy, it bursts out of me and I hug myself, squeeze my body and hold it tight. I won't allow this unbridled joy to escape, this joy that knows no reason, has no reason to be, not now I won't.

And as I scream in joy with the children from the bus, a group of orange-clad sadhus glides past, not looking at us, not even speaking a word to each other as the jawans and a few passengers rush to get bananas and chapatis, place them in their hands.

One of them peers from the far end and waits for someone to come to him, but when he sees the puncture of our bus has been fixed and all the passengers have climbed inside, he walks on with the others, limping his way to the highest mountains.

And reaching my intended village in the mountains – up flat stones, through towns with slate roofs and women with babies tied on their backs, through oak and birch, and higher up the fresh sting of pine, and then the land flattens and then a meadow where only cattle graze. Where at night there is song by the fire, and further into the night the howl of the wolf, the desolate cry of a bird from the valley, I sink further into the sleeping bag, eyes shut.

I fall asleep.

---

And me on Harleys or Yezdis with bikers all the way from Bangalore, from Cochin, from Trivandrum. Arms swooping, cutting through mountain ranges, clenching fingernails into shoulders at the deathly turns, screaming my name into the deep valleys, parched lips that scoop ice water from the rushing rivers.

More gravel, more dust, more mountain ranges, clipped and jagged and mighty, from one end of the earth to the other.

Now walking on the baking highway – barefoot, hair matted, eyes blazing, glorious and naked and haloed by the sun, leaving a trail of wet footsteps that vanish with every step, now finding myself at high noon in the desert of crumbling rock and sand, this undulating land guarded by mountains of snow that graze the sky.

And when I glance backwards, when I turn to gather all the miles that have been tread, all the paths relinquished, all that has been accomplished, I see that the whole world ends behind me and the only journey is the one onward.

And onward, climbing the gentle incline, surrounded by school children, round faces and red cheeks, who want to know everything – where you come from, how big the city is – by mountain goats that hide in the ravines, monks with their prayer wheels tossing a football and pulling a cat's tail, and the inner monastery with the smells of burnt oil and gehu, wooden camphor incense and a chiselled monk serving me salty tea and honeyed chapatis.

Waking up from deep sleep to sit in the dark basement before dawn. Sitting along the corridor where the daily prayers and the prostrations will commence. But now, all is silent, and stepping out on the terrace, I see *Nam-myoho-renge-kyo* in bold letters on the mountain front. I think of him for a moment, and then I let go.

Now higher up the valleys and ridges and mountains, until finally I am on top of the whole world.

And here I am, where nothing grows, where no ash-smeared sadhu levitates, where no monk from the mountains meditates, higher than the crystal blue glaciers, this land, where no mystical beast grazes, where not even a sapling can grow. Here I sit sifting the stone crushed into gravel over aeons more vast than man could ever dream, sifting the fine earth through my fingers, watching slate slabs piled on each other – appeasing the souls of the dead, in gratitude to the cosmos – the red, the yellow, the blue prayer flags flapping as the winds roars.

I sit here, leaving the world's valleys and plains, its megalopolises, its corruption, the property scams, its stark inequalities. Leaving him, leaving my dead daughter. Leaving Muniya and the Nepali too after blocking them out all these days on the road. Leaving all the frantic Google searches about that night. Leaving them and all that I saw and did not see, all that I refused to acknowledge that night. Muniya and the Nepali, who once consumed my waking and dreaming life, now forgotten.

The next day inside the nunnery, high noon outside but dark and cold here, I sit cross-legged on the stone-cold floor. And I am rolling back and forth with the others, chanting in loops, meditating on the Nepali, on Muniya thrown into the pit again, the same body slumped on the toilet, that child's cry, cold peach iced tea, the listless swabbing of the line of luxury cars, meditating on this and offering it all to Mara the black goddess of death – wrathful and frightening, vengeful and lusty, and she is cutting my body into a thousand little pieces.

I am sitting in this nunnery meditating on this all morning, meditating for detachment, knowing this sin will remain inside no matter all this groping.

Later I go to lie in the desert. Clouds white as light rush in, their shadows flow in and out of the land, then disappear. The sun dashes pink through dawn and dusk, rising to high splendour at noon. At night the dark spreads and is awash with a billion stars.

I lie in this desert.

Days pass in the sky. In the desert all around horses flock and graze and race each other; wild, short grasses grow tough and wither, the nomads with their yaks roam the plains, move on to greener pastures.

Years pass, whole centuries, a hundred million centuries. I lie still, listening to the mantra of Avalokiteshvara, the lord of compassion.

All is right, I tell myself. All is forgiven. My alienation from my family. She dead and gone. Muniya and the Nepali and what I did not do for them.

What I did to him. What I did to Muniya.

All is fine. All exactly as it should be.

Here, the pilgrimage now complete, here, finally, I rest.

Now come days of guest houses, days of shady motel rooms in Thimphu, in Shillong, in mountain towns like Nagar, bargaining with the fat lady playing cards for fifty rupees less, please aunty-ji, for a dirt cheap room. Past rooms on the ground floor with plastic curtains, rooms of young boys and younger girls in glinting imitation jewellery, rooms on rent for the kids to make out in after college, rooms for girls on hire for the night, past all this to my room on the first floor, the creaky flap-jack door, the hard bed and thin mattress.

Lying on this mattress, looking up at the wall, a circle for a face, a round body below, ripe round breasts, pubic hair and a uterus, slender fallopian tubes, a delicately drawn vulva, a perfect vaginal opening – the genitals still-life, the body a child's cartoon. I look at all this in this dank little room drunk out of my mind, fighting panic as I listen to the cries of the women from the whorehouse below and the old fear floods in after these days adventuring. Nothing but a show of bravado, the voice tells me.

I fling the torn sheet off, get up from the bed, go to the bathroom. In the bleak yellow light from the lone bulb, two cockroaches creeping along the pipe, the drunk and fearless singing in the streets below. I peer into the cracked mirror.

Then I gather the leftover mashed green Lifebuoy soap, smear it all over my face, a line on my outstretched tongue. Look at myself.

A Kali Maa from outer space.

Waking up in panic in the heat of 11 a.m., this alien ceiling, this bright, noisy world outside. Already mid-morning and the children return from school, the mothers have made lunch and planned dinner and here I am, lying on this worn bed, three bus journeys, two more hotels, a dirty train ride left till the next place called home.

Now brush teeth, hoist backpack, a quick scan across the room, time to bolt the door, time to leave. But wait, wait a little bit, why the hurry always, you are on a holiday after all? Stay another minute, another hour.

So I cover my face with the musty sheet, feel my heart beat strong and thick and alive.

---

I step out in the evenings of every little town in India, I put on my poker face, I ask the men on the streets, the men in the shops, the paan-walas and the istri-walas and the raddi-walas where the thekas are, the cheap wine shops. I nod earnestly, say thank you and walk away quickly to the shops, gliding, but excited, wild, nervous inside.

I stand behind the men jostling and fighting on a Saturday night at the wine shops and clear my throat and shout out for angrezi sharaab, for cheap Indian liquor, for something high and fast and dirty and smooth, and most importantly Indian, and the men stop their talk and their jostling and I'm ushered to the desk and I rattle off names and prices, rattle my knowhow, and when I'm given what I want, the men part as I leave, and I walk home with this dirty bottle of daaru hidden in the inside pocket of my black leather jacket, feeling a minor victory, conquering a speck of an island.

I rush back to my room, get very drunk on the dirty daaru in the blue, cheap lights of a dirty room, watching an eighties Hindi movie, the gyrating rhythms of the thousand-petalled dancers. I get so drunk that I go to the bathroom and vomit and vomit, and when I come back to bed I think of my old love from back when we were young, another life that, listening to Jim Morrison on the terraces of Bombay buildings, high out of our minds, looking out at the grey sea. He looks at me and croons – so tell me where your freedom lies . . .

I think of my old love and I look around at this filthy bright-green room, this white tube light, this derelict little place in this dirty wayside tier-3 or tier-4 Indian town that I am in only to catch the Shatabdi Express, that anyone only ever comes to to catch the Shatabdi Express.

I look around at all this and I say to him in my head, here babe, here, here. It is here that my freedom lies.

---

In the trains, inching through the rubbish dumps that masquerade as towns, pools of toothpaste and shit on the morning tracks, leather towns that smell vile. Train rides remembered through late afternoons, the chugging, the whining, the train groaning to the depths of nowhere.

The loo rises from the plains of this great country, gathers momentum as I lie stuck on the leather seat – a slug, a vegetable, a mollusc giving myself up entirely to the train that traverses inch by inch all over the land.

Boys thin as rails, fly-abouts, layabouts selling teddy bears in a hundred fluorescent colours with matching coloured caps and ties, selling nail clippers, saris, selling time-pass snacks, selling everything and anything, stomping through the corridors up and down, annoyed when passengers stop them to ask the price but never buy.

And outside is India where the women still beat wet saris against the earth, where buffaloes lie in the sun – this India that will always remain, this pastoral in denial, from long before the jolt and throb and thrust of the city and for long after. And then the rag-picker kids, blind or pretending to be blind, walking barefoot, singing nasally aye malik tere bande hum, flies on eyes leaking, noses leaking, clicking at their clickers, arms outstretched and pocketing a few rupees, which they throw into their half-torn shirt pockets.

Bihar, Mandya, Uttar Pradesh – I climb onto the upper berth in the sleeper class, and backpack as a pillow I don't get up for three days straight. Through murmurs of delay, derailment and workers' strikes. Through gundas that hop on and off at night and frisk the sleeping passengers.

And at night, feeling a finger running slowly, tracing a river down my foot, whistling a heart-breaking tune, this man, spitting paan, talking to his friend, and before I have gathered the courage to scream he is gone.

Jharkhand, Mandya again, inching through every second town of this country, down south now, finally.

I turn to my right. The man with red henna in his hair is still staring at me. He seems to have not stopped for three days, his stomach drooping over the berth, listless, save for the hand that disappears under the thin IRCTC sheet.

This degree of otherness, this exoticism I evoke for them. This privilege, a young woman roaming because she can, because she has the money to – leftover from Sainsbury's so long ago, leftover from whoring, I remind myself, but nobody has to know this. A woman on the loose. In this train not to return to her village to get married or to her college to complete her degree or to her hometown to see a dying grandparent, no.

They are confused by it, they can't understand it at all, how my parents have left me like this to travel for no specific purpose at all, more and more like those young angrez with their cluelessness and cursory understanding of our country, no matter how much they think they know.

They don't like it, a woman on the loose going just where she pleases, doing just as she wants. They envy me for it, my easy money thrown into cheap motels, nursing rambling loneliness with stacks of potent hooch, into monuments they see only during Diwali vacation with the entire family.

Travelling for months on the road, travelling for travelling's sake, who would have thought such a thing is possible.

They don't want their sons, but especially daughters, to have anything to do with me.

They don't like it, are confused by me, but still they can't stop staring.

---

Bombil fry on hooks, sugar rum down the throat, the breaking of waves. Down the highway speckled with pristine coastal towns – Tungareshwar, Ratnagiri, Ganpatiphule . . .

Welcome to Goa.

Climbing the craggy hillsides, dancing through full-moon nights on half-moon beaches, discovering sites of night-time raves and routine morning salvation in clearings so deep no sunlight can filter in. Making commune with eternity while crushing the hashish, that ancient smell of pine and earth, something sinister in how it clings to the inside of your head, its viscous remains that stick to the hair, the skin, buried as half-black moons inside nails.

The morning after, always the morning after. And that old familiar sinking as time becomes a heavy thing again and choices have to be made, responsibilities addressed. But sprawled face down on the beach I wonder about last night – when and how the chaos of each mind knew itself to be in community, a thousand ears drumming the same frequency, neural explosions in unison as this tribe that existed on just that beach, amidst that very wilderness, for those few hours – when exactly did this community feel ancient and sacred unto itself.

And when the mornings stretch on and the community has scattered and all bonds have been rendered transient, I still wonder if every night will pass into mornings like these, into afternoons that slumber on.

Evening in my new life with the wandering band of Israeli acrobats, fire-eater sunsets that twist around hula hoops, neon frisbees careening through space, selling sangria by the glass, healing crystals from Morocco, dream catchers woven from feathers that fly across Peru, Ecuador, the forests of the Amazon. Spanish baja by the sea, the women swaying to the red moon rising, one-way footsteps to the sea.

And what will it be like, I wonder, this new-found life that could be forever – the squawking gulls, the curtained shacks with Jimi Hendrix, Bob Marley opening lazily for banana pancakes and Nescafé, the women from the drought-riddled interiors selling beads, offering to paint our hands with henna, whispering hushed secrets to tourists while excavating mounds of earwax, as yogis stretch palms to the sun, the chakras a-bloom, bejewelled kundalinis slithering to the sky, mandalas awakening the inner eye from its thousand-year slumber.

And how and when did it come to this I wonder, staring at the tip of torchlight in this forest, the braying wolves, the silent cattle, the frightened birds, the rushing streams, hearing my trembling voice – where are you? Are you OK? John, Jerry, Margo – trailing rumours set out from town, from Tosh and Kasol, the porches of cafes and shoddy homestays of the routine murder of tourists, looting, rape, a deal gone sour too soon, bodies thrown into the undergrowth in snake pits. And trailing the rumours of friends rooting themselves to the earth, losing themselves in the wilderness as we lose our minds and bodies and trail deeper into the jungle.

Three gunshots at night, running out into the streets chased by dogs snapping at our ankles, jumping to fleshy thighs.

Now finding my allegiances in urine-stenched cop houses all over the country, over stacks of Gandhis, everyone smiling sheepishly, a minor expected inconvenience, all negotiable. Now finding friendships through no will of my own this night, on the side of the Russians, or the Armenians, the Israelis, the Nigerians, bribing our nights to freedom in the sunniest paradise on earth.

And encountering saucer plate-eyed women and saucer plate-eyed men, ribcages poking through emaciated chests, repeating phrases at grocery stores, making odd demands, locking themselves in rooms, lying naked on the foothills, muttering in self-fabricated tongues in the high noon on the beaches of Goa, Gokarna, in Vagator, in the mountains on the roof of the world.

O sun-hazed days, O afternoons of semi-stupor, O moments in between sleep and wakefulness, awaiting the drama of the night that could lead us to any distant dimension, but now seeing us sprawled on sacks of jute under fans in their achingly slow revolution. I lie like this for an hour more and only then realise that I am still high out of my head.

I look at the fan, eyes fixed on the blades, and wonder – for how much longer does the road run? How much longer, the intrigue of its call? How long then, its constant beckon?

---

Sitting in the Himachal Pradesh public bus at night, travelling from somewhere to somewhere. Alone now, fellow travellers dropped by the wayside of their own plans. Curled against my backpack, leaning against the window so I don't fall on the four others and one baby crushed against me. I'm trying hard to sleep, blocking these Bollywood party beats.

And then the soft melody plays and suddenly she's singing, the singer full of truth.

How is your selfishness?
You choose neither sun nor shade
Neither salt nor sugar sits on your tongue
You became your own God, travelled the seven seas
But remain just a dry shell inside

I open my eyes.

Clutch my backpack tighter.

Listen to the song.

And listening, it comes back to me, those moments of hesitation before the open road, and now this. Wanting to stop but not knowing when, pulled by the intoxication and adventure of the moment, always wanting to do more, go further, one hit more.

But wondering always, how much longer, this constant beckon of the open road?

All that, and now this.

My father and grandfather, the last time I thought of them – four weeks ago? Five? Back when I sent my father an SMS telling him I needed some space, I was fine, I had money, I was just taking a break and travelling, that's all.

I kept his promise to send him one message every day, rushed through his calls, ignored most, only saying to him like a broken tape recorder – I'm on the road, on the road, yes I have money, I'm fine, I'm travelling with college friends, school friends, university friends flown in from England. OK then, take care, gnight – and back to the heady haze of the moment.

I think of them going through the motions of normal life – the morning newspaper read cover to cover. I think of their prayers through the day, the quiet breakfasts, the daily emptying of my grandfather's urine bag, filing the monthly bills in this office or that, even though it could be done so easily on the app, as I once tried to show my father. My father putting the vessels back into their rightful place in the cabinet every night after the maid washed them.

Their strange, absent, self-involved, isolated child distancing herself further. Their daughter, this selfishness of hers, how her feet don't stay still, how she travels the world with no concern for her family.

How did she become this?

I pull my legs closer, put my head in my lap.

My mother, whom I had not seen for so long, not since the Nirula's airport outing before England. This mother, too proud to pander, who had stopped calling or messaging after I stopped responding. This forced distance between us. My mother, who obsesses over her house, the contrast between her and my father and me. She didn't want me, always made me feel like I didn't possess enough personality, but perhaps it's just a notion I have harboured through all these years. She never spoke to me of it.

She was fast disappearing to me, this mother of mine, hurtling like an astronaut lost in space. I miss her hard, I realise now, now that I have given myself a chance to think of her. I need to know if she is OK.

I look at the black-as-night world outside. Lean my head against the window as this rickety bus ascends the mountains.

I close my eyes to him singing still – that broken cot, that cream on top of the milk, that earthen pot, they all stand still and beckon, O pleasure seeker, O wanderer, O travelling saint.

Come home, O Kabira, your shadows call you home.

---

The gate reaches my waist now. I push it but it is locked from inside.

There's a new bell on the new wall, but nothing else has really changed here.

I wait.

Take in the house – the roof caving, the coconuts fallen on the shed cover, the vines through the veranda trellis. The grass as unkempt, varnish peeling off the balustrades, still those damn stray dogs that snap all the time. The bungalows around that have transformed into six-storeyed buildings, the buildings that have added floors, shadows that block the sun into her world.

A two-storeyed bungalow with a small attic, a shed in front, a garden to toil in. In a constant cycle of decay and renewal from the first day it was lived in. Growing wilder after my grandfather died, after my grandmother's accident that paralysed her, after which my mother took over.

Every summer vacation spent undoing and redoing the tiling, repainting, shaking out mattresses with dead moths, hunting for the rats that gnaw through the pipes.

Monsoon in this house of my childhood.

In our home the electricity goes, and from the entrails of the clouds the thunder roars. By candlelight and in flashes of lightning we tighten the taps with spanners, drag buckets under the roof, lean on the railing of the balcao and watch our garden bloom. Then my mother and I, we sit with my grandmother in the purple dark in our white nighties, gossip about the family crazies and gather on the bed. Dreams seeping into each other, soaking the sheets, a coterie of women cocooned from the world by soft drapes of mosquito netting.

This house I was born in, that my mother was born in, that she fought her whole life for, is still fighting in, that will be mine one day, that I won't know what to do with, how to live in. And mother knows I have neither the strength nor will to keep it and has grown to despise me for it. This is why she despises her own daughter so much.

Inside, the street kids are having a ball – Mintu, PriyaGold, I remember them even though it's been at least five years since I was here. Taller now, PriyaGold with small breasts that swell under the lilac salwar kameez Ma gave her as Diwali baksheesh so many years ago. She sits with Mintu in the garden as though she owns it, carrying a sleeping baby, drugged probably. There are a few others I don't recognise. The kids slope down the tiles, fall on their feet like cats on the old beige family fiat, shriek into this Sunday afternoon of scratchy cawing, blaring Bollywood party hits from a passing auto.

A miracle, this relative Sunday silence in this city of twenty-something million.

I stand still, look past the house. Drop my backpack and shade my eyes against the sun. Behind, the sea shimmers grey and coral, flickers with gold.

It's beautiful really, just this.

I turn back to the house, ring the bell.

And so it has come to this, after all.

After all my days of endless wandering, restless itching for new lands and people, escaping the creeping past, escaping myself, wandering through plains of red earth, shrines of ice and glacier tied with frozen sacred threads, forging through rivers, waiting at the ghats till my lamp trickles into the river of lights. Through the overflowing cities, the million towns of grease-reeked bus stations, driving through this country of sun-toasted children, crisp and golden-haired, shrieking for 'one chocolate' behind our jeep, through fields of green and gold grain rotting on waysides, of India waving past, women blushing beneath sheaves, peeking through baskets, the brightest pallus. Behind trucks heaving with lifeless young men travelling from village to town, town to city to find some, to find any work.

And walking with naked saints of a million sects, the sub-sects, followers of a hundred babajis, on their way to do darshan to this god or that, clapping in unison with pilgrims narrating stories of their thousand gods, thousand-headed, thousand-handed. Hitchhiking despite all odds, sitting with my legs dangling out of the train as the wind blows against the piss-stenched toilet and I screech with the children through every tunnel. Bumping against my backpack on the bus, a merry-go-round of fellow travellers, of babies dumped on laps, vomit spewed out at hairpin bends, a quick exchange of a bottle, of cones of channa and bhel and slices of tart mango slathered with magenta juice, of dabba-loads of mukhvaas and hajmola, of Cadbury éclairs and loose change through railings as the seller jogs along the whining bus, the train.

And dozing, and dozing, and waking up with a start on the roof of the bus, only the sky for cover and always the open road ahead.

And on and on, stopping only when the land ends at the shore, on my knees before the sea, in gracious respite.

And so it is that after all these days of wandering everywhere, of wandering nowhere, of wandering a hundred miles away, I come back home to my mother.

And my mother, she sits in her sleeveless nightie rocking herself to sleep in the sultry heat of this city, losing herself in the wilderness of her own home.

---

Mother and I race into the sea at Juhu Beach on a July afternoon. The open beach our own. That first instance of being afloat, aloft, the sea in the pit of your navel. She holds my body to her own, tells me I am a fish now, any fish I'd like to be, and I kick my feet in glee.

And in the grey-green haze beneath the water, pink plastic bags drifting like jellyfish, I reach my hand out to feel the jut of bone beneath her cheek, the outline of her mouth, the softest, blackest hair, my mother.

Running across the stretch of Juhu Beach, my mother and I, she drags a stick behind her to make waves and I run behind her, jumping, crashing into her back as she swoops me into the sky and I stick out my tongue to the first burst of rain.

And my father, in his trunks and chest hair, embarrassed by this nakedness, these relentless kisses, at all this embrace.

He watches us from a distance clutching the paraphernalia of this Sunday picnic – two yellow arm paddles, the lavender water bottle strung around his neck. Taking photographs of us as unobtrusively as he can.

He had it folded, single-folded first and then lengthwise, this photo, it lies in his drawer beside his bed. Black and white, my mother scooping me up and lifting me to the sky. I have never seen him take it out, but I know it's right next to him when he sleeps at night, the first thing when he wakes.

Now beach night, a free-for-all fun fair on any one of those holidays of my childhood, as only a night on a Bombay beach can be. She bickers with the balloon man, dashes through sprays of sparks from a bhutta cart, blows bubbles into our faces, raises the pinwheels to the sea breeze, licks pista kulfi and throws the melting sticks to the dogs as they tear into her billowing skirt.

She laughs at them, talking to them like long-lost friends – aye Montu, Shontu, oye Gomati, where were you all last week? I searched for you all over this damn beach, it's every nook and cranny, Gomati, don't tell me you're pregnant again! So soon? Lordy Lord! Laughs at the beggar children that serenade her, buys falooda for them from the shacks, gives them whichever flavour of gola they want from any number of the magenta, lemon yellow, electric-blue bottles of the gola carts that line the shore. She jumps on the weighing scale that doubles as an astrologist, palm reader, face reader, its neon lights blinking. Sirf pachpan keelo, it says, and a few passing women in burqas turn to marvel at her figure, as the machine proceeds to offer some notes of caution about her health in the coming months. She hears this and throws her head back and laughs so wide I almost count all her teeth, even the three fillings.

At Juhu Beach, Aksa, Malad Marve, she drags me to the Ferris wheel, pays no heed to my remonstrations but parks me on a seat of the queen of Ferris wheels, shuts the gate chalo bhaiya! And off we go, arey jaldi karo, fatafat, faster and faster. And then we're high up, and there's a whole city below, a city of Ferris wheels with broken glinting lights, a city of merry-go-rounds whose scratched-out yellow horse saddles fling off with a toddler, and just beyond the curve a city of glinting towers, and beyond that only the sea.

We watch the city, mother and I, a turntable scratched beyond its years. The city's poor and rich like harried mice scurrying below. She turns to me and gives me a tight hug without a word, and finally looking at my pale and alarmed face, laughing let's go.

Christmas parties in this old Bandra house. She turns me around as she leads me in a jiving jamboree to 'Walk of Life', to 'La Bamba', to those classics. As we twist and turn and trip, someone lifts me, Aunty Roxanne or Grandma Melanie or Daddy, and plants a kiss on my head and puts me on the lacy table groaning with kalkals, with blocks of marzipan. I grab handfuls, stuff my mouth as I watch Uncle Godfrey or Uncle Melville or Ryan point at her, as she at him, as they twist to Elvis grooving you're the cutest jailbird I ever did see. Or my mother jiving to Dire Straits with a strange man who holds her waist tight as they dance and I jump down from the kalkals and rush to them and push them away from each other as the strange man laughs and the aunties laugh and my mother looks down at me and smiles and say, arey, why men, baba?

Summer vacation in Goa, my father and I in full gear, sunhats, dark glasses, oversized 'Go-Ah!' T-shirts.

Now mother, three glasses of port wine down, in her absolute element. On the fairy-lit deck of the tourist ferries that ply up and down the Mandovi, she bolts from the seats and joins the performers – the men in top hats and the women in bandanas with puffed pink sleeves and aprons. She spins her long skirt, claps her hand in tandem shouting Ya Ya Maya Ya, Ya Ya Maya Ya . . . to the tune of the song as some of the dancers stop to watch her, unsure what to do next, as the tourists watch, a little amused, some turning back to look at us, as my father and I, sitting at the edges of our seats, look at her and pretend we can't see the others, always embarrassed, always riveted by the performance that is my mother.

---

And so, standing outside my mother's home, I ring the bell.

She can't hear it, crooning to Little Richard through the first-floor veranda. But I can see her through the jaali door, on her rocking chair. I put my bag of unwashed clothes on the street, look around.

The baniya-wala next door gives me a smile, makes circles in the air with his finger, thodi paagal hai, he's telling me. Not knowing I am the daughter of the madwoman inside.

I smile back, hoist my backpack higher and open the gate as the kids yell and scamper out of the compound and Mintu and PriyaGold walk out imperiously, Priya giving me a serious hello Didi.

Nothing has changed here.

I open the door and lean against the doorway. Watch as she croons with her eyes closed, getting up from her rocking chair and kicking at the industrial-sized Harpic bottles, the broom and pan set, the old vacuum. Even from here I know she is drunk, even though it's two in the afternoon and there's not a bottle in sight.

I watch her for a few minutes, her eyes closed, in a half trance. Mama, I say as the song changes, and run to her, hug her tight.

She pauses, held hostage by this uncharacteristic exhibition of feeling from her daughter. Then a few seconds later pats my back, clicks her tongue and says all right, all right baba, come on now, don't be so silly, in her raspy voice, reeking whisky breath.

That evening, waking up with a jolt to the drums in the dark, the loudspeaker blaring the latest Marathi hit. I wonder what it is – a wedding, a political procession, the latest gunda freed from prison? And realise it's the Ganpati pandal.

Of course. I've been so caught up in my own travels, in my own affairs, I've forgotten it's Ganpati time in the city, when the city is at its most raucous, its most glorious.

The beat is too much to stay still, to keep lying in bed. So I jump out, wear my chappals, skip down the staircase from my bedroom attic, kept exactly as during my college days as though she was expecting me to return. Out through the hallway, the dining room, passing the TV to see her bending over the balcony balustrades, fingers in mouth, piercing shrill whistles to the beats.

She's so crazy I can't help but laugh. She turns around and grabs me and shakes my shoulders, my hips, come on, she yells as we watch them, the men drunk and dancing with abandon, the women dressed in their finest navvaris – purple blocked with gold, red lined with silver – as Ganpati sits on a cart decorated with satin and silks, flowers and tinsel, hobbling on the narrow pot-holed road outside.

They hear my mother's shrill whistle through the techno beats, look up at us in the blue house, wave and call us to join.

And my mother, she is already dancing down the stairs, whistling and hopping over the stray dogs. Already out of our barely standing rusted gate, one with the crowd.

At first I stand outside, self-conscious as always, dying for someone to pull me in but not wanting to be a part of this. And then she pulls me in of course, as though this crowd is her crew, as though she is part of the organising committee of this pandal, as though she was born to dance wild at Ganpati visarjan.

She holds me tight and pulls my arms around in circles and screams as 'Zingaat' plays and the singer sings dhinchak zorat, techno varat to the song. I laugh with everyone, and when I look around I see we have already reached Linking Road, then Khar, now Juhu. I close my eyes, my mind a vestibule of no thought, nothing at all, only these mad beats.

I move to wherever the orchestra takes me.

Standing at the barricade of Juhu Beach, fighting tooth and nail with the cops that whistle and beg us to go back as the clouds pour down on us. Jostling with the crowds, pulling, pushing, shouting morya, screaming ganpati cha jai jai kar, we watch our Ganpati carried out to sea among all the other Ganpatis, grand, homely. We stay despite the falling, the heaving, the noise, the downpour, the cops pushing us back. Despite marigold petals and tinsel in our eyes, in our hair, despite the crush of free vada paos from passing building residents caking our shoes. We stay and squint till all we can see is his tusk still poking out of the sea.

Walking back shouting for him to pudchya varshi lavkar ya, walking the ten kilometres home because no rickshaw will ply at this mad hour when the whole city is one big street party.

Finally we reach home. The doors still flung open, lights beaming, we walk up to the living room and scrape mashed masala potato and half-strewn garlands from our bodies, kick off our shoes. The faint beats of another Ganpati going out to sea in the distance.

She drags the second rocking chair from her bedroom, flops into hers and looks at me as I flop into mine, put my feet up.

Gives me a wide smile.

Then jumps up, walks to her cabinet, pours out two glasses, hands me a rum with very little Coke and three fat ice cubes, just the same as hers.

Want to jive? she asks after taking a sip that is really a gulp, and before I can say anything she puts on 'Crazy Little Thing Called Love' as I give her a half smile, gather my breath. Then reach out for a coaster, place my drink gingerly on it and stand up and offer her my open arms.

The next day we go into town because she wants to show me something.

Monsoon, with my mother riding the local trains.

The men from the passing trains whistle at my mother, they do now as they did then, know the strength of her striking beauty, even in this flight of a moment, want a little of it for themselves. And my mother whistles back, all four fingers in her mouth piercing through the air.

Vacations in the Bombay locals with my mother. She grabs my hand and pushes me with the rest of the crowd. We inch our way to the doorway. Malad kya? the others ask, Borivali? to establish whether we obey the unspoken hierarchy of the local trains which determines who gets to occupy how much square inch of space, depending on where they need to get off.

My mother shrugs, and when Malad comes, or Borivali, Jogeshwari, the heaving mass of ladies behind us assumes we were getting off and now realise we are not. She holds on to the metal rod for dear life and crushes me with her force as they descend, ascend, outwards and inwards, a swarm of abuse around. All is war – every station, this is what happens. She shouts back, hollers like nothing I have ever heard, aey mad o what, as she smacks a wayward arm or thigh, as though waiting for this for days.

Tereko itna phod dungi na, someone shouts from behind on this train ride here and now, and my mother shrieks.

My mother, relishing these arguments, this daily entertainment, throwing herself into the fights of other ladies, who grabbed whose fourth seat, who was right to push whom, lending her opinion on the marriage proposals and family affairs of strangers. Everyone took everyone else's opinion seriously here, it seemed, secrets instantly revealed to strangers. Everyone intensely involved in each other's lives. She turns around and asks the women sitting behind her their advice, and they invite others, until the whole compartment is discussing the merits and demerits of the potential grooms for Priya or Padma or Parvati.

Chalti hai kya, someone shouts at her from the men's compartment – nau se baarah thrusting me out of my reverie.

Later that evening she takes me to Worli Seaface, opposite Haji Ali where boards have been put up blocking the view of the shrine. Mumbai is upgrading, she says to me excitedly as we stand beside the boards, and I can see a curved interchange slowly emerge. Over strawberries and cream at Haji Ali Juice Centre, she shows me videos of smooth, simulated highways being built along the coast of the city with green extensions and parks. Like Dubai, like Singapore, the comments read.

Mumbai is upgrading, as I grumble over the mess all this construction has made in this city of twenty-five million with village-loads, town-loads of new entrants every day coming to live in Bhayander, in Agripada, in Nallasopara, to buy a 200-square-foot flat with one balcony that can fit all of three potted plants.

Mumbai is upgrading. Inconvenience regretted, she shrugs, and looks up at me, her face full of glee.

---

Once a month they visit our house as part of a heritage tour, part of the Celebrate Bandra festival, the MumbaiJio Live festival.

A host of people – retirees from Bandra, Khar, Juhu, a few from further down the western suburbs, some elderly couples from the Catholic colonies of Malad and Borivali my grandparents knew. Hipster youngsters, sporting the same large glasses as me. They write articles in obscure art journals and blogs no one quite reads, post grainy pictures of our roof and mildewed walls and the broken grotto outside in sepia tint on Insta, avoiding the kitchen with its veneer cabinets and state-of-the-art top table Ma got done a few years ago.

An enthusiastic young tour guide, a history student doing her MPhil at Bombay University, explains the design of the house to the rapt audience – points out the gabled rooftops, the balcao tiling, the delicate wrought-iron pillars of the ground-floor veranda. In the living room, all sit politely, Ma like a duchess on her rocking chair front and centre. And immediately they fire off all manner of questions – as though they've been waiting for this for years. For how long has she been living here? Who are or were her father and mother? How did he acquire this property? How does she maintain it now? Pointed, well-researched, well-thought-through questions about the Portuguese interiors and architecture she didn't know much about. And so, again, she recounts her family history, gesticulating wildly, relaying every detail to this rapt audience she seems to have locked in a cage of her making.

And she makes up stories too, producing aunts and wayward cousins, hackneyed stories, half-truths, half borrowed from this book or that, a movie she caught late last night on MGM. Some stories made up on the spot, pouring out like the rain now outside. Stories of how her father inherited this house from his father's brother, how the brother's son, the rightful heir, turned out to be a useless drunk who was thrown out by his father and spent the rest of his days drinking himself to death in the nooks of this neighbourhood of Ranwar.

He probably haunts the attic, she adds, as the thunder roars, and to her delight the electricity goes and the audience is left in the dark.

And so my mother entertains these studious folk who have traipsed to her house to discover some architectural and historical obscurity. And to give them their time's worth, she makes up stories. Every cliché thrown in from strands of hearsay and neighbourhood gossip she grew up hearing. A non-stop mishmash till she ceases to care that it stopped making sense a long time ago. Doesn't really care if she is found out, comes to be known as the MumbaiJio Live festival fraud. Doesn't believe these people take her seriously anyway. Not the old-timers who have known her family for years.

She wonders why they come at all.

But there they are. I turn around and see them, their spectacles clouded, wearing looks of mild bemusement, but beyond that, expressions I cannot quite unpack.

A rapt and silent audience that is the mother of all anti-climax.

And just as she is about to ramble off again, the guide takes over, thanking her profusely for her legacy, for sharing her stories, for her hospitality, for her utmost regard for history and community, always; before ending on a dismal note – a beautiful home like hers needs to be preserved, she might not believe it but it's pure heritage, really. Such a rare thing in today's world. And taking the lead the others pitch in, muttering at first, then slowly a singular collective, a chorus of crows – she's doing the right thing, it must be so hard but she must stick on.

And in this moment I know my mother thinks of the others. The Rosarios and Braganzas and Castellinos who have sold their own bungalows last year, or the year before last, who now live in penthouse apartments on the site of their old properties, using all that extra money for cruise holidays to the Mediterranean, to visit relatives in Australia and England. The chorus of crows gets more grating, croaking now about the voracious appetite of property developers.

She shakes her head dismally, lowers her voice and tells them darkly of how she wakes up each morning to the land sharks on the far horizon and wily cousins swimming closer, presenting her with newer, cleverer litigation as the days wear on. In fact, she overheard the neighbours discuss how her life might be in danger, and she tells it so well that really in this moment it might just be true.

That evening, we go for a walk and then step into the neighbourhood Yacht Bar. We sit at her usual table by the corner as she orders her quarter of rum and Coke. After a round or two, she interrupts conversation at the next table, almost always only men – two or sometimes three, asks for a light. I watch as she walks slowly out to have a smoke by the entrance, feels the eyes trailing her back.

Now she is looking up at Christ the King at the entrance of St Andrews church lit white as she takes a long, deep drag, knowing that right now at least one of them has already stood up to approach her, making his way to her while considering the least pathetic excuse, the most glib opening line.

---

*After I hear his retreating steps but cannot see him any more, the housekeeping man through the keyhole, I turn and go back inside the room. And the first thing I do is to put the godforsaken AC off.*

*It feels weird, unreal, to be free of his clasp and back in my clothes, all the agency to do what I want. But a long time ago, this stopped being real anyway.*

*I pace up and down the thickly carpeted room, looking at the pointed ends of my shoes.*

*I sit on the plush chair by the window looking at the dim lights of corporate offices.*

*I want to run, to do anything else would be entirely foolish, but something remains unfinished. And so I wait. Put on the TV, flick through FTV, the wellness programme on NDTV, Shirodhara therapy as a sitar plays in the background.*

*I could just leave now, so easy, so smooth, no one would ever know. But something is missing, a niggling something. Something needs to be done, but I don't quite know what and so I wait.*

*And then it occurs to me – in the drawer of the bedside table. Underneath the lamp, where he always keeps his things.*

*There it is. He left it there on purpose while he knew I was watching. Teasing as always, just out of reach.*

*I pick up the gun, familiar but still heavy, cock it, hide it in the back of my jeans. I pace up and down the full-length mirror, practise slinking the gun out, point it at my reflection.*

*Then go to my purse, take out the dark cherry red lipstick, slather it on, smack my lips. To the minibar, grab the salted peanuts and cashew nuts, the miniature bottles of vodka and gin. Park myself by the window, draw open the flimsy white curtains. Take a swig of the vodka, then another. Flick a peanut into the air, open my mouth wide, grind it to a pulp with the first crunch.*

*I lean against the wall, wait for something to happen.*

# Four

*He's faster than I expected. A second and he's already in front of me, boring down. The click of the door key, that look of surprise, the rushing to the side table, pulling open the drawer looking back at me, coming close, very close now.*

*All this before I realise what is happening, what has already happened. Before I have decided what to do. I look up at him staring down at me, stand up gingerly. He pushes me against the wall, one arm blocking to the left, the other to the right, jamming me in place.*

*Come on he says, that stare that bores. Come on, don't play with me.*

*I back myself against the wall to get away from his boozy breath, his face, his cologne, his hold and power that made me nothing for so long.*

*Back up like a gazelle, but there's nowhere to go.*

*I keep my eyes locked on his as the icy gun tucked into my jeans pushes into my spine, scrapes against the wall.*

---

Scraping mould from the balustrades in Ma's house in sunny Bandra, I get a message one day. Come home, my father says, not even bothering to call any more, as my mother did not so long ago. He's almost gone.

Just this, nothing more, nothing else. I look up at my mother. She's on the phone with him now, inside the house. She comes out and looks at me. Her head shaking, and I know I have to leave.

But she won't come, not even for her own husband, for her own father-in-law.

Now back to Delhi after weeks, nearly a month but really decades, having travelled the continent of India to escape that night.

I don't ring the bell. Open the door cautiously with my own key. Walk into his room. The sun is white outside, but the maroon curtains are drawn thick and it is cool and dark in here.

The male nurse sits on the floor by the bed giggling at a WhatsApp joke. As soon as he sees me, he jumps up, shuffles about. Baby kidhar thi itna time he asks, masking the awkwardness of my absence for so long now with fake familiarity. I give him a weak smile, nod and look at my grandfather on the bed and my stomach sinks.

He is still, cotton balls stuffed up his nostrils, eyes shut. Skin damp with a faint layer of perspiration. The time of death recorded in the doctor's report on the bedside table – 4.10 a.m.

My grandfather's ghazals play from his old player, from the cassettes my father taped for him from the late late show on the radio through the years.

I sit beside my grandfather, feel the sticky shock of his white hair, still thick and alive. His skin not yet icy, still heat and life left inside him, extinguishing cell by cell.

Everything is exactly the same, the soft ghazals, the curtains blocking out the day, the white walls of shadows. My grandfather is lying on his bed the same as he always did, but he is dead, and that is as clear, as plain as the body that lies before me that once was my grandfather.

My father watches me watch him, says nothing to me, not how have you been, not where were you for so long, not how is Mama. I say nothing back. Not how he felt, not how he would cope now, I don't even ask my father why or how my grandfather died.

And then he goes away to do something useful, probably take care of all the necessary paperwork, organise the funeral.

I missed him. Missed my grandfather by just a few hours. He went away without seeing me, didn't care to wait.

But then why would he, I remind myself. I wasn't here these past many weeks. Backpacking around the country in a mad haze. And later, cleaning, cooking, catching up on jive and gossip sessions with my mother in the old house in Bombay as he lay sick and dying, clinging to his hallucinations.

And even when I was here, I wasn't really here. Meeting strange men in five-star hotels. Meeting him. Walking among the malls like a ghost. Having her die inside. And later, distributing stolen quinoa and quiches to the poor, daily revolutions with spray paint. The truth is, I was never around. Not there to help my dad clean his bedpan, make his breakfast. Barely even making conversation with my grandfather through all these months, although chiding myself every other night to ask him about his school days, his first job, his old hometown the next morning. What his favourite colour was, the first movie he ever saw. The more I thought about it, the more I realised how little I knew, how a lifetime contains so much that others – even those you live with – don't, can't ever know. Just anything I could have talked to him about, everything.

But now he was gone and it was too late. My grandfather had forsaken me in death, just as I had him in his life.

So why would he have waited for me? Here I was, wracked with guilt, making even this, his life, his death, about myself again.

Suddenly there is a flurry of activity. The ambulance staff from the hospital barge through the door. Along with the male nurse, they place a white sheet on my grandfather, lift his body. When he's wrapped inside, they tie each end – knot the top and bottom like a sweet wrapper – lift him and take him away as I catch myself wondering if he might be suffocating inside.

At the funeral, the electric crematorium is full and so we have to burn him instead. I stand with the others – the dutiful male nurse, a neighbour from the next building my father occasionally goes on his evening walks with, and my father's old colleague from the ministry who has made the trip all the way to Greater Noida. I can't believe my mother wouldn't come, that she would abandon my father in his time of need. Just when we were beginning to resolve our differences, this happens and I pack my things in a hurry, storm off, tell her how selfish she is as she yells from the first-floor balcony to believe it or not, but everything does not revolve around you!

Now here the priest circles my grandfather lying inside a broken forest, chanting mantras, dripping ghee over the logs. Then he looks back and calls on my father to go and light the pyre. And my father is about to light him but then stops abruptly and stands still. He's blanking out, I realise. He's blanking out except for his hands that shake as the fire at the end of the stick shivers.

Go, someone whispers, Daddy ka madat karo. The male nurse, the friend, shove me from behind and I gather my nerves and place my arm on my father's, steady his hands in mine. He turns around to look at me as I nod and edge him closer. Come on Daddy, I whisper. Come on.

Slowly we set one log alight, then another, and as it catches the ghee my father says under his breath to me, so quiet I can barely hear well, I guess he is gone now.

And it takes everything inside me, every muscle I am made of, to hold on to him, my father. Alone now except for me. I was all he had.

I hold my gut tight. Look at him, squeeze his hands in my own. Full of grief for my grandfather, for him. Full of grief for the world in which all things live, and then must die.

Soon the calls come in from the second and third cousins and the next-door neighbours drop by for a condolence visit, my grandfather's long-lost school friend from the city visits. They all sit around, sip their chai in silence. Then they say let us not mourn but instead celebrate his life, he lived a long and glorious life – eighty-seven years, my God, what a long time, what a full life, our own parents died of heart attacks and kidney failure and strokes at God knows what, at fifty, at sixty! How wonderful that medicine has advanced. I look up at them from peeling the edge of my nails and say yes, yes you're right, he really did live a long life. It really is wonderful. Wondering what they even knew of him beyond the bare bones that made up his life – his name and family name, that he opened and shut several unsuccessful businesses, his one son and this son's recent, unfortunate divorce, after close to twenty-five years of marriage. They never came to visit, these last few years. Did not know of the urine bag he tagged along for years, the pain in his joints he complained about less and less over time to make life easier for us. About his weak but passionate ghazal singing when the world lay asleep.

They didn't know about Shahbanoo. But then, neither did I.

I smile the appropriate amount, wondering when they will leave and allow us our grief, the loss of my grandfather, gone, his life ended, even if he was eighty-seven, even if it was expected for a long time, even if greater griefs have come and will still befall the world, bigger losses, legitimating more defensible sorrows – earthquakes killing thousands, wars murdering tens of thousands of civilians, terrorist attacks, serial killers killing children.

My grandfather is no more and will never be, I want to shout to them. But go to the kitchen to get the samosas and sweet imli chutney.

That evening after everyone has left, my father pays the male nurse his dues, shakes his hand. I watch his surprised face as the nurse gives him a sudden hug. Then he turns around, waves at me and says Baby, Daddyji ka khayaal rakho. Help him around the house, take care of him, listen to your parents, not quite telling me what a spoiled brat he thinks I am.

In the silence that follows, we shuffle about. I go to my grandfather's room to clear his cupboard, because it is a task that must be done and my father has taken his telescope to the terrace after days and I do not wish to disturb him.

From the cupboard, I take out everything that remains of my grandfather's life – eighty-seven years and this is what it amounts to, a lifetime locked inside an old Godrej cupboard. Stacks of adult diapers – three-for-one economy pack size ten–twelve – piles of papers and plastic files. Warranty certificates for speakers, Titan watches, Samsung microwaves. Dull pink, ochre and blue paper folders with test papers from hospitals my father took my grandfather to, which I was barely there for – CBC, urine, CT, MRI, PET, liver and kidney function. A file of papers charting the deterioration of a body in micrograms of lowering protein counts and lipid profiles and potassium levels. Health insurance papers filed and stamped, stapled and photocopied, receipts of spectacle bills, dentist's records from forty years ago, eye check-ups. A pile of stained and faded off-white pyjamas, the one cream silk kurta he wore every Diwali and every year on his birthday.

And at the back of the safe his old Nokia 1100. I open his SMS inbox. Happy New Year from Sydney! Log on to travistra.com and enjoy spectacular views of the Sydney Opera House Harbour and the fireworks display! And in the sent items, my grandfather's reply to the same number, Happy New Year to you and your loved ones. And then a follow-up message, May God bless you all. I look at this, and something breaks. Something breaks at this, my grandfather's, sweet, meaningless act of kindness, and I mourn the loss of his passing.

Later, I look through the safe in his cupboard – an unused chequebook, a passbook not updated for years, and behind it all a blue leather-bound diary. I open it, struck by the beautiful ink writing, and trace my fingers on its curved sprawl.

By the upper right corner, the date – 7 September 1947.

At first there was light, a wave through the doorway – the precise silhouetted geometry of pentagons and stars. Then there was her, standing on the red plinth, facing the tents in the symmetrical gardens beyond. She feels someone, something, brush against her neck, and when she turns she sees a man in the shadows looking at her through the doorway and covers her face with her niqab.

He's embarrassed for her, and so he lowers his gaze, and when he looks up again she is gone, lost in this camp, most likely back to the Muslim quarters of this makeshift refugee town of Humayun's Tomb, separated from him by a canal and a country.

As he steps out of the tomb to look for her, he sees more refugees arrive by the droves, having walked a hundred miles, some with pushcarts, sacks, babies. Most with nothing. He looks at them and recognises the bewilderment in their faces as his own when he first stepped in here, having walked all the way from Sindh, now Pakistan.

It must be a dream, they tell themselves as they look all around at the vast symmetry of the courtyard, and then at the grand tomb. It had to be a dream.

The last days and weeks, as they walked further and further away from home, further towards Delhi – this promised city of reserved land and housing, where all said it would stop, the murder and pillage and rape, neighbours wary overnight, hostile and suspicious, like in some forgone world. How could it happen in this day and age, they wondered, as people do when barbarism shows its familiar face again.

What came over them? Over people like them? What came over their communities, their families? How did slaughter come so easily they wondered, they shuddered, as they walked to Delhi, but couldn't understand it.

So it must be a dream after not knowing who will be dead tomorrow to stand now before this grandiose tomb they had heard so much about – a scene out of the Arabian Nights surely – as they gaze at the curved archways and stars on either side of the gateway, the white dome, the pigeons that descend like a wreath.

It could only be a dream.

And this moment, although weighed down by the larger narrative of the wreckage raging across a country in the throes of an arbitrary Partition, this narrative that is to shape India and her forever evil twin, her shadow-self nation of Pakistan, her raw nerve beneath the superstructure of her syncretism, this moment when the refugees, Hindu and Muslim alike, first walk through the gateway and this monument appears suddenly before them – just this moment, a small one certainly, but significant nonetheless, surpasses all political rhetoric as the Partition-torn refugees encounter the sublime.

A dream, they tell themselves.

A dream.

She must be a dream. He searches everywhere for her – in the gardens, through the Hindu and Muslim camps, peeping into tents, men and women sleeping, children sucking thumbs. And finally he sees her sauntering into Neela Gumbad, behind Humayun's barber's tomb. She is inside sitting cross-legged and looks up at the intricate design, at each leaf, each flower. She pulls off her niqab, and when he comes to sit next to her, does not budge. She lets his knees touch her own, and he cannot believe it.

He, from Hyderabad Sindh, City of Wind Catchers and Orioles, will go on to set up several petty businesses in the city. He will join his cousins in business, and they take him because he is family and they must, but he proves to have no head for business, neither accounts nor sales. He will have no understanding of the stealth needed to become rich. Every morning he will make his own sandwiches for lunch, pack them in a tiffin as his family slept. Then wait for twenty minutes in the mist for the bus. Travelling across dusty roads to warehouses and factories, looking for jobs, trying to make sales. Taking a break, he will carefully unpack the Amul butter sandwiches in the park, eat them cold.

He will travel across the country – to Calcutta, Bombay, Bhopal and Madras – to sell spare auto car parts, plastic containers, and later yard lengths of suit pieces and dress material, but will remain more or less unsuccessful. He will leave his family business, look for jobs, set up a clothing import business on his own, but that too will fail.

She from Shahjahanabad, the thick, dark crosslanes of Purani Dilli, where everyone was leaving to follow Quaid-i-Azam's will, or so she had been told. At first her father did not want to leave, but every day came news of more killings, and fearing for his daughter they reluctantly made the trek to Humayun's Tomb, their last pit stop in India.

Shahbanoo lies now with my grandfather in Neela Gumbad, rotting now and blue no more.

Soon she will go on to settle in Karachi, later Lahore. She will read Urdu literature, become a college professor of the junior division of the university, marry a general and produce three children. She will teach the polemics of Faiz, the brutal modernity of Manto. But her own short nazms, which she will write in secret throughout her life, many of which explore the loss of losing him, which she would only realise as she wrote them, she will show nobody. They will remain undiscovered, even after she is dead.

My grandfather and Shahbanoo, they would both partake in this geopolitical game of musical chairs in which a million or more had and still awaited slaughter for no known reason, for the convulsions of the time that brought forth the most barbaric nature of man. And history would paper over this time and they would not look back once, but each, both, thrust headlong into their respective lives and the lives of building their new-found nations.

But now they both lie in Neela Gumbad, where no one else ventures, craning their necks and gazing at the designs, wondering about a time long gone, so leisurely, so eternal as to grant the painting of these million motifs, each curving around the other. A time when the highest form of living was to gaze at the changing shapes of drifting clouds.

Aeons passing in dreamy lassitude.

Three days later it's time to leave – she to newly formed Pakistan, he to a refugee colony set up three miles away where he and his cousins, his uncles, have been granted land. The new nation has been born and there is a lot for a young man to do.

But three days is a lifetime. They know everything there is to know about each other, and so when he asks for her hand, sure they are in love and so they must marry, he is taken aback by the scorn in her large black eyes.

How foolish, she thinks, he is Hindu, and she born into a Muslim family, although she has other ideas having read most of Manto and she's spoken with her father about the commingling of religions and her growing curiosity about Sufism. Still, all that is just talk.

When she sees his watery, over-eager eyes she's surprised, because she didn't even once entertain this idea these past few days. She was making a friend, biding her time, although ensuring her friendship was hidden in this camp full of family and relatives and neighbours from Shahjahanabad. And even though sixteen with no prospects yet, she does not want to marry him, does not want to marry at all in fact, not for a few more years so she can complete her matriculation at least.

She cannot believe that a few days with this man and he is asking for her hand in marriage. How lovelorn, how pathetic. Who does he think he is? Some badshah courting a begum under this moonlit dome? The only just out-of-war country split into two, violence and mayhem all around, how could he be so foolish, afford romance at a time like this.

After she leaves without a trace, he will throw himself into his future, rushing headlong into his life. But his longing for her will always walk alongside him. And overcome with it, rendered weak and ineffectual by it, he will remind himself over and over again that he must hate her, must hate her brother she spoke of so lovingly, castrated and killed by Hindu mobs just outside their mohalla. Whenever he thinks of her – her sharp tongue, her slender wrists, he will force himself to revisit all he saw on his way to the tomb.

He will sit with his cousins and neighbours after work in the newly built barsaatis in the silent colonies of the city, and they will share horror stories of someone's aunt raped on the way here, someone's cousin's friend, although it was never spoken of openly, only among these men on terraces on evenings such as these.

He will hear of this family shame, and he will be filled with hatred for Shahbanoo.

Before knowing why or how, he will secretly hate all Muslims – thinking of them all as one and the same, one community, one person, housing historical resentment that accumulates through the years like fat around the body. He will overhear at family gatherings, at his keertan meetings, and later in the news – Hinduism isn't a religion, it's a way of life, it's a way of being. We lived here peacefully for centuries, they plundered and looted us. Destroyed our temples to build their courts. They came from there, we have always been here. They built their mosques and palaces and tombs over our temples, our land, our kingdoms.

And now look, they've left us with a graveyard of a city.

And slowly, like the rest – his uncles and cousins and a visiting friend – he will believe that Muslims are here to take over India, in a race against us Hindus to produce offspring and take over the country. When he hears the news anchors and panellists say matter-of-factly why they don't go to Pakistan, which was created just for them, he nods and wonders why indeed not.

With his distant family, his wider groups of friends, and in the keertans through which he will increasingly seek respite, he will say the word 'Muslim' – Musalmaan. He reserves this word only for conversations with his closest. Instead, he uses the 'M word', like the others. Ms are dirty, they whisper to each other, Ms are fanatical. Ms don't care for science or progress, their youth are reckless, so rude. Ms will lead to the downfall of this nation, our civilisation.

Of Shahbanoo, he will tell no one his whole life. Two years after her, he will marry through an arranged match, a Sindhi like himself, righteous and staunchly Nehruvian. She never talks of the horrors of Partition or Pakistan, even though from an elite Karachi family herself. He will crumble under my grandmother's shadow, still pining for but hating Shahbanoo and everything she has come to stand for in his life. And hating her, pining for her, hating that he still pined for her, he will feel vindicated, finally redeemed, when he watches mobs ascend the decaying dome of Babri Masjid, thrust their orange flags when the papers declare victory at Kargil.

With his son, his only child, who inherits his inner defeatism in manner but his mother's pragmatic brand of nationalism, he doesn't speak of Shahbanoo. Of what happened, of how he felt about losing her, of how he feels about Muslims, about how this hatred of her, of M's, is secretly consuming him.

From my grandfather's silence, my father, who does not possess the imagination to believe that people have secret lives, impossible demons wrestling inside, gains nothing. Instead, he takes after my grandmother in her ideological veneration of institution building, the need for a strong bureaucracy, a thousand doing their work in offices and cabinets for the venerable project, the building of this great nation.

And so, in the currents of time and the winds of change it brings, Shahbanoo remains forgotten, like pages from a history book full of splendorous monuments and tombs. Her memory weighs under the river of bitterness that curves through the country, simmering through Indian society – Hindu and Muslim – brought forth to dinner table conversations, to fervent WhatsApp discussions, asides at shaadis and at PTA meetings, even after my grandfather dies.

And only in the last stages of my grandfather's life, when he is already senile, is she remembered. Not as an invader, the shadow self he must hate. Not even as a lover, so quick to jilt him. She is remembered only as the light that falls like a wave through the filigreed stars, the divine geometry of the first and only love of his life.

And does it ever cease? This cycle of desire and longing – a half sentence scribbled as though in the middle of the night, ending with a long dash – desperate for an answer, the last entry on the last page from my grandfather's diary, seven months ago.

---

Now yeh, akashvani hai.

Sitting on the grey-blue leather seats of the Shatabdi Express from Mumbai to Delhi to my almost gone grandfather, to take care of my father.

The breakfast laid out before me. A cold cutlet on the left, potatoes and peas popping out. The perfect mini boxes of jam and toast, the Amul butter to be peeled from the top with the tip of your finger.

Passengers walk through the first-class compartment to the toilet leaning against the side of the train as it lurches to the capital. Uncles read the papers as I eat my breakfast and block out any assumptions about what could or could not, what may or may not, have already happened to my grandfather. Furious with my mother who has left my father alone, even at a time like this.

I block them out, overhear the conversations. IAS aspiration stories – UPSC entrance exams given, cleared, failed, several attempts made, of private service only when all attempts at UPSC have been exhausted.

Private service as backup, but still there's such pride at Tata's takeover of Jaguar, such pride tinged with repulsion at Ambani's residential tower in Mumbai. At the Indians in the Fortune 500 list. The uncle is reading aloud his WhatsApp joke of how Apple phones are dismantled, remodelled and sold for a quarter their price, the street-side genius of our local jugaad, flummoxing even Tim Cook.

Men discussing the latest municipal elections in UP, quipping about corruption in the BCCI, their wives crossing over the conversation to discuss the success of their children in America, online recipes for matar paneer, chole, moong dal ka halwa.

Diabetes, hypertension, hyperacidity, and everyone joins in. Fervent discussions over digestive Ayurvedic tonics – even as they wolf down their omelettes or cutlets – miraculous concoctions of haldi and tulsi. Baba Ramdev's success shows that Indians are a proud people. We will build our heritage and traditions that have lasted thousands, millions of years. And then the talk moves to the reverse brain drain – thousands of young people moving back after studying in the best universities abroad, they want to contribute to their country. As if our IITs and IIMs are any less.

Listening to all this, half listening, half not.

But then, yeh akashvani hai.

At first, the usual haul – the prime minister's international visits, climate-change summits, working group committee meetings, ministry shuffles, hundred-crore scams. But as I am about to doze off, the newscaster in her usual impassive tone –

A former brigadier and his house help of ten years have been booked for sixteen counts of murder and thirteen counts of sexual assault in a fresh case in Noida, New Delhi. All India reports.

And then the police commissioner's crackling over the clamour of the media – case is under investigation, accused have been taken to sessions court, I cannot comment any further.

I look down at the pea I was about to eat poking through the fork.

Sixteen counts of murder, plus thirteen counts of sexual assault. Sixteen.

Muniya and the Nepali among them.

I look down from the top berth at the others. They're chatting about how the Indian economy is sure to take over China's any day now, about the poor quality of Chinese goods flooding our markets, how we have the potential to take over manufacturing for the world, how India must and will become a five-trillion-dollar economy in the next five years.

I look at my phone. Through intermittent signal Google murder-Noida-children.

And the articles fill my screen like an avalanche and I realise how much has happened through the night, how much I have missed.

I click on a YouTube link. A reporter outside the brigadier's house. Placards by the mansion, 'No religion says to kill human', 'children stay safe', 'baby killer', in bold red with paintings of flowers and children and blue birds flying out of bouquets. And then the reporter reports – nine children, six teenagers, one young woman in her early twenties have all disappeared in the past two years from the slum colony nearby. And one by one they flash the identities of the missing children and woman – an Aadhaar card, a torn birth certificate, a passport photo, a name. The shocked face of the small girl I had seen on the blog of a citizen journalist almost a year ago now.

I pause and zoom in, not Muniya, I would have recognised her the first time.

Next shot, a man looking straight at the camera. Dazed, distracted. When the reporter shoves the mic into his face and asks him what her name was, he says Shefali.

They came to offer us all kinds of things he says – pandits popped all around and said give us money, wear these gold rings, tie these sacred threads, change your house address, do this type of havan at seven-thirty every morning and the universe will lead you to your daughter. And later, all kinds of guys came around said give us ten lakh we will find your daughter, lawyers came – the brigadier's lawyers came around and said give us twenty lakh, we will take you to your daughter's killer. As though we have that kind of money!

And the fanatic ironer from the video I last saw before all this, before I skipped town, when things were still coming to a head. She says – I went ten times to the brigadier's house, ten times, twenty times again and again to ask, have you seen my girl? Have you seen my daughter? She was just here! I just gave her an errand to run you know, she was to get me some dress material and then she just disappeared, and he kept saying, no no, no, I have no idea what you're talking about.

I'm telling you, they should be killed the same way our children have been killed.

And the video stops, the report ends.

The next day, after my grandfather's funeral, I search again, murder, Noida, children, rich man is evil, and a whole host of articles appears.

Articles detailing what All India had skipped the previous day on the train. Details of slum dwellers who grew suspicious over time. Over months of these disappearances, the police failing to file FIRs, suspecting the parents of being lax, of the kids and teenagers having run away. But all the while rumours grew thick of something evil inside the house because so many children had gone missing from the area. The house was either near the black hole or in the black hole where all the missing children, the girls and a few boys, seemed to have disappeared, the articles say.

And moreover, the house gave off a terrible stench.

Two fathers of missing girls, who were not allowed to file FIRs, managed to convince an MLA of a neighbouring ward that there was something shady about that house. So they all went in. And as they looked through the drainage ditch behind the house, they found a broken leg and called the cops.

That night, as I tried to fall asleep on the train that rattled to Delhi, the cops rushed to the mansion, a few hours too late. They tried to control the mob – the parents, the relatives and neighbours of the missing children – which was in a frenzy now, crashing the windows with sticks, overturning sofas and flat-screen TVs and tall glass vases, breaking the latches, the brigadier and his manservant hiding in the barsaati.

Early the next morning the digging began across the courtyard, all over the drainage ditch. They found jeans, shorts, chappals, sandals, plastic hair clips dug all over. And along with that, huge bags buried, the ground full of bones. Limbs in one bag, severed heads in another at the other end of the ditch. Fingers crunched below the shoes of parents, relatives, neighbours in frantic search of their children.

I read and watch, disgusted, full of fear, enthralled. But there is no mention of him, nothing at all. Only the brigadier and Karni Singh, his Man Friday, as the papers call him, both immediately arrested. I listen to the news again, I Google incessantly.

I read every article I can find online, sometimes twice, thrice, but there is no mention of him, or me, at all.

---

Karni Singh. He revealed everything in his interrogation. They discuss him incessantly in the press. From a tiny village in MP, a Dalit from the Budhik caste, the butcher caste.

Like so many young men, he came to Delhi for work to escape the land on which nothing grew, to escape poverty, moneylenders, drought, debt. To make money for his young family – his wife in the village, his young son, another baby on the way. His family were farm hands, although his father worked at the butcher's from time to time, taking the young Karni to observe, occasionally help.

Karni Singh found his way to the brigadier's a few years after he landed in Delhi. He became his second-hand man, his house help. He cooked and cleaned, made the beds, took care of his master's basic administrative tasks, delivering parcels and letters. Although the brigadier was divorced and lived alone in this house, his daughter and granddaughter came to visit occasionally.

In the day, all was routine and dull, given over to tasks the day demanded if you were just a servant. But at night the brigadier threw parties – with call girls, with women and drink and drugs, women such as myself with rich men such as him. And Karni was there for all this. Although he was shocked at first, he ignored all this, putting it off to the ways of the rich, a world that would always remain alien to him, although he lived to serve them. He was a servant, and would always remain one.

So he locked himself inside his barsaati on the terrace, falling asleep to traces of music from the parties far below.

Only rushing outside when called to get more whisky, more food.

But slowly, he grew agitated, irritable, locked up like this inside his room. He could still hear the music, had to clean up the mess the next morning, and his desire to throw himself into the parties, the orgies, would grow unbearable. He would sit by the door through the night, and when he turned there she would be again – the woman in the flowing white dress standing in the dark of his barsaati, this woman who taunted him and told him he was a mere labourer, just a servant from a low caste, and that's what he would remain forever.

He grew restless in the day too, so when the brigadier was out on work, leaving the house to Karni Singh for whole months at a time, he began to lure children over. He couldn't of course use the same call girls as his boss, some of whom he knew were particularly special to him, so one evening he called out to a young girl playing hopscotch in the lane just outside the mansion.

At first he raped her, but it didn't work, he couldn't excite himself enough. So he killed her, it was easy enough. She was just a small child. And when urged by the interrogator – why did you do it? Why kill? Why? He blinks as if it's the first time he has considered this.

Something just came over me, he says, I can't explain it. I just, I felt the urge to kill, he says plainly. And then proceeds to tell the interrogator that he strangled her body, and then had sex with it. Finally this mad desire that was consuming him for months now subsided, somewhat. And the lady in the flowing white dress left him.

But they returned, both the desire and the lady, as though one and the same. Two days later, three weeks later.

With greater intensity, more than anything he had ever experienced. And so he raped again. He killed again. He killed and then raped again.

---

Karni Singh. I see him now, on that Friday night that broke it all. But it takes me a while to remember him. I'm amazed I have forgotten him all this time. He was the other man standing with Muniya in the kitchen whom I had dismissed as just another servant.

Karni Singh, I remember him now from earlier in the evening when I went to put my glass in the basin. His hand caresses Muniya's neck gently. A grown man with a hand around the neck of a ten-year-old, and it never elicited any suspicion in me.

More than Karni, what comes back is the fat man, the brigadier walking towards me. He has clearly had too much to drink. He eyes me now and dawdles from the far end of the room. As I watch him I am thinking how I'm sick of it. Nights like these, at parties with his builder friends, his friends who are steel magnates and media tycoons, CEOs of chemical plants in OKhla. He brings me to farmhouses a long drive out from the rest of the city, to houses such as these. I sit here with the other builders and their wives and girlfriends. I sit with them and listen to them but I am alone. Sick of pretending to like what I don't enjoy. But wishing so much to be a part of them, to not be an outsider, just this one night.

The fat man arrives. Sits down, and before I know what's happening he places his hand on my thigh like he owns me. Disgusted, I leave my flute of half-drunk wine, my fourth already, and get up to go look for him.

Why does he bring me here, if he is going to spend half the night with the men on the balcony, out in the driveway smoking, talking acquisitions, deals.

I push myself through the passageway crowded with the well-heeled, people laughing and talking and drinking and nibbling, brushing off the waiters hired for the night.

I go from room to room looking for him.

Back in the party room and I see the winding staircase in front of me, consider going up. I hold the rail and climb up one step at a time, careful not to trip here like the last time. Each step at such a distance from the next, a test for the drunk on nights like these.

I finally reach the top and survey the ground floor, sick of but mesmerised by the rich, their asymmetrical jumpsuits and their fine linen. Such a pleasure to survey them from this distance.

And then I remember I am looking for him. I turn around. This floor is surprisingly dark. And empty. I go from room to room until finally I enter what seems like the master bedroom.

The brigadier's bedroom. This has to be it. Teak flooring, teak cupboards, an enormous blue bedspread. Military regalia on the wall. A curved wooden basket for the laundry.

To the left is another door. The bathroom probably, and even though I know he can't be inside here, not inside the door, not in this dark bedroom, nowhere on this whole floor, he's probably on the ground floor at the far end of the car park smoking with the brigadier's son-in-law, I open the door anyway.

That's when I see him.

The Nepali slumped on the toilet, low groaning, an open slit for a mouth.

Hiding, always hiding. In the library, in the university, at home, in this room in the new apartment.

I catch my breath and shut my mouth, stop myself from making a sound. Tiptoe out the bathroom, back through the passage on the first floor, down the winding conch staircase, not believing I haven't tripped, finally out of the house. Needing to not believe what I saw.

Out of the house now, in a garage I find in the far corner, I shut my eyes tight.

Five years old, shutting the dickie of the grey ambassador we all knew to be haunted. Curled like a baby, I listen to the sound of my name, high and low, again and again, the chorus of the rescue party. My mother hysterical, my father's hollow ring as they search around the colony with the others. The uncles and aunties and their children too, the ones who abandoned me at hide-and-seek a few hours before.

Hiding from no one, no game, no other children, in the corner of the yard in the house in Bombay these days of strange, finicky tantrums. All around the city sounds, the aeroplanes, someone's chopping vegetables. The salt-white fat of pork sizzles in the pan, a coconut falls and splits open. Every afternoon after lunch, when they go to their locked rooms to sleep, I walk out of the dining room, barefoot, down the steps to the corner of the garden, to the wall with the wet moss, and sit against it for hours. The heat is sweltering at this time of the year, in the summer vacations when I come to Bombay, every other year.

I sweat in my frilly bloomers, the light cotton dresses my grandmother stitches for me with the smocking and Peter Pan collar. The sweat and Johnson's baby powder cake the creases of my neck, under the chubby arms. I am a melting cream bun. I sit on my haunches and dig up the mud with a poky twig, the fat worms, and hold them in my finger and try to split them in half. Or I interrupt a line of ants, and when one dares to climb up my thigh, I place it on the mud and smash it with a rock. And then the city sounds barge in again, the neighbours shouting, another bike accident and the people rush to watch.

Only much later, am I found. Alfredo, who tends to the garden and the hot house, passes me in the late afternoons and says, Baby, what you played today? Why you sit alone in the corner? And before I answer he is already gone to tell my mother or my grandmother where I am and they come chuckling and clicking their tongues holding a belan or a broom.

Hiding here too, because I don't know what else to do. The conversation in the distance, men and women smoking cigars and cigarillos closer. But for how long can I sit on my haunches in the dark behind this gleaming golden Porsche like a petty thief.

Finally I get out, back to the party. Inside it's like nothing has happened, no change at all. My seat at the corner of the sofa still empty. The fat brigadier who has had too much to drink thankfully not around. I go to my place, sit down.

Look up at the ceiling where the Nepali sits slumped and dying.

---

The next day, sober and scared as the night before hits me. But I can't just sit around at home.

I drive alone to the neighbourhood of the party. I can't believe how far it is from my house, it seemed so close at night in the dark, when you are high and distance and time collapse. I enter the colony gates, give the watchman the house number made up on the spot, which he writes down in his ledger tediously. When it miraculously seems to work, and he lets me pass through, I drive down the main driveway not knowing which way to look, my mind having blanked out all these crucial, most practical details. I drive up and down the empty colony streets, not remembering the number of the house, its shape and size, the make of its door.

I drive around parks on either end of the colony, round and round. Children in monkey caps, their eyes lined with kohl play on broken swings, the maids watch over them and gossip about their madams. I look at them as I drive past, look up at the water tanks perched on top of every house.

And then I spot him peeping through the curtain. The fat man who had too much to drink and placed his hand on my thigh like he owned me. He looks straight at me and goes away as quickly as he came, but I know he is hiding behind the thick beige curtain on this dead winter afternoon.

I park my car in front of his house, defiant. I watch the maids come and go, I watch their children slip in and out of his house. It's at the end of the road, this house, just by the reserve forest and water tank, and there's a lock on the outhouse outside.

I get out of my car instinctively. Ring the bell, its trill unexpectedly loud.

And even though I hear no steps, no sound at all from inside, I run back to my car, drive away in panic, sure that he is waiting just on the other side of the door with his big hands, waiting to slit my throat like he did the Nepali's. And the muffled scream of the small girl I heard too, clamped shut, the girl I threw in the pit like a soiled and soaked sanitary napkin.

The girl who would be Muniya.

And what the media will focus on for months to come, what will become the mainstay of this case – in the kitchen, right after the excavation of the bodies on that first night when the mob came crashing in, they discover flesh that is a piece of a young girl's thigh, long cold now, rotting in the pan on the gas burner, flies hovering all over. The psychiatrists from the best mental health institutes of the country on the news programmes will say that Karni Singh couldn't stand the poverty all around him, he couldn't bear to be as poor as they were, couldn't stand to think he could never have, could never be, what the brigadier and his friends were.

And so he had to eat the poor to feel rich, just like the brigadier and his friends, in their own way, ate the poor too. Swallowed them whole. Consumed them as they pleased to do their bidding.

And I see him, a man, like any other man, any other house help, in the kitchen with Muniya.

Earlier in the night, before I escaped the dawdling brigadier, before I saw the Nepali slumped, before I ran out to the garage, before I came back and sat on the sofa and saw the butterfly patch from the Nepali on the ceiling, before I wailed with the Nepali and was shushed and put into the room, before I woke up and found myself in the courtyard next to Muniya's body, before I threw her in the pit, before we drove home, before all this, while passing the kitchen, I saw Karni Singh, with his hands around Muniya's neck.

Karni Singh killed Muniya and the Nepali, and then possibly ate them. Did only Karni Singh kill Muniya and the Nepali? Did Karni Singh kill and eat the others too? Did only Karni Singh kill and eat the others? I saw one dead body that night – Muniya's – and the Nepali so far gone he was as good as dead, but I didn't see any of the killings. I assumed the brigadier, along with my lover, did the killing. But maybe they didn't, although they were certainly covering up Karni Singh's tracks. Why cover up for his servant, if he wasn't part of the killing, as the brigadier proclaims, as his lawyer proclaims, as his daughter proclaims. Even Karni Singh stresses that he did all this alone, that the brigadier wasn't involved.

Two children were murdered that night, but if there were sixteen in all, the cover-up must have been massive. Who else was killed? Who else did the killing? Who else covered up?

Head spinning, turning round and round, one after the other they appear, these questions spinning deeper and deeper.

Until they reach the deepest question of all, the most important, the most confounding.

Why?

Why did the brigadier cover up, if as he claims he wasn't one of the murderers? Because he didn't want blood on his hands? He at least knew about these murders, which had been taking place for over three years in his house, even if he wasn't part of the killing. There was no way he couldn't have known. Or was there a way he couldn't have known?

But even if he didn't kill, why did he cover up for his servant? Because the reputational risk was too high? Because the brigadier's sex orgies would be revealed? His parties with call girls, with rich businessmen, politicians, bureaucrats, policemen. Was he covering up for them all? Were they covering up for him? Were they all in on the killing? Were the rich and powerful just covering up for the rich and powerful, their associates, their allies, their agents, their PR machinery, till no one knew who was covering up for whom, although it might have all begun with this killer, who was very poor?

And as before, and as it has haunted me through all these months, I wonder again, why did my lover help? He who has everything, why cover up for the brigadier, covering up for Karni Singh?

And I am part of the cover-up too, of course, I face myself finally. Like the brigadier, like my lover, like the higher-ups in the police service, the courts, among the politicians, the media – as the poor were shouting on the screens on TV saying the rich are all part of it, just watch, a parent of a missing child tells a reporter, the brigadier is going to go free, the cops, the judges were all at the parties in his house. Karni Singh is just taking the blame for his boss, just like the poor always have for the rich in this country.

I read the headlines. And I realise if I couldn't answer myself as to why I helped him, them, that night, why it felt so easy, so necessary, even though I had seen the Nepali on the toilet and run away from him, even though I could have done something; if through all these months I didn't know why I did what I did, why I shut up and didn't dare tell a soul, why I became so numb to the reality of burying a dead girl, why I didn't even once confront him even though I harboured his baby inside; if all this, how can I possibly begin to understand why he did it, why the brigadier, two men who were nothing more than masks to me the whole time, why Karni Singh?

And for the first time I face the possibility that the answers to all, to any, of these questions would never actually come, that life would go on without even the hint of an answer, with no clarity as to what happened that night, and why it did. As to who was really involved in the murders, and why. As to who the hell he was, who I am.

That night would disappear as a wisp of mist in the winter.

Two weeks later, the brigadier is acquitted.

I read the headlines again and all I can think of is a phrase I have heard from a book, from a movie, a web series, I can't remember where exactly, but all I can think of is this phrase that says it all, that sums up that night and everything since – the phrase that says this is a world in which nothing is solved.

---

*Come on, give it to me he says.*

*I wait, think of something to say.*

*I saw you help the major dig the pit, finally I mention that night that changed everything.*

*Nothing.*

*The brigadier, I mean.*

*Ex-brigadier, sorry, killing the children?*

*Nothing.*

*That Nepali boy sitting on the toilet seat.*

*A hint of the tiniest smile.*

*Was he even the Nepali? Or was he from Arunachal Pradesh?*

*How does it matter? I say.*

*Because, I say, responding to myself, and then nothing.*

*And the girl –*

*Now you tell me, he says, why did you help us?*

*I look up at him.*

*Why did you help us carry her, throw her in the pit?*

*Nothing.*

*Don't act so helpless, he says.*

*Tell me why you helped.*

*That question finally. The one I have been avoiding for so long, skirting around for months now.*

*Why?*

*Why did I do it?*

*Looking at my faint reflection in his pupil I know the answer – the one I couldn't face, but have known all along. I did it to be closer to him, to be closer to power. Closer to power, however amorphous, however far away, out of reach. No matter all my rebellion – spray painting across his advertisements, stealing from the rich and giving to the poor, even bringing down websites of the largest government agencies and corporations of the country. But inside, if I were to really strip myself down, I was just as power-hungry as the rest of them – his sycophants, the rest of this city.*

*I covered up a murder for this, buried a murdered child. Was I capable of even killing one?*

*I don't kn – I say, and then stop.*

*Silence. Locked like this in a Mexican standoff that lasts a century.*

*Suddenly, he pins me to the wall, hands around my throat, reaches around me for the gun, hot, impatient, wanting to trample me. It drops to the carpet.*

*I look down and kick it to the side, run and pick it up. I climb on the bed, can't believe all this is happening.*

*You're part of it too, he says smirking, if I'm in, so are you.*

*And I know he's right. Accomplice to murder? Abetter?*

*I load the gun, point it at him.*

*Backing, backing slowly on the bed still facing him, always facing him, I jump to the floor now as he approaches, saying under his breath you're part of this, if I'm caught, you're caught, you know this, you're fucked . . . until I reach the door and there's nowhere he can go, nowhere I can go, and I pull the trigger, only thinking it's too late for subtleties, for secrets, for suspicious minds, there's only this, I think, as he runs at me and I pull the trigger.*

*He cavorts and falls.*

*Slumps below me, his leg starting to bleed. Like the Nepali.*

*I freeze, can't believe it.*

*Then gather myself, know that I must take my chance now. I place the gun on the floor just out of reach.*

*Walk slowly to the door. But before I pull down the handle, I turn around and walk back to him. Sit on my haunches beside him.*

*I want to tell him everything, but he might bleed to death if I begin. So I say, I hope your son is doing better.*

*He looks up at me. I reach out for his face, caress his eyebrow.*

*Then get up, kick the gun further away, march to the door, open it, walk out. Turn back to look at him one last time. Shut the door, turn the DND sign so it's back in place.*

*I walk through the long passage, the carpet absorbing the click of my heels. Instead of taking the elevator, I walk down the stairs, three, four at a time. Say good evening to the housekeeping staff who stop their work, their unloading of floor detergent, their folding of clean white towels and smile at me as I pass by, sort of bow.*

*And when I'm in the lobby, I dawdle along, cool as a button. Just up for a late late drink after a hard day clinching deals.*

*But it's only as the Uber speeds through the city and I'm telling the driver to go fast, faster, faster, do I realise what I have really done. Left a powerful man for nothing, his secret still on my lips, my secret on his, in the suite of his own hotel, right beside his gun.*

*He's probably screamed for help by now, speeding his way to the hospital in the ambulance. Would he survive? Would what happened that night finally get out?*

*And then I turn around, gazing at the headlights behind. Would he have sent someone to get me?*

*And as we drive through the dark towards home, I know I need to get out of Delhi, as soon as possible, that it's time for me to hit the road.*

---

The night I skipped town, the night I shot him, weeks ago.

Nothing since, no news of him through all my travels, through my time in Bombay. I Google searched, spent hours poring over the *Times of India*, *Indian Express*, *The Hindu*. But nothing. No news of whether he was dead, alive, arrested, acquitted. Nothing. Even though he was so big, a big property tycoon who had been shot, if only on the leg, one would think this would make the news. Delhi's real estate poster boy missing for weeks.

But no, nothing.

His PR team on overdrive, nothing else could explain this.

As I travel, I call his number, once, twice, but there is no response, I call his landline, his wife picks up. I cut the call.

---

And now, I watch as my father holds three brown paper bags full of groceries in the underground parking lot of the mall in our neighbourhood, the one with the bowling alley on the top floor I played in quiet terror with him in, so many months ago.

But now I am with my father, my father who is alone, now that my grandfather is dead and he has no one to take care of. No bedpans to replace, no weekly dialysis appointments. Alone, now that his wife has left him. In the blue light of this netherworld he is lost, a little drunk after his first, then second drink in years.

After our grocery shopping, I insisted that instead of going home as usual we have dinner at the new craft beer pub with its in-house brewery. My father squirms as he enters and asks the waiter to turn down the music. Settling in, I order the mango-brewed pale ale, and after some goading a pomelo-infused ale for my father, which we sip along with our double-loaded burgers and pasta arrabiatas, our crispy potato wedges, insisting to him that a side dish was crucial to every meal.

Now we are walking across the curved driveways and looking for our car, happy in the knowledge of our tipsiness.

For a few days after my grandfather died, I watch my father at squash practice while creaking on the swing in the children's park. He puts on the light, bounces the ball a few times and is off, playing against himself. Hitting the ball with a hard force, more ferocious with every serve. I have never seen him like this before. At home he drifts as usual, but here he hits the ball like his life depends on it. I sit outside and watch my father wage battle with the wall.

And then suddenly, he throws his racket down.

And we both watch as the racket, the ball, fall to the floor.

I decide to take him out the next day.

And now, as he walks ahead looking for our car in this giant car park, I see the grocery list with each item cross-checked spilling out of each paper bag he carries in each arm, coupons saved plucked from beneath the fridge magnet now redeemed, the free dishwashing rags, the five-rupee-discounted goods falling out of the bags that he now bends to stuff back in.

I know we are two floors below our car. I have taken a picture of the number on my phone, but I let this moment be and walk beside my father as we wander around the cars. I give my dad a hug from behind as he stops in his tracks and then puts his arm around me, pats my back absentmindedly.

Over dinner, I help him remove the auto download feature from his WhatsApp so his memory does not get full. Then tell him that a QR code is nothing to be afraid of, it is just a link and that no one can steal your pictures or personal data, Daddy. And finally, I answer his questions about what an influencer really is and how much money they make, the best I could, to his great shock.

At home the next afternoon, I help him input the OTP from his SMS inbox in time to get his UPI ID started. Watch as he excitedly scratch the scratch card.

'Better Luck Next Time!' it says, and he looks up at me wide-eyed and shrugs.

And when I begin to receive the almost hourly WhatsApp forwards, the WhatsApp good morning messages with sunflowers and hazel-eyed cocker spaniels, the platitudes of wisdom on how to live a good life from him every single morning again, even though I have told him a hundred times not to send them to me, I let it pass.

A few nights later, we go to the terrace. He sets up the telescope, we watch the universe through the haze in the night sky.

The buildings have mounted higher, blocking out the moon, but there is always deep space, backwards and forwards, as he told me when I was young, space is endless and we are inside it, forever.

---

The boy with the All-Star sneakers with the theories up his brain, he sits on his computer all day. He and I had drifted apart through these months, after the night I shot my lover, after I travelled across the country, after Bombay, but I see him from my window in his apartment, when I poke my head in the refugee area, he is still there, his makeshift office.

Hey, he says one day to me, where u been?

Around, I shrug.

He gives me a half smile and nods to himself, his attention shifts back to his laptop. Cool, he says drop by sometime, and then turns around and has a long argument with the wall about the most effective guerrilla formations for the raid tonight, or the right heading for the pamphlet that needs to be printed and posted now, like now bro!

And then before I leave, he places his hand on the receiver of the landline on a call he suddenly needs to make, looks up at me searchingly and says, so you thought revolution was a dinner party? before he gets back to his conversation, straight to his hotline with the president.

---

So, content writing as they predicated, goaded me towards. Not even the creative impetus of advertising. A communications intern in a multinational company manufacturing body scrubs and conditioners, face masks and all manner of personal care products the world was in dire need of.

A message from Siddhartha 'Sid' Ramaswamy Iyengar Ananthamurthy on Google chat. Heeyyyyy, sup, so . . . quick question. And then, after I have told him what he needs, sent a mail, several files zipped and sent through WeTransfer he bounces, Imma bouncing, he says with a cool, sorted, yo, layder.

Days pass like this, engaging in brand identity management strategies, in an endless tussle to claim the other division's brand properties as one's own. In audience targeting and evaluation strategies, client acquisition strategies. Eventually, I sell my soul, but it isn't as bad as I imagined.

Slowly, I begin to sit with my colleagues in the cafeteria. Come Diwali I even volunteer for the rangoli competition, and the following Friday to conduct a well-being session on mental health.

Some months after the happy night with my dad in the local brewery. He's taken to craft house beer now, experiments with lemon and orange and offers impromptu recipes from the internet to amused waiters as they serve us our frothing mugs, our spare pork ribs glazed with barbeque sauce.

We go for a beer every other month, sometimes twice when he is up for it.

Mama came to visit soon enough, to offer her condolences. I insist on taking her to the new brewery. Getting drunk with my parents on a Saturday afternoon in a part-empty restaurant in a huge mall, I think all is well with the world.

But after she leaves and we don't hear from her again, I realise just a death in the family, just a new craft brewery in the neighbourhood mall, just a drunken afternoon cannot amend the damage of a whole life, and I realise how little I really know about my own parents.

This afternoon, the junior-to-mid-management employees are huddled inside the boardroom named 'Leverage'. The CSR head gives a presentation about the company's many projects. Water harvesting in three districts of rural MP, targeting local adivasi populations. Partnering with local NGOs on social and emotional education programmes focusing on the girl child. Livelihood generation schemes – a bag business designed to showcase local heritage and artwork for their mothers, a dual-income generation scheme to supplement their meagre agricultural income.

---

And Muniya? And the Nepali? I think of them when I see these CSR presentations, when I don't. At the back of my mind's eye, when I wake up in the morning, step into the metro to get to work. An invisible film, the click and reel that will probably never go away.

After it all came to a head, after the brigadier's acquittal, the papers listed down the names of the victims, where they were from. Muniya was Shamita Singh, from Katautia village, near Patna. The Nepali Tenzin Jomrang, from a village just outside the capital of Itanagar, Arunachal Pradesh. The other victims were all from Karauli village near the house, only these two from out of Delhi, living with the brigadier and Karni Singh, without family.

That's it. Nothing else. I frantically search online for more information, but there is nothing. There's more I can do, of course, I could go to their villages and try to find their families, I could go back to the brigadier's house, I could pretend, forge a press ID and interview the investigating officers, but I do none of this, afraid these investigations might lead to me.

And so I shut up, go to office, come home. More and more sure as the days pass that it was best to lie low, and this too shall pass, that the public anger would die, the country's attention on prime time news would shift to something else.

And eventually, it sort of does.

And in time, I shut the searches, although I still glance at the articles bookmarked on my browser every time I open it. His website, and interviews, replaced by press coverage of the murders.

I see these, I don't see these. I wonder if I will ever face the consequences of what I did, and if I do, what form it will take – private grief? Public punishment? Something worse?

If not in this life, then surely in the next, or the one after?

---

Sitting at Chaayos in the office complex. Just a 3 p.m. office break before the chai-and-smoke-break crowd descends. Still shy about breaking the ice with my new colleagues, even three months into this job.

I sit here, looking out at the city, wondering if I should speak to my reporting manager to transition me out of my current role and into CSR.

Meanwhile, I keep scouring websites such as this one: 'Deep Green Resistance starts where the environmental movement leaves off: industrial civilisation is incompatible with life. Technology can't fix it, and shopping – no matter how green – won't stop it. To save this planet, we need a serious resistance movement that can bring down the industrial economy.'

And I wonder when I will begin to do something that really matters with my life.

Sitting in Chaayos, not really listening to the chatter around, I think when does real life begin?

And that's when it comes back to me, an image flashing, seeding doubt. And I think, could it be? Really? Him all along, and I never once realised it all these months!

Travelling in the mountains, a few months but really a lifetime ago. Bones rattled and frozen in the Himachal Pradesh bus as it breaks down, gives way after twenty-six hours on the boulder-gashed roads. After two hours wrapped inside sweaters, jackets, two shawls and a monkey cap, I get out. Stand by the side of the road, watch the men change the tyre, wrap my hands around a glass of chai.

And then I see them, walking in deep contemplation towards us. Beards to their navels, mangled hair, some naked and sunburnt. Unaffected by the sun, the crushing cold. They pass us in silence, not a care in the world. Not stopping to ask what happened, just walking silently from the ghats of burning flesh in Varanasi up the valleys where the river roars, walking to the highest passes to sit in the caves with Shivlings for ice spears.

We watch them pass by and a hush takes over – the men working on the bus, the driver and the other truckers who have stopped to help, the convoy of army men, the passengers.

But then, one from the very end of the group limps and stops in his tracks.

He turns, walks back, looks at me. And even from this distance I can see his smile. His tall frame, the right amount of fat worn down. He raises his chillum to his mouth, gives a crazed laugh and turns back and walks on with the others to the summit of the universe.

# Acknowledgements

I want to thank Namita Gokhale for all her support throughout this book's journey and for all the years of friendship. I also want to thank Smita Khanna and Jayapriya Vasudevan, my agents at Jacaranda, and Chirag Thakkar, my publisher at Bloomsbury India, for believing in this book.

# About the Author

Anisha Lalvani has lived in Mumbai, Delhi, Bengaluru and London. She has a master's degree in English literature from Mumbai University. She has worked in publishing and on various literary projects, including the literary television programme *Kitaabnama: Books and Beyond* and the Jaipur Literature Festival.

She currently works in communications at a leading think tank that engages with the nexus of environment, economic opportunity and human well-being. She posts on Instagram @anisha.lalvani.54 and on X @AnishaL_Writer. This is her first novel.